Alan Scholefield

© Alan Scholefield 1977

Alan Scholefield has asserted his rights under the Copyright, Design and Patents act, 1998, to be identified as the author of this work.

First published in Great Britain in 1977 by William Heinemann Ltd

This edition published in 2017 by Lume Books.

Table of Contents

Part I	5
Part II	52
Part III	76
Part IV	118
Part V	151
Part VI	180

Part I

Friday, 2.10 p.m. – 6.12 p.m.

Philip was so close to the animal that all he could see was its teeth. Only inches from the wire they appeared huge: they curved down to a serrated edge, flanked by two sharp incisors that looked as though they could pierce case-hardened steel. They were yellowish with dark brown stains at the roots and shone with a film of saliva. He was so close that his depth of focus was isolating them and turning lips and hair into an amorphous grey blur. They were rending teeth, tearing teeth, teeth that could chop and cut, rip and worry. Philip saw himself in a sudden waking dream on his back under a … under an acacia tree. Yes, that was it, an acacia tree. The lion had its paws on his chest and he was looking up into those same yellow teeth. In a second the jaws would close on his face, tearing away his nose and eyebrows, removing the front of his face as though it were a rubber mask, leaving only red meat and livid white bone. But his fingers had touched the gun. It had fallen when he tripped. A .375 magnum. The most useful gun in the bush, Dick had called it.

With his right hand he had swung the rifle until the muzzle was pointing into the lion's mouth. Then he had pulled the trigger. 'The damn thing fell flat on top of me,' Dick had said. Philip could momentarily feel the weight of the dead flesh and smell the foetid air from its open mouth. Then, as Dick had done, he rolled the lion away and stood up … the dream of Africa faded and he was once more back in the house off Eaton Square in London, standing in front of the cages that held his pets.

He put his finger through the wire mesh and touched the guinea-pig on the nose. 'Hullo, Sweetypie,' he said. Sweetypie turned its rounded bottom towards its owner and defecated. Philip turned away from the half dozen cages that lined one side of the small room that had once been a dressing-room but was now the Great Ngorongoro Crater Menagerie containing his gerbils and his white mice and a soft brown rabbit called Mr Magoo because of its habit of peering near-sightedly at him when he came to clean its cage.

He walked towards the window and as he did so he felt the strange feeling in his back that meant he was being watched by someone. It was a physical thing, as though the watching eyes projected twin rays that touched him. He paused, pretending to look at a book lying on the table. Whose would the eyes be, he wondered? His mother's? The maid's? Dick Howard's? He had surprised them all at one time or another. In the past week he had seen the maid three times as she looked in on him, and twice the dead white face of Dave the chauffeur. That was odd because he was certain Dave had never looked in on him before. He swung round. But there was nothing, no one. Except for the faint scratching of the caged animals, the interlinked rooms were still; the curtains over the windows giving on to the landing, motionless.

He continued towards the outside window and stared at the traffic flowing west along the King's Road and Eaton Place, before entering the filtering system of Sloane Square. It was odd seeing the cars move without hearing them. That was the double-glazing; it cut out most noise from outside. 'Cuts out the fresh air too, if you ask me,' Dick had said, when the men were putting it in a few weeks earlier.

Philip's mother had heard him and said sharply, 'If you think that's fresh!' She had waved at the square, which lay at the end of the short cul-de-sac. 'Anyway we're putting in air-conditioning.' And they had.

The misty streets were almost empty except for the traffic. Usually at this time, just after lunch, there would be several people in the square, and on mild days most benches visible to him would be occupied. But now the few passersby hurried along the pavements muffled up, scarves trailing, woolly hats pulled well down over their ears. According to the television the whole country was in the grip of a north-easterly airstream which was bringing icy conditions from northern Russia. There had been snow in Scotland — the A9 was closed between Perth and Inverness — and some of the roads in the Pennines were blocked by drifts. Before the one o'clock news the weatherman had said that the temperature in London at noon had been minus two degrees Centigrade. 'What he means is twenty-seven degrees Fahrenheit,' Dick had said with irritation. 'Can't think why we've changed.'

Whatever the scale used, he had only to look out of the window to see it was freezing. Even if there had been no hurrying figures it *looked* cold. The north-easterly wind was blowing leaves and dust across the King's Road and the plane trees were waving their dark bare branches; the mist seemed to be getting thicker, but in the room which held the Great Ngorongoro Crater Menagerie Philip was wearing a thin cotton shirt. That was another thing they had put in, the finest heating system available. There had already been a central heating system in the house when they had bought it but his mother had not considered it adequate, so she'd had it ripped out and an air-ducted system installed. It had cost a fortune and it wasn't finished even now though you would not have guessed it by the temperature in the rooms. He walked into his bedroom, which led off the small dressing-room, and looked at the thermometer by the door. It read twenty-five degrees Centigrade, or seventy-seven degrees Fahrenheit, as Dick would have said.

His bedroom had been furnished from the Habitat catalogue, in white, orange and a bright grass green, the combination of which helped to bring warmth and a certain excitement to the drab afternoon. It had been designed more as a bed-sitter than a bedroom and the bed itself was a studio couch smothered in big squashy pillows. The room had only three proper walls: the fourth was not a wall at all but a long glass window of the kind sometimes found in hospitals. This had been his mother's idea so that she could look in to see if he was all right. Even though it was curtained he hated the consequent lack of privacy. At the foot of his bed was his desk, a white melamine top resting on sets of drawers; above it was a set of shelves, some of which contained books, others single items like the Masai spear-head which Dick had given him, the big round sea-green paper-weight which his stepfather had bought for him at Biot in Provence, and the block of clear Isopon which he had made himself with the treble link of gold chain trapped and suspended inside it. Six months earlier, when he had been in bed with an asthma attack he and his mother had chosen each item from the catalogue during long evenings.

That had been at the beginning of autumn. As far back as he could remember autumn had been a bad time for him: bronchitis, pneumonia once, influenza, head colds, chest colds; mainly chest colds that had developed into other things. A week ago he had gone down with another cold and his mother had kept him back from school. The moment he began to wheeze he had expected the usual visits from his private doctor, the pills, the antibiotics, the inhalants.

But for once the course of treatment had followed a different pattern. It had begun with an argument between his mother and Dick Howard. '… he's got a weak chest, that's all,' he had heard Dick say. 'You coddle the boy, Ruth. And if you go on he'll have a weak chest for the rest of his life.' His mother said something which he could not make out, for they were in the drawing-room on the far side of the stairwell and he was on the landing outside his room. Then Dick had said, 'Lots of boys grow up without fathers. Doesn't necessarily mean they ... all right, but you know what I mean. What he needs is a couple of years at a good boarding-school. That'd make a man of him. Rugger, swimming, cold showers ...'

Then his mother's clear, irritated voice: 'That's what's wrong with the British! Too much rugger and swimming and cold showers at school. I'm not having Philip grow up ...'

'What about your military academies, your military schools in the States?' Dick had said. 'Same thing. Anyway, I'm only saying leave the doctor, just for tonight, and let me —'

'All right!' his mother had said angrily. 'Just tonight.'

In a little while Dick had come into Philip's room. 'Hello, old son,' he had said. 'I've come to do in that cough of yours. Track it down, hunt it, and bang ... finished!'

Philip loved it when Dick came into his room at night. He loved the rich tobacco smell that permeated his clothes and even the smell of liquor on his breath was not offensive, for this was how he imagined white hunters to be. Usually Louise, the French maid, would bring him a cup of warm milk at bedtime and then his mother would come in and talk or read: night after night after night. But occasionally Dick would pay a visit from his flatlet on the ground floor; it was something to look forward to, something to spin out as long as he could; it broke the routine. On this particular evening Dick had knocked on the long glass wall that looked into the corridor, waved, and had then entered the room. In one hand he held a tumbler of water and in the other a small bottle. 'First an aspirin,' he said, giving Philip the pill and the water to wash it down with. 'Now the camphorated oil. Might tickle a bit.' He had warmed the oil and he poured a little into his right hand, lifted Philip's pyjama top up to his neck and began to rub the oil into his chest. 'Lovely smell,' he said. 'This is what my mother used on me when I got chesty. Best stuff in the world.' The smell entered Philip's clogged sinuses and for the first time that day he began to breathe more freely. 'There ...' Dick had said. 'That should do it.' He wiped his hand on a towel and screwed the top back on the bottle.

'Don't go,' Philip had said.

'Well —'

'Can't you stay a little?'

'Just a little. What shall we do?'

'You know.'

'Good Lord, Phil, I've told you every story I know, everything I ever did. You know more about my life than I do.'

'Tell me about when you were a district officer in the Colonial Service. When you were in the Zambesi Valley.'

'You've heard it all before, you know.'

'I know.'

'Any particular story?'

'Just after you'd gone there. The one with the dog.'

Dick had sat down on the edge of the bed, a tall man in his late forties with dark hair going grey and a narrow face seamed by sun and wind, networked by patterns of tiny red veins.

For years he had appeared younger than he was, now he was looking his age, shrunken, as though from an illness. He wore an old but expensive Donegal tweed suit in a heather mixture, a yellow Tattersall waistcoat, soft checked wool shirt and a club tie, and on his feet a pair of handmade buckskin desert boots. There was something slightly old-fashioned about his clothes. To Philip it was exactly how a white hunter should dress in London in winter; but to the casual passerby in the street he looked like an ex-officer wearing mufti made for him twenty years earlier.

'Well, I was about twenty-two then and they'd given me my first district. Place called Chirundu —'

'You said it was near Livingstone. You said you used to go out and look at the Victoria Falls.'

'That's right. Chirundu's downstream from the Falls. I had a launch, you remember. In those days I had this small dog. Terrier. Mixture really. Called ...' He paused for a moment and Philip said, 'Dinner. Because he always wanted something to eat.'

'Right. Dinner. Din for short. On this particular day I had gone out into the bush by myself with just a two-one-six Rigby, nice little gun, light, but all I wanted was a small buck for the pot. We were going along a path near the river, hot as anything even though it was late afternoon —'

'When the buck come down to drink,' Philip said.

'You know it backwards.' Howard paused and pushed himself back so that he was more comfortable and leant against the wall. Philip was lying with the bedclothes up to his chin staring at the ceiling, seeing the grey bush of the Zambesi Valley, feeling the sticky heat of the late afternoon, hearing the cicadas and the raucous screeching of the birds. As the story proceeded along its familiar lines the two people in the room were drawn together by the web of memory and imagination: Richard Howard, middle-aged, slightly tipsy; and the boy, Philip Blanchet, ten years old, but young for his age, dark, said to resemble his dead father; pallid, big-eyed, thin.

'... and then?' Philip said, prompting.

'Then the dog must have smelled food, perhaps from a nearby village. It was the time of day for the evening meal. Can't say what started him off. Unusual really, because he was an obedient little fellow.' Philip smiled to himself. Dick was spinning out the story in just the way he liked. He knew the ending; what mattered was how it was told.

'So off went Dinner up the path. I remember as though it were yesterday. A little black and white terrier lolloping up the path ahead of me and then putting on speed and disappearing round a bend.

'Well, I didn't think much about it. I'd more or less given up the idea of a buck. I didn't have a gunboy or a tracker with me, which meant that if I shot one I'd have had to carry it home or put it up in a tree. Didn't fancy either. So I let him go. Then after a few minutes I heard yip! yip! yip! High-pitched. Not like his usual bark at all. Sounded frightened. So I stopped and stood there, looking up the path. I was about to shout, "Here boy!" when around the bend of the path comes Din at full lick. Fast as any cheetah you ever saw. And right behind him a lion. Not quite full-grown. A young male. But big enough.

'Didn't take more than a couple of seconds to work out what was going on. The lion was after Dinner for *his* dinner. And Dinner was making for me as hard and fast as he could. Coming back to master for protection. Came shooting down the path, past me, then stopped just behind my legs as much as to say, "There now. You can't touch me. I'm in block." Ever played block, Phil?'

Philip shook his head. He had seen it played at school but had never been asked to join in and it wasn't exactly a game one played in Eaton Square even if there had been other boys of his age to play it with him, which there weren't; nor would his mother have permitted it, if there had been.

'It's really a game of touch with a special area where you're safe.'

'I know how it's played.'

'Good. Pity the lion didn't. He'd never heard of it. Came straight for me. He wanted the dog, you see. So I shot him. Took a hell of a chance with a light gun like that but what else could I do? Shot him through the brain at about fifteen yards and he dropped at my feet. Dead as mutton. Absolute fluke, of course, couldn't have done it again for toffee.'

'What about Dinner?'

'Oh, yes. It cured him of running off all right. After that he never went ahead of me. Always used to walk just at my heels. He was a good dog. Had him for years, four or five, I suppose, before a snake got him. Now what about a little shut-eye?'

Philip's dreams that night had been of the wide Zambesi River and lions which hunted small terriers. When he woke he could breathe more easily. Now, six camphorated-oil-rubbing-nights later he was almost clear of the thick asthmatic breathing. Dick had been right; his mother wrong.

He had been standing at the window for some time as these thoughts passed through his mind. Like the sleeping dreams he had at night these waking dreams were all bright colours and rich narrative. It was the area in which he spent most of his time; his imagination. Weeks, months in sick bed had created an imaginative world frequently more real than reality. Again he had the sensation in his back as though something was lightly touching him. He turned abruptly. This time he saw the curtain on the landing window twitch, then there was a knock at his door. Louise put her head round as he crossed to his bed.

'You are bad boy,' she said, shaking her finger at him.

He dropped on to the bed. 'I don't feel like resting,' he said.

'Madame will be very cross with me.' She spoke English with a heavy accent and pronounced words like 'with' as 'wiz' and often spoke in a jumble of English and French simply using the first phrase in either language that came to mind. Sometimes he had to stop himself from laughing at her. She was a big woman with a sallow, yellowish skin. At one time she must have been attractive, but now her features were too sharp and she was beginning to lose her figure. She was dressed formally in a black-and-white check shirtwaist dress that served as a uniform, and a small frilly apron. Philip and his mother had never had a maid before. She was one of the changes that had overtaken their lives when his mother had married Michel Blanchet. *Blanchet*. The name still did not seem right to him. Philip Blanchet ... 'You're lucky,' his mother had said. 'It's not everyone who gets to use a French name.' But he had liked his own name: Warren. ('As Idaho as potatoes,' his father used to say. Or was that what his mother had told him his father used to say? He could not remember his father.)

Louise pulled the aircell blanket up from the bottom of the bed and tucked him in. She stood for a moment, her face pinched, an expression almost of sadness in her eyes. He was so young; so defenceless lying there. Then, as though gathering herself, the expression hardened and hastily she looked away lest he see a change in her.

She looked at her watch and then at the Mickey Mouse alarm clock on his bedside table. She picked up the clock, set it right and wound the alarm.

'Another half-hour for you.' She put the clock back on the table and walked softly to the door. She stopped, turned, and arranged her face in a pleasant smile, but Philip was lying on his back staring up at the ceiling; again, as though a cloud had passed over the sun, the warmth drained from her eyes and her expression became cold and hostile. Then she closed the door behind her.

There were moments when Philip was so bored he could feel tears of frustration begin to prick the back of his eyes. It was for times like these that he would save a series of thoughts, spin them out, exploit them, fantasize. Now was such a moment. The Mickey Mouse clock showed 2.30 p.m. He had to rest until 3 p.m. His mother was not leaving until 3.15. At 3.30 he would … he felt his stomach contract from a mixture of anticipation, pleasure … and apprehension.

Again there was the flick of a curtain at the corridor window and he watched with half-closed eyes. His mother's face was framed by one of the glass panels. The curtain fell back into place and the face vanished.

*

Ruth Blanchet stood by the curtained passage window of her son's room for a few moments and then made her way back to her own room on the half-landing above. He hadn't been asleep, she was sure of that, but at least he was resting. Rest was everything, Dr Tremlett had said: rest, warmth, a balanced diet, 'and don't let him have too much time to think of himself, give him an interest. Part of his trouble is psychological.' She had done it, she told herself; everything that had been asked of her. Rest: there was a rest period after lunch at his private school and she had been insistent to the headmaster that he should, in fact, *rest*, and not use it, as such periods were so often used by schoolboys, for horseplay and games and, though she did not say so, unpleasant sexual experiments. Warmth: she couldn't do more than she had done. Michel had raised his eyebrows when he had seen the bills for the new air-ducted heating with the automatic humidifier. She had not mentioned that it had been specifically installed for Philip's benefit. Instead she had said, 'Michel, you come from Provence, I was born in Florida; the British think their climate's semi-tropical, we know it isn't.'

He had not been amused. He was a small man, slightly shorter than Ruth. She had always thought that the southern French were extrovert Latins, but Michel was quiet, withdrawn, cold. When she had made the joke about the British climate, he had pursed his lips and tapped the bill on the top of the table and finally nodded and said, 'If it must be.'

A balanced diet. She could certainly claim that, for who did the cooking if not she? One of the first things Michel had asked when they were married was whether she wished him to send over a cook from France with the maid, but she had rejected the idea. Cooking had been part of her hotel training and, apart from that, she enjoyed it — especially as she had someone to clean up after her. It seemed to be working out. She was able to keep Philip on the sort of diet Dr Tremlett had outlined and she was also able to cope with more elaborate meals on the rare occasions when Michel was at home and not flying halfway around the world to make an unexpected (and therefore unwelcome) lightning inspection of one of his hotels.

As for an interest, there was Philip's menagerie, the Great Whatever-it-was Crater Menagerie. She had Dick to thank for that. He had made the boy interested in keeping animals. Give him his due, he had done that.

She went into her room, sat down at her writing desk and looked at her watch: 2.53. She had nearly twenty-five minutes before Dave would come round with the car and only the notes left to write. She nodded with satisfaction: her timing was right. Her dark hide suitcases, neat, shining, stood by the door of her bedroom, her coat lay across a Victorian spoon-back chair in the corner, and by its side was her make-up case. Everything in its place. As her eyes came back from the suitcases she saw herself in the long, gilt mirror on the wall. She was wearing a black and brown mohair tweed suit with a fawn silk blouse, and wondered whether she should have worn something slightly less sombre. But Michel did not comment much on her clothes. He expected her to buy the best and she did so. Once, when she was wearing a murderously expensive Chanel suit he had said, somewhat shyly, 'You look very *neat, chérie*.' It was a strange word to use but she had known what he meant and was oddly gratified, as though he had called her ravishing. She saw a woman in her mid-thirties, dark, with a pale face, broad Slavic cheekbones, strong competent hands and eyes so dark brown they were almost black; they were like her son's, slightly larger than normal, with shadow-smudges beneath them; in them she could read uncertainty, doubt, anxiety. Well, she thought, why the hell shouldn't I be anxious? I've got a son who sickens with every goddam germ known to man and now I'm flying off and leaving him. She reached for her paper with the words, 'from Ruth Blanchet' at the top and wrote 'Louise', underlining it with a fine stroke of the pen. Louise was to do the cooking for the two-and-a-bit days she would be away and she wanted to be certain she got it right: no heavy French sauces, no cassoulets, no spicy Provençal dishes. She wrote:

'1. Dinner. Consommé (there is chicken stock in the fridge). Followed by ...' She had been about to write down an omelette but then she remembered that Dick Howard would be having all his meals with Philip so she wrote down lamb chops instead, with mashed potatoes and a green salad followed by yoghurt for Philip; (she had a childlike faith in yoghurt because she had once read that people who ate a lot of it lived to astonishing ages) and a creme caramel for Dick. She had left several cremes caramel in the fridge and half-a-dozen yoghurts and there was fresh fruit for Louise and Dave if they wanted it.

2. Breakfast. Philip liked cereal, she would have been happier if he had eaten porridge. They compromised on muesli. She wrote that down. Dick could order what he liked. She wondered if he usually ate breakfast. Sometimes he looked ... she had seen enough hotel guests with the morning trembles to recognize what they had been on the night before. And once again her heart began to flutter in her chest like a small trapped bird. She told herself not to be stupid, but the panic got worse. What if something happened? What if Dick got drunk? How could she leave Philip in his care?

But what if she didn't? The cable telling her that Michel would be in Vienna from Friday night to Monday morning before he flew off to the United States had been a simple statement of fact. There was no request that she join him, just the facts. Too often in the past she had answered the telephone call or the cable with excuses. Some had been real; there *had* been builders or gasmen or electricians in and out of the house all day, but gradually she had found herself making up excuses not to leave Philip. Michel's messages had grown fewer. In the past six months she had received none. Then, two days before, had come the cable from his secretary telling her where he would be that weekend. She had sat down and worked out that he had spent a total of twelve days at their home in London during those six months. She knew there was no alternative: if she kept refusing they would become strangers. She looked round the room, seeing the richness of its furnishings with a new eye. She *had* to go. And of course Philip would be all right. It wasn't as if Dick was alone, she told herself, there was Louise and Dave in case anything went wrong.

3. Lunch. Veal. Louise could do the escalopes in a little butter: no cream, no marsala, simply *naturel*. She underlined the word. Louise had not objected when they had first discussed it; but she had seemed uninterested. Her eyes had slid away and she had listened as though it was none of her business. There was something odd about Louise. Ruth could not put her finger on it but she felt as though Louise was constantly sizing her up: not only herself, but the house, the furniture, her clothes, her jewellery. Once she had found her jewellery case disturbed, but when she checked nothing was missing and she guessed Louise had tried on one or two items. She decided to say nothing and it had not happened again. Louise was like a dealer or a tax inspector: that sofa must be worth X pounds and that painting Y and the silver Z; it was that sort of feeling, but underneath Ruth caught a faint hint of something more. Envy? Well, that was not hard to understand. Ruth herself would have been envious in Louise's place. But she did not have to stay if she didn't want to. There were English servants to be found, though God knows what Michel would say. 'The English are not a service people,' he had said when he first mentioned giving her a French maid. 'They do not like to serve. When have you seen a good English waiter?' And she had to acknowledge that he knew what he was talking about. Even Dave, the chauffeur, with his long blond hair and his dandruff, had a knowing manner. He called her Madame and when Michel was there he was perfectly respectful, but when she was alone there was an undertone to his 'Good morning, Madame'. It was as though it were a tiny joke between them that she, an American and no better than he, should be addressed in this exaggerated fashion.

4. Dinner (Saturday) … She wrote quickly and neatly and soon she had finished the menus and had written another note about laundry and about the thermostat on the central heating: 'It is not to go below 22 degrees C,' she wrote, and underlined that too.

She clipped the notes together with a small hand stapler, then pulled another sheet towards her and wrote 'Dick'. She had been tempted to write

'Richard', but Dick sounded more friendly and at that moment she wanted his friendship.

Sometimes she resented the way she had been manoeuvred into first-name terms.

From the day he had moved into the flat on the ground floor, he had treated her with an avuncular — sometimes, she thought an almost paternal — air. She had known that the flat was being prepared for a ... she had supposed a sort of glorified concierge, a companion, someone who would be in the house, even if hardly seen, to keep her company when Michel was away. In her mind's eye she had visualized a woman, a comfortable body, Scottish perhaps. Then one day Michel had telephoned her from his London office in St James's Square and told her that someone was coming that day to occupy the flat — and Richard Howard had arrived. The first thing she noticed about him was his grey eyes, eyes that should have been steady but were instead filled with a kind of bewilderment. Then she saw the gun-cases. Six of them. Four rifles and two shotguns that now hung on the wall in his sitting-room, and she knew that Michel had more than a concierge in mind, Richard Howard was a guardian.

But he had been so weak and frail then that he seemed hardly able to look after himself. He had made no effort to pick up any of his belongings, leaving everything to the taxi driver.

'Sorry about the junk,' he had said. 'Always thought a man should be able to put all he possessed into one suitcase. Travel light. But I can't manage without three. And the guns, of course.' Then he had followed her into the house and she had noticed that he limped, or not so much limped as shuffled. His pallor was unhealthy, the shade skin goes when deep suntan has been kept inside for a few weeks.

She had wanted to ask Michel about him but he had flown away about his business and she was left in the house with a strange man. He had started to call her Ruth at the end of the first week.

'You're too pretty to be called Mrs all the time,' he had said with heavy-handed gallantry. 'You call me Dick and I'll call you Ruth. Agreed?' How could she not agree?

When her husband came back three weeks later another factor had entered the relationship. 'How do you get on with Howard?' Blanchet had asked, removing with precision the fine dorsal bones of a Dover sole.

There were several things she might have said: that Howard was a drinking man, that Howard had seemed too frail to have watched over a sparrow (though he was stronger now), that she didn't like the idea of a man living in the downstairs flat ... But she said none of these for the one outstanding success had been Philip. From the moment Howard had joined the family, for that is what it amounted to, Philip had undergone a change. Until then he had been withdrawn, introverted, sullen if challenged, moody and often bad-tempered. Within a fortnight of Dick Howard's arrival he had blossomed. She had watched the two of them at first with suspicion and then with a measure of relief. She had often told herself that Philip did not need a father; that she was capable of giving him that sort of masculine discipline, but when she saw how he acted with Howard she knew this had been a rationalization born of the knowledge that Michel was never going to be a father to him. And so when her husband had asked her how she got on with Howard she thought of Philip and told him the experiment was a success.

'I'm glad,' he said. Then he said something she would never forget. 'They can always get at me through Philippe.' (He always gave the name the French pronunciation.) It was as though a cold wind suddenly chilled her. 'Get at you?' she said. 'Who? What are you talking about? Who are they? And why Philip?' But the telephone had rung and when he came back from a discussion with one of his directors in Paris he was preoccupied and unwilling to explain.

She pulled the notepaper towards her and began to write.

1. Philip is not to go outside.

2. Please see that the house is kept warm.

3. Louise has instructions about food.

4. We are staying at Sacher's in Vienna. (She phoned the International Exchange for the number.)

5. Dr Tremlett's address is 94 Collingwood Square. Telephone number 711-967891.

6. Bedtime is 9 o'clock, except tomorrow when he can stay up to watch Starksy and Hutch.

7. He must rest between ...

... she wrote quickly and concisely and in a few minutes the list was done. Then she went downstairs.

*

Richard Howard was dreaming. He sat sprawling in the big chintz-covered armchair in his sitting-room, his mouth half open, breathing heavily and jerkily as the horror of the dream caused his heart to race. He always slept for a little while after lunch, specially on *jours avec*. Today, however, was a *jour sans*, tomorrow would be a *jour avec*. Nothing hard today even though it was a Friday. *Jours sans* were days when he should have had nothing at all. He excepted wine. A little wine never did anyone any harm. 'Take a little wine for thy stomach's sake.' Someone in the Bible. Couldn't remember who. But if it said so in the Bible, who was going to argue? So he had taken a little wine for his stomach's sake. He sometimes thought how aptly ironic the aphorism was in his own case, for it was in the abdominal region where the muscles had been ripped and the flesh mangled and the actual lining of the stomach torn open. Later, when he could understand what the doctors and nurses said to him, he had realized how lucky he was to be alive: doctors don't often use the word 'miracle'.

The wine, while comforting the pain, had made him sleepy. He had slept and now he was dreaming. It was the same dream he had had on many occasions. He was lying on his back under an acacia tree and the lion was on top of him. He could smell his breath and see his teeth, stained brown at the roots; feel his weight. He knew the gun was somewhere near his right hand and he stretched for it. But before his fingers could reach the butt the lion had disembowelled him with his churning hind legs and his entrails had sprawled all over the dusty veld.

He jerked awake, heart hammering in his ears, sweat lying cold on his forehead, and rose shakily to his feet, the dream still clear and terrible in his mind. Automatically, he crossed to a low table on which stood several modern Swedish decanters and lifted the one containing brandy, reached for a glass and was about to pour himself a measure when he paused. It was a *jour sans*. But he needed *something*, that was damn certain, after a dream like that. Just one. He poured out a drink and swallowed half of it, feeling the heat of it in his throat and then his stomach. That was better. God, if he could only stop dreaming. If he could simply sink into black oblivion. He knew the doctors would have a name for what was going on inside him. Time, they'd said at the hospital. Well, time was putting right the wounds of the body; what about those of the mind? In the novels he'd read it was a matter of baring your secrets, talking about the things you didn't want to talk about or didn't even know were there. Once you let them out, talked about them, confessed, opened up your inner self — why, then bingo, everything was all right. That was nonsense. Why had he told Philip if not to exorcise it from his mind? Admittedly he had varied it slightly from what had actually happened, but he didn't want to frighten the boy and in any case he, Richard Howard, knew what had happened; wasn't that enough?

Thought of Philip reminded him what day it was and his mind thankfully grasped at a different subject. He wandered over to the window and stood watching the powdery granules of snow smack against the glass then bounce into the area below. It wasn't the best day for Philip to be going out but you couldn't choose your time, you had to grasp the opportunity. And the opportunity was today, this afternoon, for tomorrow was Saturday and Saturday was the Jewish Sabbath and Loewenthal's was closed. It also closed on the Christian Sabbath and Ruth was due back on Monday, which only left this afternoon.

The wind pushed and pulled at the branches of the plane trees but the double-glazing kept out all noise. Should he, he wondered, go with Philip? But they had been over this together secretly and it had been agreed that he go by himself. The other times, when they had bought the gerbils and the white mice and the guinea-pigs he had accompanied Philip in the Citroen with Dave driving. This time it was to be by taxi.

Philip by himself; an adventure. It was high time he learned to do things for himself. If only Ruth would let the boy alone, go and join Blanchet whenever she could, then they could really have some fun. He could take him to the Zoo and to Whip-snade and let him see animals in more or less their natural freedom. They could travel by bus and train like ordinary people and not in an overheated limousine with a chauffeur at the wheel. How did she expect Philip to grow up like an ordinary child and into an ordinary — or put a better way, a *natural* man, when she was bringing him up in a hothouse atmosphere like some rare tropical plant? Asthma. Bronchitis. Rot. He had a weak chest, that was all, and it would never get any better if she went on like this. Not that Howard was against the warmth of the house. Coming as he did from the tropics it was the one thing that made a British winter bearable. There had to be a balance, as there was in nature. What Philip needed was a school like Gordonstoun with its emphasis on hardihood and the outdoors. Memories of his own youth in Africa crowded into his mind: of freezing mornings in the Highlands of Kenya, when the water in the rain barrels was frozen and frost covered the English garden; the huge fireplace of mountain-stone and his father standing almost on top of the fire in the early winter mornings sipping his hot coffee and shouting at old Luke, the major-domo, for shaving water or more coffee, or where the hell was his breakfast, and Luke who seemed, in Howard's memory, always to have been the same age, about seventy, irritated and irascible and constantly mumbling under his breath at all the trouble he was being put to. And then out on the horse to ride the cattle fences before the sun was up. *That* was cold. It was what Philip needed.

There was a knock on his door and Ruth came in with the note she had written.

'It's all down here,' she said, handing it to him.

'Oh.' He put the brandy glass behind him but he was aware that she had seen it. He took the note and read it. 'You've forgotten one or two things,' he said.

'What?'

'You haven't put down Scotland Yard's telephone number. Nor the Prime Minister's. And what about the Archbishop of Canterbury, in case we need him?'

'Very amusing.'

'Well, it's true. Everything here but the kitchen sink. You're only going away for two days, Ruth. And there are *three* of us to look after him.'

She stared at him.

'Sorry,' he said. 'Just teasing.' Too often their conversations turned into dialogues underpinned by tension.

'Well, don't.'

'No.'

'Don't blame me for worrying.'

'Certainly not.'

'I can't help it.'

'No.'

'I know you think I imagine Philip's illnesses. But you don't know us all that well. You don't know what it has been like.'

'No.'

'You think I worry too much, don't you?'

'I think you've got to let the boy stand on his own feet. You can't live his life for him.'

'But these illnesses were real. You don't think I imagined asthma, do you? You don't think bronchitis was just a cough and a sneeze?' She paused and the brisk, competent façade cracked. 'I wish I wasn't going. I don't have to, you know. I can easily cancel. Michel doesn't care one way —'

'Don't be silly. Of course you're going. And you're going to have a marvellous time. Vienna! Good Lord, most of us would jump at the chance to get a break from London in February. Worst damn month of all with its fogs and its cold. No, you're going to let Dave drive you to the airport and you're going to get on the plane and Bob's your uncle, you'll soon be sitting down in Vienna and having some of that chocolate cake with cream, what do they call it?'

'Sachertorte. We're staying at Sacher's. I've written the telephone number down just in case.' She pointed to the note. 'Ring any time. Doesn't matter when.'

'You're doing it again, Ruth.'

This time she ignored him. 'Please put it away safely,' she said. It was an order; she was the mistress of the house once more.

He waited until she had gone upstairs before he finished the brandy, then he took the note to his bedroom where there was a small writing table. He opened the right-hand drawer and immediately saw the letter. He put in Ruth's note, hesitated, then took out the letter and read it for the sixth or seventh time. It had come at the beginning of the week and he supposed he must have read it once a day at least. Was it because it frightened him? Nonsense. All he had to do was say no. But did he want to say no? Or, put it another way: did he have the courage to say yes? He stared at the letter as if to gain some hidden clue that would help him to make his decision. It was an excellent notepaper, and so it should be, it belonged to the Georges V in Paris.

'Dear Mr Howard' (he read). 'Forgive me please for writing to you in this way but I am here only a day no more and I heard you were in London at M Blanchet's home.' (That was an odd thing. *How* did he know? There had been a long article about Howard in the *East African Standard* when he had left Kenya, recalling his life and adventures and his final accident, but nothing in Europe. Still, he'd been pretty well-known in Nairobi and he supposed these hotel safari people were in and out of the place once or twice a year, especially someone looking for a man with experience. Anyone in the Stanley Bar could have told the writer he was in London. Perhaps he'd even met Blanchet.) 'As you may have heard, my company, Hotels Belgique Trans-Africain, is expanding once more in Africa ...' (No, Howard thought, he hadn't heard, why should he?) '... and we are building a new hotel with safari park on the west bank of Lake Kivu.

'Although we have many hotels in Africa we do not yet have a safari park. This is why I write. Would such a venture interest you? To come and create something new, and then to make it a success?

'I do not talk about such things as salary or conditions at this early stage, but rest assured we are not ungenerous. There is also a pension plan.

'I go from here to my head office in Brussels and I will be in London about the middle of next week. I shall telephone you and perhaps we could meet. I look forward to it.' The signature was not clear; Howard thought it was 'Barbot', but could not be sure.

He dropped the letter back in the drawer on top of Ruth's note and closed it. Did he want to or not? He wandered into his sitting-room and stopped by the liquor tray. His hand went out to the brandy decanter but instead of picking it up he took his empty glass into the kitchenette and washed it. He felt a small glow of virtue. He rinsed the glass, dried it and put it away carefully. He didn't have to make up his mind at that moment. Barbot, or whatever his name was, had said he would be in London the middle of next week. There was plenty of time. He returned to the window. A mist was blurring the outlines of the houses on the far side of the square; the whole picture was one of dank depression. Suddenly he yearned for Africa, for violent changes in colour, in the quality of light; for heat and dryness, for night air that washed over one like warm new milk, for strong sunlight, for food that stung the palate with chillies and spices, for all the violent contrasts of that land which was so unlike the one in which he now found himself.

His mother had always talked of England as 'home' and she had tried to keep one foot in Africa and one in a kind of Cheltenham-England to which she clung through the *Illustrated London News*, *Country Life* and *The Lady*. It had never been 'home' to Howard even though he had spent all his school years there. Africa was his home and he still longed for it even after what it had done to him.

Now he was being offered a chance to go back. He would have his own little empire again. Like Kivu. He had never been there but he knew it was on the border of what he still thought of as the Belgian Congo, and Rwanda-Burundi. It would be different from Kenya, and from the two Rhodesias which he had known in the days he had worked in the Colonial Service. It would be new, it would be a challenge, it would give him the chance to regain his place in the scheme of things instead of sitting about here drinking too much and pretending he was actually *doing* something for the money Blanchet was paying him.

For a few seconds he felt buoyant, almost euphoric. There seemed nothing he could not do. And then, abruptly, as though the air had gone out of a balloon, he felt flat, assailed by apprehension and doubt. He was too old to start again; that was the bloody point: too old. But even as he formed the thoughts he knew they did not comprise the complete answer.

In the distance a bell sounded. At first he thought it was the telephone, then he realized it was Philip's big Mickey Mouse alarm clock. He looked at his watch. It was three o'clock. Not long now, he thought, and Ruth would be gone.

*

The black Pallas Citroen stood at the kerbside. Dave was holding the rear door, but Ruth was still in the front hall of the house as though unwilling, finally, to leave. Louise, Philip and Howard were all there. 'Now, don't forget,' she was saying to Philip. 'I'm just at the end of a telephone line. Dick's got the number. Any time you feel —'

'Yes, mother, I will.'

'And remember, no going out.'

'No, mother.'

'And Louise is going to make you escalope. You like escalope. I've made it myself —'

'Ruth, you're going to be late,' Howard said.

'Goodbye.'

'Goodbye.'

'Goodbye. Have a super time.'

'Look after yourself, darling.'

She hugged Philip and then, almost without thinking, she raised her cheek to Howard and received a dry and somewhat abrasive touch.

'Goodbye.'

'Goodbye, Madame.'

''Bye, darling.'

'Have a good time, Ruth, and don't *worry*.'

She went down the steps and into the big, waiting car. In a few moments it was lost in the traffic converging on Sloane Square. Dave was usually a reasonably steady driver but today he whipped the Pallas in and out of the slow-moving traffic until Ruth felt as though she were in a ship and not a car. He had not driven like this since the first time he had gone to the office to fetch Michel. Then he had used The Mall as a speedway. Michel had ordered him to stop at the end of Birdcage Walk, ordered him out of the car, told him that if he ever drove like that again he would be fired, and had then driven himself back to Eaton Square, leaving Dave to walk.

Now he shot along the King's Road, turned into Sloane Avenue and made for the Cromwell Road. She thought of ordering him to slow down but decided against giving him the opportunity to argue with her or try to ease the chip which he sometimes wore like a martyr's crown. Each time she looked up she met his eyes in the rear-view mirror. She was glad to see that they lacked the knowing expression he often wore; instead they were preoccupied. She shifted her position to avoid them and was able to look at them without being seen. He was not bad looking, with blond hair and a strong body. As a youth he had suffered from acne and this had left a roughened face. She supposed he was about twenty-five and there was no doubt he had a strong animal attraction — though not for her, she hastened to qualify.

She wondered if he and Louise were having an affair. Louise must be fifteen years older but that wouldn't matter if she fancied him. She stared out at the seemingly endless line of semi-detacheds that spun past her and thought, as she always thought, when she saw them, that they represented some sort of record in ghastliness. But behind her thoughts lay the picture of Philip at the door of the house in the grey afternoon light.

At the airport Dave stopped the car outside Terminal One and signalled to a porter. Then he had her door open. Usually he did this with a flourish at places like airports and hotels, sometimes giving her a look which said *we* know it's all a game; but now, as she thanked him, she noticed that he did not meet her eyes. That was odd. It was unlike him. In a moment she was in the crowd making for the departure lounge.

Dave stood on the pavement, the open door still in his hand, watching her enter the terminal. Good legs, he thought. His eyes travelled upwards and rested on the grey mutation mink coat. Rich bitch, he thought, with a sudden spurting of hot anger. Rich American bitch. He slammed the car door and went to the driving seat. The anger had made him tremble and his hands were unsteady as he lit a cigarette from the lighter on the dash. He took off his dark navy-blue cap, tilted the driving mirror so that he could see himself, then he brought out a comb and ran it through his hair, enjoying the sight of himself, cigarette in mouth, eyes screwed up against the smoke.

There was a tap on the driver's window and he swung round. A policeman was leaning down. Dave's heart gave a sickening lurch. He touched a button and the window slid open.

'Excuse me, sir,' the policeman said with heavy emphasis on the 'sir'. 'This is a no-parking area. Would you mind admiring yourself somewhere else.'

'Sorry.' He touched the button and the window rose again. He started the car and swung away from the Terminal building. Once again anger rose. 'Must have seen the cap,' he thought. 'Never would have spoken like that if he hadn't. Not to a bloke in a car like this. Bastard.'

He drove on and turned, into one of the car parks. He looked at his watch; he could hardly see the numerals for the darkness that had seeped into the grey afternoon. Fifteen minutes before the Madrid plane was due to land. He threw the half smoked cigarette out of the window and lit another. That copper had unsettled him. Well, fuck him. No problem. He hadn't done anything. He leaned back in the seat and began to think about the money.

*

Philip was in the Great Ngorongoro Crater Menagerie. He had cleaned out the gerbils' cages and now he was finishing the guinea-pig's. He had wanted to leave these chores until he returned but Dick had said, 'You don't want to bring him into a dirty menagerie, do you?'

'How do you know he'll be a he?'

'Instinct. Thought of a name for him yet?'

'But what if he's a she?'

'Don't know that I could tell off-hand. Never really examined them before. Always think of them as masculine. Anyway, try and think of one that would fit both.'

He finished sweeping the bottom of Sweetypie's cage and put her back in the fresh sawdust. 'It was easy with you,' he said to the guinea-pig. 'You just are a sweetypie.' He took the droppings in their sawdust and emptied them into the rubbish bin that stood in the dumb-waiter in the kitchen. When he returned to his room Howard was sitting on his bed.

'All done, Phil?'

'I'll give them another clean-out tomorrow morning.'

'Good boy. Ready?'

Philip found that his heart was racing. 'Yes,' he managed to say. For a moment he thought his breathing was going all haywire but he did what

Dick had told him to do, closed his mouth and breathed evenly through his nose, and the spasm passed.

'Get your coat on and I'll phone the taxi rank in the square.' He heard Dick go downstairs to his own flat to phone. He supposed that was because of Louise. It was their secret — his and Dick's — and there was no reason to share it with anyone else.

He heard Dick coming back up the stairs but even as he did so he saw the curtain over his passage window drop back into place. Almost immediately the bedroom door was thrown open and Louise came in. She looked flustered. 'What do you do, *chéri?*' she said, pointing at the coat.

'He's going out,' Howard said from the doorway.

She turned sharply. 'Madame say —'

'I know what Madame said. Taxi's on its way, Phil.'

'You cannot do this. The child is —'

'He's only going out for a short time, don't worry.'

'Yes! It *is* I who worry! You —'

'Come on, Phil.'

'No! Madame say he must not go!'

'Madame isn't here now,' Howard said, with a slight edge to his voice. 'I'm in charge and I say he *can*.'

'You! You are in charge! *C'est impossible!*' She gave a short barking laugh without mirth. 'You! Who is going to look after Philippe if he is getting sick again? You?'

'He's not going to get sick. That's the trouble with all of you. You keep on talking about him getting sick. No wonder it affects him.'

There was a ring at the door. 'That's the taxi,' Philip said.

'Fine. Ready?'

Louise threw herself between them. 'Philippe, your mother say you must never go out in cold like this. You will get sick. You *know* —'

Howard caught Philip by the arm and led him from the room. 'For God's sake keep out of this!' he said viciously to Louise. 'You're only the bloody servant. Remember that!'

She chased them down the staircase to the ground floor making small but ineffectual grabbing movements at Philip's arm. 'Stop!' she shouted several times. 'You must not let him away.' Her English, never good, began to disappear.

Howard pulled open the front door. An elderly man with a grey-yellow tea-strainer moustache stood on the front step. 'Taxi, sir.'

'That's right,' Howard said. 'Got the money, Phil?'

'You cannot!' Louise shouted, pulling now at Philip's collar. 'It is too cold.'

Howard tried to smile at the taxi-driver. 'She thinks it's too cold for the boy.'

'Nasty sort of day,' the driver said, stepping back down the steps.

'Off you go, Phil.'

Philip jumped into the back of the cab and heard the door close behind him. He looked up. Louise's face was at the window, distorted by the glass, the mouth twisted, the eyes bulging. She looked frightful. She was signalling with one hand and trying to open the door with the other. He saw Dick come up behind her, take her by the arm and pull her backwards on to the pavement. As though in fear of his life the driver pulled away from the kerb and drove two hundred yards down the square before he reached behind him and slid open the dividing window. 'Where to, son?' he said.

This was the beginning of the test which he and Dick had gone over several times. He gave the address of Loewenthal's shop in Camden Town and sank back with relief against the seat. Again he could feel the irregular beating of his heart and the constriction at his chest. He closed his mouth and began to breathe evenly through his nose. 'You all right?' the driver said with some concern. Philip nodded, keeping on with his steady breathing. 'Warm enough?' Philip nodded again. 'Don't you worry, son, you won't catch cold in my cab. It's got heating.' He closed the hatch and drove across the square, heading in the direction of the park.

It was a longish drive from Eaton Square to Camden Town and Philip had time to calm down and look about him with fresh eyes. This was an historic moment, the first time he had ever been in a taxi by himself. He always travelled with Dave, to and from school. He did not like Dave, they never spoke and Dave never got out of the car to open the door as he did when either his mother or Michel was there. He sensed a cruelty in Dave that frightened him and he was glad when the holidays came so that he would not be alone with him. His taxi-driver, on the other hand, had seemed a friendly man. He stared out of the window, still breathing regularly, but without conscious effort now. This had been the first thing he noticed about Loewenthal when they had bought the original pair of gerbils; the wheezing breath and the size. He was a very fat man who wore a black skull cap, and Philip had wondered if he too suffered from asthma, he wheezed so much as he moved about his shop, but Dick had said, 'It's all that fat that's making him wheeze. My ... A girl I once knew used to have a dog like that. Dachshund. Kept on feeding it chocolates and biscuits, and finally it got so fat it could hardly move. It wheezed.' Dick did not often mention the girl. Once Philip had asked him about her and he had said, 'Jane? Afraid she got lost in the shuffle,' and changed the subject.

They got caught in traffic crossing central London and Philip had a chance to see the lights. He loved being out in the gathering darkness, loved the lights all round, loved being snug in the corner of the taxi, it was like being a lord or a king. He should have experienced the same feeling when Dave drove him in the Citroen but instead he always felt like a child: vulnerable and somewhat apprehensive.

'Here we are, young sir,' the driver said, leaning out and opening the door. He seemed to have recovered his composure.

Philip stepped out on to the pavement and then remembered the next part of the test. 'Please will you wait?' he said. 'I've got to fetch something and then will you take me back.'

'Right you are. I'll be here.'

The shop was as he remembered it. Above the window was a hand-painted sign that read: A Loewenthal. Pet shop. On a board next to the door a second sign read: Guinea-pigs. Gerbils. Rabbits. Hamsters. White mice. Budgies. Goldfish. Tropical fish. Fighting fish. A third notice on the other side of the door read: Importer of Exotic animals since 1934.

He paused and looked into the window. Often Mr Loewenthal had a basket of King Charles puppies or black and white kittens in the window which drew old ladies and young children, but today there were only a few cages containing mice and a pair of West African cane rats. He pushed open the door and heard the bell ring above him, but the small shop was empty. He stood there for a minute or two not knowing what to do. Then he thought of the bell and he opened the door and closed it again. Still no one came. He felt a slight flutter of panic. What should he do? What would Dick have done?

He went out to the taxi. 'Finished already?' the driver said, folding up the *Daily Mirror*.

'There's no one there.'

'But it's open, innit? You went in.'

'Yes, but Mr Loewenthal isn't there.'

'Did you give a call? A shout like?'

'No.'

'Ah, well, that's it then. Probably in the back. You'd best shout.'

Philip went back into the shop but still the bell brought no one. A door behind the counter led into another part of the building. When they had come for the other pets, Mr Loewenthal had disappeared into the back each time and come back with a box. 'Mr Loewenthal!' Philip called softly. 'Mr Loewenthal!' A parakeet in a cage near the door shrieked with laughter and he felt his heart race. Somewhere in the room behind the shop he heard a noise of boxes being pulled about.

'Mr Loewenthal!' he shouted, this time louder.

The noise ceased and he heard footsteps. The door behind the counter opened and a woman came into the shop; she was holding a small crocodile in her right hand. 'Yes?' she said. 'Is there something?'

'I've come for —' The combination of the woman and the reptile momentarily confused him for she, too, appeared to be an exotic specimen. He guessed she must be Mr Loewenthal's wife for she was almost an exact replica. He was reminded of a large plum over which had been draped a fur coat. She was much younger than Mr Loewenthal but just as rotund. She wore a collection of thin gold chains around her neck and a ring on each finger. He had the impression of great untidiness from her dark hair that seemed not to have been brushed that day, to her clothes which hung on her as on a washing-line. He stared first at her and then at the crocodile. It was about a foot long, and she was holding it so that he could see its yellow belly. It didn't look like any picture he had ever seen, for the long jaws seemed to spread out at the very tip.

'Yes?' she said again.

Philip had come halfway across London and now he found he was unable to speak. She frightened him. There was something not quite normal about her. And it wasn't because she had a reptile in her hand. It was her eyes; they had a wildness in them, a sort of madness.

'I've come for …' He dried up again.

'Get out!' she said. 'Go away!'

He felt himself about to be attacked and, turning, would have fled, had he not seen, behind the counter, against the back wall, half a dozen labelled boxes. On one was his own name. He paused and pointed.

'I've come to pick that up,' he managed to say.

She bent and looked at the label. 'Blanchet?' she said. 'Eaton Square?'

'Yes.'

She put a hand to her head. 'I'm sorry. Please ... My husband is sick.'
'Mr Loewenthal?'
'You know him?'
'Yes.'

She tapped the left side of her chest. 'They took him to hospital at lunchtime. In an ambulance. And Harold, the boy who cleans, doesn't come until tomorrow.' Philip saw that it was not so much wildness as a mixture of despair and harassment that filled her eyes. 'Forgive me for shouting.'

She pulled the ticket off the box. 'Take it then.' He picked it up and found it was much heavier than he had imagined it would be.

'Can you manage?'
'There's a taxi outside.'
'Do we send you a bill?'
'Yes, please. Mr Loewenthal knows.'

She opened the door for him and Philip carried the box out to the cab. He put it down on the seat beside him and thought he heard the faintest scratch-scratch.

'Home?' said the driver.

'Yes, please,' Philip said. There was more authority in his tone than before.

*

Dave stood just inside the entrance to Terminal 2 watching the incoming passengers from the Madrid flight. He had never seen Jacmel before but Louise had described him in detail and Dave was certain he would pick him out. But the speed with which the passengers came through the Green exit made it impossible and instead he left his position and drifted towards the inquiry desk. The announcement came almost immediately.

'Would Mr Jacmel's driver please come to the central inquiry desk. Thank you.'

He pushed forward towards the desk but had not gone more than a few steps when he felt someone grip his arm from the back. He winced and turned angrily. He saw a short thickset man in his late forties or early fifties with steel grey hair cut *en brosse*, a heavy moustache and pale blue eyes. He was dressed in a grey suit and grey topcoat and wore a grey hat. In the light of the Terminal his skin seemed grey, a dry dusty grey, granitic.

'You are Dave.' His voice was surprisingly soft for his build. He looked as though he might have been a tough ex-paratroop sergeant and Dave had expected a grating delivery. The man moved his hand from Dave's arm and said, 'I am Jacmel.'

Dave was disconcerted. Louise had said nothing about a moustache. He would never have recognized Jacmel. Now he was not sure whether to shake hands with him or not. The French were always shaking hands, weren't they? But Jacmel did not extend a hand.

'You have the motor?' he said, and glanced at his watch.

'In the car park.'

'Let us go. We are late.'

Dave drove back the way he had come less than thirty minutes earlier. He had expected Jacmel to sit in front with him and again had been slightly disconcerted when he had got into the back seat. Who the hell did he think he was? He was no better than Dave himself. Maybe the French didn't know no better. As he turned on to the motorway he snatched a glance into the mirror, twisting so that he could see Jacmel. Once he had managed to see Ruth hitching up her tights and had nearly gone into the back of a lorry. Now all he could see were Jacmel's hands resting on his crossed legs. They were square and blunt and in keeping with the rest of his frame. There was something about the Frenchman that gave him what his Dad had once called 'the disquiets'. All the way along the motorway Jacmel had remained silent and he felt an increasing need to break the tension by talking. Manners, he thought angrily. No bloody manners. But what did you expect from Frogs?

''Ave a good flight?' he said at last as they neared the Chiswick flyover.

'Thank you,' Jacmel said.

Dave waited but nothing further emerged. What the bloody hell did thank you mean? He hadn't given him nothing. He swung down Earl's Court Road and then along the Embankment past Chelsea Bridge where he turned left and made his way into the maze of Pimlico streets that lie between the river and Buckingham Palace Road. He went north and stopped near the BOAC air terminal. Jacmel got out and came to the driver's window.

'I will see you at the house,' he said.

'You know the way then?'

'Well enough.'

Dave reached into his jacket pocket and took out two bunches of keys. 'Yellow Cortina estate,' he said, giving him one set. 'Everything as you wanted. Hired for a week. All above board.' He handed over the second set of keys. 'Third floor Keats. Rent paid in advance for three months. Nothing overlooking it.'

'I shall see you at the house.' Jacmel turned away, a grey figure with a lightweight grey suitcase in his hand, and disappeared in the direction of Alderney Street. The winter evening was drawing in and the street lamps were haloed by misty vapour. Dave watched him until he disappeared around the corner and then with an irritated shrug drove off towards Eaton Square.

Jacmel continued for about a hundred metres before turning into a National Car Park in the basement of a block of council flats. The West Indian attendant was in his small wood and glass office reading a tattered copy of that morning's *Sun*. He looked vaguely at Jacmel, nodded, and turned back to his paper. Jacmel walked along the parking bays until he came to the yellow Ford. He unlocked the tailgate, swung it up and dropped his suitcase into the back, closed it, unlocked the driver's door and got in, closed it, and sat in the cocoon of cold silence. He sat like that for a few moments as though almost unwilling to move; as though the next move would begin a chain of irrevocable events. But he did move. He reached over to the glove compartment, unlocked it and opened the flap. The revolver was pushed to the back and all he could see was the butt. He looked over his shoulder but the West Indian was engrossed in his newspaper. Jacmel slid out the gun and placed it on his lap. He flicked open the breech and turned the cylinders. Five full chambers. He closed it, allowed the hammer to come down slowly on the one empty chamber, then tucked the gun into the top of his trousers and buttoned his jacket and topcoat. He started the car, paid the overnight fee, and turned in the direction of the river.

Shakespeare Close had been built soon after the Second World War and for a number of years had been the largest block of apartments in Europe. It was divided into six 'houses', separate blocks with their own entrances, all named after poets: Shelley, Wordsworth, Byron, Coleridge, Tennyson and Keats. Keats House faced on to the plane trees of the Embankment and the black waters of the Thames.

Jacmel drove into Keats House parking area. The block was oblong in shape and had four entrances, two along its length and one at each end. It also had four sets of lifts, two centrally, one at each end, to correspond roughly with the doors. But the building had only one porter who sat in a small cubicle just inside the main doors. The cubicle was in a lobby and from the lobby it was impossible to see the doors at each end of the building. Tenants could reach any of the four floors without the porter ever knowing. It was for this reason that Jacmel had chosen Keats House.

He left the car, walked to the end of the building and entered the small side door. It was exactly as he remembered it from his visit a month earlier. He pressed the button at the lift in front of him and went up to the third floor. He looked at the key. No. 309. He turned left along the corridor, opened the door of 309 and let himself in. He had seen no one and no one had seen him.

He was in a two-bedroomed, furnished flat. Immediately facing him was a small kitchen and bathroom, to his right two bedrooms, to his left a large lounge-dining-room. He went first into the bedroom and then the lounge. In each room he bent and felt the central heating radiators, then he turned up the thermostat. In the second bedroom he switched on a floor humidifier. He went into the kitchen and opened the fridge. It was filled to capacity with milk. He opened a store cupboard and saw the usual staples as well as a dozen large packs of muesli.

When he had gone over each room with care, checking the windows — the drop was sheer to the Embankment, there were no balconies — beds, towels, television, he glanced at his watch and sat down at the telephone table in the lounge. He did not need to look up the number; he knew it by heart. He dialled and heard the brr-brr at the other end of the line. He touched his forehead with his fingers and they came away wet.

*

In the house in Eaton Square Dick Howard was cleaning a rifle. The thoughts about Africa, the letter from M Barbot, the unpleasant scene with Louise, had all helped to unsettle him, so he had turned the day into a *jour avec*. He'd already had one brandy, which meant that the fast had been broken, so he had poured himself a whisky and soda and taken down one of the rifles from the wall-rack. He had always found that handling the guns had a calming effect on him. He had brought out the oil, the brushes, the rags and the pull-through, and was busily cleaning the gun. He loved the smell of gun oil.

He was so absorbed that he did not at first hear the telephone. Gradually its insistent ringing worked its way into his mind and he found himself waiting for Louise to answer it. When she did not he put down the gun and the cleaning cloth and went upstairs wondering where she was. He could have sworn she had not gone out.

He picked up the receiver. 'Hello.'

''Ullo. M'sieu 'Oward?'

'Yes. Who's that? Mr Blanchet?' It didn't sound like Michel's voice but there was no doubt that it was French. 'Here is M Barbot. I wrote to you a letter. Did you get it?' Howard's heart gave a lurch. 'Yes … yes, I got it.'

'Good.'

'I thought you said you were coming —'

'Yes. I thought so too. Next week. But I must be in Athens. So I am here now. Can we meet?'

Howard paused. 'I expect so.'

'When?'

'You mean today?'

'It is inconvenient?'

'Well … '

'Tonight then?'

He had promised Philip to help him rearrange the menagerie. He couldn't disappoint him the moment their weekend got under way. 'I'm afraid tonight is impossible. What about tomorrow?'

'Alas, tomorrow I am gone. It is only for fifteen minutes. Have you thought about what I suggested?'

'Yes, yes, I have. It's only that —'

'And then I must go to Nairobi and Mombasa.'

Nairobi. Mombasa. There was Hutchins in Nairobi. Willis in Mombasa. Richards too, probably. Any one of them could run a two-penny ha'-penny game park on the edge of Lake Kivu. And they'd probably heard about it already.

'I am not far from you,' the voice said. 'The Carlton Tower Hotel. You know of it?'

'Yes. It's not far.' He looked at his watch. Philip would be well on his way.

'I am here now if that suits you.'

'Well, I suppose. Yes. All right. But I'm looking after a child, you see, and I can't be long.'

'I understand. We have a drink. Ten minutes. We look at each other. I tell you one or two things. Then back to your child. *Bien.* I will be in the cocktail lounge. A window table. It is on the first floor.'

'I know it.'

'I leave my name with the *maitre d'hotel.*'

'All right. I'll be there in … ten minutes?'

'*Tres bien. Au revoir.*'

'Goodbye.' Howard put the receiver down. 'Louise!' he called in the direction of the kitchen. 'Louise, are you there?'

The maid had been standing just inside the kitchen door, listening. Now she walked to the table and moved some crockery, made a noise. 'Louise!'

'*Oui?*'

He put his head round the door. 'Louise, I have to go out for half an hour. Philip may come back while I'm gone. Tell him not to open the box. Follow? Tell him to wait until I get back.'

She did not answer and he thought she was sullen after their argument. 'Comprendo?' he said harshly.

'*Je comprends*!'

He closed the kitchen door with a sharp bang and went downstairs to get his coat. As he closed the door of the house behind him he began to feel the fluttering of panic. What was he going to say? How was he going to answer Barbot's question? Should he say yes? Should he say no? Maybe? Perhaps? I'll think about it? These people didn't hang around and he wasn't the only ageing white hunter looking for a cushy number. But was it a cushy number? That's what he had thought about Gametrails Safari Hotel in Kenya — and look what had happened. Anyway, there was more to it than that.

There were no cabs in sight and he began to walk as quickly as he could in the direction of Cadogan Square, trying to keep his head up, trying not to shuffle.

*

In apartment 309 in Keats House, about a mile and a half from Eaton Square, Jacmel pulled open the A-D section of the telephone directory and riffled through the pages until he came to the number of the Carlton Tower Hotel. He dialled and asked for reception.

'My name is Barbot,' he said. 'I have a message for a Mr 'Oward. I will meet him in your cocktail lounge, a window table, but I am held up for fifteen minutes. Please ask him to wait.' When he had rung off he walked to the window and stared sombrely out at the water. So far everything was perfect. His hand went to his jacket pocket and he pulled out a crushed packet of cheap Spanish Celtas, lit one and picked several strands of tobacco from his tongue. He looked at the badly made cigarette. Its tobacco was loose, some had fallen out into the pack. Not long now, he thought, and he'd be able to afford a better brand; he'd be able to afford a lot of things he'd not been having lately. He'd be able to eat sucking-pig at Botins again. Be able to buy a new suit — the one he had on was all that was left of the palmy days, in fact his whole outfit, while it gave an air of some wealth, was all he had left. He'd have a couple of suits made in Paris, and a shirt or two from Sulka ... he caught himself. Not Paris. Never Paris. Rome then. And shoes. And he'd be able to take Isabel to Puerto de Naveccerada for a weekend's skiing. That would be good. But thinking about Isabel reminded him of Louise. God knew what he would do about Louise.

He looked at his watch. Six minutes since he had spoken to Howard, time enough for him to have got clear of the house. Once again he checked the revolver, then he put on his coat, let himself out of the flat and went down in the lift to the car. He saw no one. No one saw him.

As he drove down Belgrave Road his thoughts went back to Louise. She *was* Algeria for him. In those last days before independence when he would have been shot by both sides if he had put his nose into the streets, she had hidden him. While Algeria crumbled into a Moslem state, while his brothers, the *pieds noirs* and the army deserters fought a last-ditch stand to save the country from being dragged away from France, he had spent days on end in bed with her. It was ironic that at the time when he had been in most danger, in the week after he had blown up the oil dumps in Oran harbour, he had had one of the best times of his life. He had never enjoyed a woman more. It was summer and she had a cool apartment on the heights above the old city. When they needed food she would go out into the warm dusk and come back with new bread, wine, *saucisson de campagne*, a few onions, olives ... Sometimes they pulled the bed to the window and made love looking out over the city, letting the evening breeze off the sea dry their sweat.

But that was 1962 and Louise had been twenty-six. Things were different now. He had been shocked when he had seen her a month earlier. He knew she would not be much more than forty but she looked worn out. Isabel, on the other hand, though only a few years younger than Louise, seemed in her twenties by comparison. That is what money could do, he thought.

He paused at the traffic lights on Buckingham Palace Road, seeing the mist swirl round Victoria Coach Station and he shivered. After Algeria most other climates were too chilly, yet he had to admit that he felt more alive, more mentally alert than he had for a long time. Perhaps he needed action and danger, as in the old days, to give life its full taste.

The old days. Less than twenty years ago, yet another age. The change had been abrupt. They had a vineyard in those days, started by Jacmel's great-grandfather a few kilometres from Miliana. When Jacmel inherited it there were more than five hundred hectares under vines and the wine they produced had a reputation that was growing to equal that of the Clos Fallet or the Coteaux de l'Harrach.

From his childhood Jacmel had worked on the great vineyard that lay under the hot African sun, knowing that one day it would be his. He had loved it with the passion of someone who knows exactly what he wants from life and that he will be doubly blessed by getting it. In 1958 his father died and he took over.

He threw himself into the reorganization and improvement of the vineyard, building a new cooling system, a new *fuloir*, putting in stainless steel fermentation tanks, replanting areas with *shiraz* vines. He was in the midst of this work when de Gaulle made his speech on Algerian self-determination and the days of the French presence in Algeria were numbered.

In the space of a few months Jacmel's dream turned into a nightmare. Early in 1960 he helped other European settlers defy the government by putting up barricades in Algiers, with the passive complicity of the French army. But it had not helped. A year later French voters approved de Gaulle's policy in a referendum and four weeks later the *Organisation de l'Armée Secrete*, the O.A.S., was formed to fight the French separatists and the Moslem community.

At first Jacmel had stayed among his vines. Helping to build barricades was one thing, making plastic explosive another. But slowly he began to realize that if Algeria became independent he would lose the vineyard and with it everything he had ever wanted. It was then he decided to fight.

Like many other recruits to the O.A.S. he started by carrying messages, arranging clandestine meetings, helping to run 'safe' houses for hunted *pieds noirs*, but soon he worked his way up in the organization until he finally reached the apogee — or as some Frenchmen said, the nadir — membership of the Delta Commando which robbed banks, blew up soft targets, kidnapped and killed Moslem leaders or French *barbouzes*, the counter terrorists who tried to infiltrate O.A.S. ranks. He had enjoyed neither the robbery nor the killing. He told himself there was no other way. Six months after joining the O.A.S. he was on the French Government's 'Most Wanted' list, and after he had blown up the oil storage tanks in Oran harbour both the F.L.N. and the French Army organized an intensive search for him. It was then that Louise hid him.

When Algeria became independent in July 1962 and the Moslems began to cut a few white throats he had decided to get out. He paid one last visit to his vineyard. He and Louise drove out in a small Panhard with false plates, stopping well away from the farmhouse.

It was warm in the late afternoon with a sirocco blowing from the south, and the vineyard was deserted. The vines were heavy with black grapes. As they walked towards the house he could feel the heat of the soil come up through his shoes. The blood-red sun was sinking behind a range of low hills casting the house and winery into dusty grey shadow. This was the time of day his father had come out on to the veranda and drunk several glasses of iced wine and soda. From a distance the house looked just the same as ever, but as he drew closer he could see that the shutters and the windows had been smashed. F.L.N. slogans had been daubed on the walls. Inside, the rooms were shattered. Broken furniture lay everywhere. He and Louise had walked through the rooms in silence. Outside, he went first to the pressing-room then to the vat house. Vandals had again anticipated him but there was evidence that later hands had tried to put right some of the damage. He guessed what had happened. Rumours were rife that workers' cooperatives had been formed to take over the vineyards once the owners had fled.

He had stood outside the winery for a long time then abruptly he had turned to Louise and said, 'Come. Help me.' They went to the shed where the tractors and the spraying equipment were housed. This was one area he had not modernized and he showed her how to operate a hand pump that raised gasoline and diesel oil from their storage tanks on the ground, to tanks on high platforms. He then brought in one of the tractors with the big sprayer which was normally used to spray the vines with copper sulphate against mildew. The sprayer's tanks were empty and into these he now fed diesel and gasoline from the high tanks.

There was a moon that night otherwise he would not have been able to do what he did, since the lights of the tractor would have drawn labourers from nearby villages. He worked without stopping except to refill the sprayer tanks. All that night Louise pumped and he sprayed and by dawn he had covered a series of strips, soaking the vines in the mixture. At first light he knew it would be too dangerous to continue so he put the tractor away and poured what remained of the mixture into the vats holding last year's wine.

As the sun's rim broke the eastern horizon he put a match to the vines nearest the house. The petrol, held by the heavier diesel fuel, had not vaporized and now it went up like a bomb, each vine exploding into flame and smoke. The fire raced down the rows and sparks were carried from one fuel-soaked strip of vineyard to the next on the driving wind. Soon, whole areas of vines had caught alight.

The wind was blowing the flames in the direction of the house but Jacmel did not wait to see it burn. He and Louise had got into the car and had driven away in the direction of Algiers and he had not looked back once at the great pall of smoke that rose up into the sky.

The burning of the vineyard marked the end of a phase in Jacmel's life; nothing was ever to be the same again.

He turned the Cortina into Eaton Square and began looking for the house. It faced north. There it was, the Citroen was outside as arranged. He stopped, went up the stairs and rang the bell.

Louise must have been waiting just inside the door for it opened immediately. She pulled him in.

' *Entre vitel Mon Dieu*! *Que je suis contente de te revoir!*'

She closed the door and put her back to it. Her sallow face was strained.

'*Qu'est- ce qu'il y a?*'

'*L'enfant est sorti. J'ai pas pu l'arreter. Je suis* —'

From the bottom of the stairs Dave said, 'Remember our agreement? You no spikada French and I no spikada Pakistani. Right?'

Jacmel looked at him without expression, then Louise said, 'Come upstairs.'

In the kitchen Jacmel said, 'Tell me.'

'The little bugger went out,' Dave said.

'You …' he pointed at Dave. 'You be quiet for a little.' He turned to Louise. 'Tell me.'

*

At this time, in Hampstead, the lights were already on in the Institute of Toxicology which lay between Heath Street and the Whitestone Pond. In the late afternoon gloom the mist had settled on Hampstead Hill and the outlines of the Institute were blurred. It was not a big building, nothing like the Pasteur Institute in Paris with which it closely worked. In the days of Empire its grant had been substantial but since then Treasury money had only come in dribbles and the Institute now barely survived and was little known outside its own particular sphere.

In her office on the first floor Dr Marion Stowe, its assistant director, was dictating into a recording machine. 'Antivenom is effective in relieving hypertension and bradycardia provided that the circulating volume is restored with intravenous fluid, preferably fresh whole blood or plasma expanders stop paragraph Antivenoms are not thought to prevent local tissue damage though four of the patients bracket cases three to six see Nigerian research BMJ Warrell, Ormerod, Davidson twenty December seventy five close bracket who had severe local envenoming —' The telephone on her desk began to ring. She looked at her watch and smiled. Susan home from school. She thought of the dark cheerless flat in Belsize Park and again — as she often did — felt a sense of guilt at the thought of her daughter returning each day from school to an empty flat. But what could she do? How could she change things? She pulled off her left ear-ring and answered the phone.

'Hello, darling,' she said. 'Everything all right? Have a good day? Stew? Oh, poor you. Anything special you'd like? What about some Chinese? I could pass the Tai Tong on the way home. Sweet and sour chicken? Good, yes, and pancake rolls. What about beef and green peppers, you like that? I'll get one of each. We'll make our own rice. Anything on the box? Blue Peter isn't on, is it? No, of course not, that was yesterday. Anyway, it's Friday so I won't be late. See you soon, darling. 'Bye.' She put down the telephone and automatically put on her ear-ring again. Ten years old, she thought. My God, in a few years she'll be gone and then what? She felt a sense of desperation. Thoreau was only half right, she thought. All women, too. She picked up the microphone and began dictating again. 'If necrosis does develop immediate extensive surgical ... debridement ... uh ... followed by split skin ... ah ...' She switched it off. She could not concentrate now. Monday would do just as well.

She sat back in her desk-chair and stretched, feeling restless. She got up and walked to the window. She could see nothing but her own reflection in the long panes: a woman of middle height, thirty-four years old, in a long shapeless white coat. Irritated, she took off the coat and threw it on to a chair. That was better, she could see herself more clearly; she had a waist once more. She ticked off the points with a lack of sentiment: hair, rich, auburn; face, good eyes, large mouth, high cheek bones — too definite for beauty but not bad. Tim had once said she looked Byzantine. It was a nice thing to say. Bosom, good, high. Hips too broad. Tell-tale creases on her skirt. Stretch marks on her tummy, too, but only she knew that. And Tim, of course. Good legs. Feet too large. On the whole B+ or, if the day was kind, A–. She decided to go home and went to the lab across the hallway. Professor Taylor-Askew, the Director of the Institute, had not been in for nearly a month and with his eyes steadily becoming worse, was unlikely to return. Idly, she wondered if she would get the job. Did she want it? Did she want to be cooped up here for another twenty-six years before retirement age? Once she became director she would have even less time with Susan, and as for marriage ... well, there didn't seem much prospect of that anyway.

It was a small laboratory, only three assistants. There had once been five, but that was before Marion's day. Joe Truman was bent over his microscope, unmoving, as though cast in bronze; Phyllis, who had taken her doctorate three months before and was getting itchy feet, was washing out some flasks and the Rajah, C. C. Mukerjee, who made the tea, drove the van, looked after the specimens in the small room next door which they called 'the zoo', was unpacking the latest batch of venom from the Sparrman Institute in Port Elizabeth. It was a scene unchanged for the past five years and sometimes Marion was grateful, for it gave her a sense of continuity and security, and at other times she felt repelled by its sameness; it was a dichotomy she had never resolved.

'Didn't Loewenthal have something for us today?' she asked Mr Mukerjee. 'Wasn't there a shipment due from Durban?'

He looked up from his unpacking. 'I have been,' he said.

'Everything all right?'

'One is looking sick.'

'How many were there?'

'Three.'

'You should have called me.' Frowning, she went into the adjoining room, the 'zoo', and closed the door behind her. It was very warm. Around the walls were fifteen or twenty small wooden crates, each with a trap-door at the top held by a metal catch. One side was open but covered by fine wire mesh; in each crate was a snake. As she walked past the cages she was aware of the jewel-like eyes and the flickering tongues. There were Russell's Vipers, coral snakes, rattlers, taipans, Egyptian cobras, puff adders. The three new crates were on a shelf on the left of the room and she crossed to inspect them. They still had their customs forms stapled to their sides and the words 'Dangerous Reptiles' stencilled on to the wood. There was no movement in any of the crates and she craned forward to look more closely. The first held a *boomslang*, the elegant green and yellow tree snake that had been thought only slightly venomous until a few years before when one had killed a famous American herpetologist. It lay coiled upon itself regarding her with unwinking eyes. It didn't look too bad after its long flight. Nor did the night adder in the second cage. But the Rajah seemed right about the occupant of the third cage. It lay limply, its head tucked into the far corner of the crate. Marion thought there was something odd about it and it wasn't only the way it was lying. The light in the room was dim so she switched on a powerful centre lamp and went back to inspect the snake. Her frown deepened. Then she realized what was bothering her: size. This was a small snake, not more than three feet long; shiny black, small head. And it looked like a ... but she wasn't sure what it was. She went back to her room and pulled down Fitzsimons' *Snakes of Southern Africa* and paged through it until she came to *colubridae*. She found the picture she wanted facing page 121. She held the book up to the light and glanced back and forth from the picture to the inert body of the snake. It matched. She was looking at a harmless black house snake of the type that was found throughout South Africa. But the Institute never ordered harmless snakes. She flicked back a few pages and under Field Notes read: 'Similar in habits to the Common Brown House Snake, but not nearly so common nor so widespread as the latter. Like other members of the genus, it has a quiet docile disposition and seldom attempts to bite, even when first handled.' There was not much more so she turned to the entry for Brown House Snake and quickly read the columns of text. Apparently they were often tamed and used almost as pets by some South African farmers who kept them to control vermin in and around the homestead. Then another line caught her attention. 'In its darker phases this species is often mistaken for the young of cobra or mamba and, unfortunately, summarily killed for such.'

She closed the book and went into the laboratory. 'Have you got the waybill for that Durban shipment?' she said to Mr Mukerjee. He rummaged on his desk, brought up a sheaf of papers and handed them to her. One *boomslang*, she read, that was correct. One night adder, that was also correct. One black mamba ... it wasn't like Loewenthal to make mistakes. 'Mr Loewenthal's got it wrong,' she said. 'He's sent us a black house snake.' C.C. stood up and looked at the waybill and then at Marion. He sucked noisily through his teeth.

'Mr Loewenthal was not there,' he said. 'I am being dealt with by Mrs Loewenthal.'

'That explains it, then.'

'Must I take it back?' There was a look of sullen resistance in his eyes.

'It'll be all right here for the weekend,' she said. 'Probably better off than in the shop. Leave it till Monday.'

The expression gave way to one of happiness. 'Very well. Very well.'

She looked at her watch. 'I'm off,' she said. 'I'm going to see Professor Taylor-Askew.' The lie slipped out easily. 'Joe, if you're last, will you see the lights are put out?'

Joe grunted and she went into her room to get her coat. ''Night everyone,' she said, passing through the lab and out on to the landing and down the staircase. The mist was much thicker now. It made everything very still. She could hardly hear the cars churning up Heath Street at the start of the Friday rush hour; there was only the drip-drip from the huge oaks that surrounded the Institute. Sweet and sour chicken, she said to herself as she crossed to the car park. And beef with green peppers. Pancake rolls. She wondered if they had enough soya sauce at home, perhaps she should stop in at the supermarket and pick up a bottle.

As she let herself into the driving-seat of her Renault coupé — the one extravagance she had allowed herself in the past three years — she began to think of the weekend. Two whole days of Susan to herself. What would they do? Her mind was a blank. She should have planned something, but the paper on monovalent antisera on which she was working and which she was to read at the International Conference in Brussels the following month had taken all her attention. Movies? No, too much like television. Theatre? Susan wanted to see *Jesus Christ, Superstar*. There would be a matinée on Saturday. That was one thing. Sunday? Lazy day just being together. Lunch out, perhaps, or brunch at the Café Royal. Susan would love that. Then Monday and school again and the weekend would be gone;

Monday, bloody Monday. She fumbled in her bag for the car keys and then stopped. Something was happening on Monday. What ... ? She remembered: she would have to remind the Rajah to take that snake back to Loewenthal's and get the one they had ordered. Incredible making a mistake like that: substituting a harmless black house snake for a mamba. There couldn't be too many house snakes in Britain. She had never seen one before herself and Fitzsimons' book had said they were rare even in Africa. It must have been a special order, probably wanted as a pet by someone who knew something about snakes. Well, whoever it was would be frustrated when they went to the shop to — She shivered violently, and it was not caused by the cold. *What if? What if? What if?* The phrase was repeating itself in her brain like a drumbeat. But it was impossible. It could not happen. Why not? The wrong snake had been sent to the Institute; why couldn't the error work the other way? Was it not possible that whoever had ordered a black house snake had been given a black mamba by mistake? No, it wasn't possible. Anyone who knew snakes well enough to have ordered such a species would know or *should* know a black mamba at a glance; the size alone would tell that it wasn't a house snake. Unless it was a young mamba. Loewenthal couldn't make a mistake like that, not with all his years of experience. But the mistake could have been made in Africa. Sometimes the snakes were packed in their travelling cages and labelled by the catcher out in the bush. And in any case, Loewenthal had not been in his shop.

She opened the car door and hurried back into the Institute. As she did so she looked at her watch and made sure there was still time to catch Mrs Loewenthal before the shop closed.

*

In the Gerald Road Police Station which lies in the heart of Westminster a long stone's throw from Belgrave Square, Eaton Square, Victoria Station and the shabby huddle of Pimlico, Inspector Alec Nash was about to go off duty when the telephone on his desk rang. He'd had a bad week. On Tuesday a parcel bomb had exploded in a parked car outside the gates of Parliament, killing a traffic warden and injuring a passing cyclist, and since then there had been very little sleep for anyone in Gerald Road. Nash, a tall man in his early forties with a craggy face and big, raw-boned frame, stood staring at the telephone, tempted to ignore it. He told himself he was off-duty anyway. Then he remembered that Mary, his wife, was going to phone about Jim, and as he remembered his heart gave a lurch. Today was the day for the meeting with Jim's probation officer; the big day, the one that Nash had been dreading ever since the magistrates' hearing. In the course of his life in the police Nash had had to deal with dozens of probation officers. Sometimes he had considered them a soft option when one took into account the number of young villains on the streets, and he had tended to treat them with a certain coolness. How ironic that now a probation officer was all that stood between Jim and prison. He dreaded the scene to come: he and Mary on the sofa, his son Jim, tall, gangling, lank of hair, probably half drunk, sitting on one of the upright chairs, and the probation officer — Arkwright, was it? — solemn, earnest, with that look of pity in his eyes which Nash had seen so many times. How did you explain to him how it was that you had a son of seventeen who was already on the way to being an alcoholic and that when he'd had a few he did irresponsible things like taking other people's cars? How did a police inspector with two commendations for bravery and a spotless record explain that?

He picked up the receiver. Chief Inspector Neill's voice came through loud and clear. 'Alec?'

'Yes.'

'Thought you might have gone.'

'No.'

Neill chuckled. 'Don't take it so hard. I know you're tired, but don't you want to be commissioner one day?'

'No.'

'Look, there's a woman on my other line. Says she's doctor someone or other. Talking about snakes. She's been through to Central and they've pushed her on to us. Probably nothing in it, but I've got a meeting in two minutes with Benson of the Bomb Squad. See what she wants, will you?'

'I've got an appointment in thirty minutes.'

'Now look, Alec, I'm ...'

'An important one.'

There was a pause. 'Jim?'

'Yes.'

'Okay. Well, just see what she wants. If there's anything to it, pass it on to Harris. He's due back from Acton in a few minutes.'

There was a double click on the line, then a woman's voice saying, 'Hello ...'

'Inspector Nash here.' He drew a pad towards him. 'Could I have your name, please.'

'Stowe. Dr Marion Stowe. I work at the Institute of Toxicology in Hampstead.'

He wrote down the word 'toxicology', and then the word 'Jim' and stared at it for a moment until he realized what he had done and blacked out both words. 'Poisons,' he said.

'That's right.'

'How can I help you?'

She talked quickly and fluently. She had a pleasant voice, he thought. Soft and low, just the sort he liked. He began to form a picture of her at the other end of the line. Soft, yielding, warm, competent. Was there humour in her tone? Did she have a child? Had she gone wrong somewhere, too? Why was there no one to tell you? Abruptly she stopped and there was silence on the line. 'Are you there?' she said.

'Yes, I'm here.' He had been half listening and now he said, 'Let me see if I've got this right. You say you work with snake poisons?'

'Yes. It's one of our fields. We work on new strains of anti-venenes.'

'Anti-venenes ... those are — ?'

'You give them like injections,' she said impatiently. 'To people who are bitten by venomous snakes. I explained it.'

'Yes, I've got it. So you work with snakes in your Institute?'

'Yes.'

'And you say you got ...' he looked at his notes, 'a house snake instead of a ... mamba.'

'Yes.' Her tone was sharpening with irritation.

'The one being harmless, the other not.'

'That's an understatement. A black mamba is one of the three or four most venomous snakes in the world. It's also aggressive.'

'I see. And you think a mistake was made.'

'I don't think. I *know*.'

'Bear with me, doctor. Snakes aren't really my field.'

'Well, they're mine, and I'm telling you.'

Nash lit a cigarette and immediately regretted it. 'You say the mistake was made by Loewenthal's in Camden Town.'

'No, I didn't say that. I said a mistake had been made. *I* don't know who made it. Don't you understand, there's no time for a discussion. Anything could happen — '

'I assure you that a few more minutes now will mean a lot of time saved in the long —'

'It's already taken me ages to track down Mrs Loewenthal.'

'He is ill, is that right? The owner of the shop?'

'That's right. They've taken him to hospital. A heart attack. But that's not what I'm talking about. She gave the snake to a boy. She doesn't know if it was the mamba or not. They had a shipment of more than a dozen snakes. Half of them were harmless small constrictors for zoos. But she might have!' Her voice had risen.

'All right, Doctor. She might have. Let's hope she didn't. Can you give me the boy's name?'

'That's just it. I can't. Mrs Loewenthal doesn't remember. Except that it was French. She does remember the address was Eaton Square or Eaton Place because it's a posh address and it stuck.'

'Can't we get her down to the shop? Or can't she get someone she knows? You say there's a lad who cleans the cages and feeds the animals.'

'Look, she's almost hysterical, she thinks her husband is dying, and he may be for all I know. He weighs nearly twenty stone. It took me half an hour to get hold of her and get some sense out of her.'

Nash's mind began to work more quickly. A French name, he thought. There couldn't be too many in Eaton Square and Eaton Place. The Voters' Register would have all the names.

'Right,' he said. 'Leave it with me, Doctor.'

'But hurry,' she said. 'You've got to hurry.'

'Yes. One thing more, have you got any anti-whatever it is?'

'Anti-venene.'

'Anti-venene. Have you got any to counteract a mamba bite?'

'I've got some polyvalent anti-serum. It's not specific against mamba venom but against several neuro-toxic snake poisons.'

'Oh.' Nash found himself groping. 'Doctor, where can we reach you?' She gave him her home telephone number. 'You'll be there all evening?'

'Yes. But get in touch with Mr Beale of the London Zoo. They have set procedures for this sort of case. He'll organize the hospital. Probably St George's. Just hurry, for God's sake. Mamba venom is terribly fast. Depending on where he was bitten a child could be dead in a matter of minutes and no amount of anti-venene would save him.'

*

Dick Howard sat in the first floor cocktail bar of the Carlton Tower Hotel and stared out over the dark area of lawns and trees that made up Cadogan Square, then he looked at his watch for the tenth time in as many minutes. Philip would be getting home now. Must be, it was just after half-past five. Unless he had been caught up in traffic. He swirled the last of the ice that was all that was left of his Scotch on the rocks and considered ordering a second drink. Barbot's message had said he would be fifteen minutes late; he was already more than twenty. One more? Or leave now? For the past few minutes he had been feeling uneasy. It was the sort of sensation he had sometimes had in the bush, not often, three or four times in all. A feeling of slight fear, not even fear, more like anxiety, a kind of free-floating apprehension that all was not as it should be. Once, up on the Luangwa in what was then Northern Rhodesia he had been hunting a leopard wounded by a poacher's muzzle-loader. It had taken to a heavy patch of scrub and the dogs from the African village near by would not go in and bay it. So he went in alone. It was a stupid thing to do with a leopard. But he had gone. There was a lot of thorn, scrub thorn and acacia trees, and he had not been in there more than a minute or two when the same feeling had swept o ver him, he had felt unsettled, uneasy. He'd been following a blood spoor but as the feeling grew stronger he had stopped and looked carefully into the bush ahead. He had not been able to see anything. Then a compelling urge had caused him to turn round. The leopard was about twenty yards behind him, standing quite still in the dappled shade, regarding him with yellow eyes. Instinctively, he had brought up the gun and shot it and only afterwards, an hour or more later, he had begun to shiver violently with the reaction.

Now he had that same feeling that something was wrong. He paid for his drink and shrugged on his coat as he wrent down the stairs. There was a queue for taxis at the door and he turned right and made for Sloane Street. It was the middle of the rush-hour and the street was filled with home-going traffic. He saw a taxi and waved at it, then realized that the light was off. There were no others in sight and he turned back, walking as fast as he could, to take a short cut to Eaton Square.

*

As he was walking, Philip's taxi was coming along Grosvenor Gardens making for Belgrave Square. Philip was preoccupied by the movements which were coming from the box with greater regularity. The scratch-scratch was quite audible. The interior of the taxi was warm and he wished he could open a window. But he might catch cold, and it wasn't far to Eaton Square now; so he sat back trying to enjoy the last of his ride. He was feeling rather pleased with himself. It had been a long ride, there had been the unforeseen circumstances at the shop, yet everything had gone off smoothly.

'Right you are, then,' the taxi-driver said, leaning back and opening the door. Philip paid him and took the heavy box in his arms. 'You manage all right?'

'Yes, thank you.'

He had not reached the bottom of the steps leading up to their front door before Louise was out of the house and running down to him. She was trying to arrange her face in a smile of welcome.

'Quickly,' she said. 'It is cold for you. I help you.' She reached out to take the box but Philip shook his head.

'No.'

She held the door open and he saw Dave on the upstairs landing.

'Come, *chéri*,' she said. 'There is something I must tell you.'

Philip stopped outside Howard's door. 'Dick!' he called. 'Dick!'

'He has gone out,' Louise said.

'Where?'

She shrugged. 'I cannot say.'

Philip frowned. 'He said he would be here. He said he'd wait.'

'I do not know about that. A telephone call and then he tell me he is going out.'

'He said he'd be here.'

'Perhaps he will not be long.'

Disappointment washed over Philip. He had been expecting Dick to help him unpack the crate; expecting them to talk about a name; expecting them to be drawn close by the revelation of the shared secret. Now he wasn't there. He stood by Dick's door for a few moments longer and then began to climb the stairs. The box was very heavy and he could feel a series of jerky movements inside it.

'What you got there, Phil?' Dave said. 'Bengal tiger?' Philip hated Dave calling him Phil. Dick called him Phil. 'That's right,' he said.

'Present from Gandhi, was it?'

Philip reached the top of the stairs and turned into his own room. 'That's right.'

'You're a cheeky little sod, y'know that?'

'Leave him alone,' Louise said.

'Well, he bloody is.'

She followed Philip into the Great Ngorongoro Crater Menagerie. 'When you were gone I had a telephone call,' she said. 'My sister is sick.'

Philip put the box down on the floor. 'Oh.'

'The doctor is worried.'

'Where? In France?'

'No, *chéri*, here in London.'

'I didn't know you had a sister.'

'Oh, yes. I must go to see her. No ... do not take your coat off. You must come with me. I cannot leave you here.'

'Dick said he'd be here. He can't be long.'

'We must go quickly. Just for ten minutes. Dave will take us. It is impossible to get a taxi now.'

'You go.'

'But I cannot leave you. What would your mother say?'

Philip touched the box with his foot and felt an answering jerk. He was very warm in his coat and began to struggle out of it.

'Please, *chéri*, don't make trouble.'

'There was a taxi outside. The one I came in. Why didn't you take that?'

She looked confused for a moment. 'I didn't think. I was glad to see you; that was all I felt. Now please. She could be serious. Wouldn't you like another ride?'

'You didn't want me to go before.'

'That was by yourself.' Anger was seeping into her tone. 'Would you not like an ice-cream?'

He thought of that. He would not mind another drive. He'd like an ice-cream. And when Dick came in it would show him that he, Philip, could break arrangements too. But then he looked down at the box and the longing came over him to see the new member of his menagerie. And for that he would have to wait for Dick. He had been told several times not to open the box himself.

'No, thank you,' he said. 'I'll wait for Dick. I'll be all right.'

'Is it because of this?' she said, touching the box with her foot.

'He told me not to open it by myself. He said I was to wait for him.'

'I will open it.'

'He said *he* would.'

'He is not a god, Philippe! Anyone can open this.' She knelt on the floor. 'What is it, a mice? *Un lapin* — another rabbit?' She began to tear at the cardboard covering. Philip watched her.

'Another of your little furry animals? Stupid things. Dirty.' She pulled angrily at the cardboard, stripping it away from the wooden crate. Philip should have been annoyed at what she'd said, instead he watched her, a slight smile crossing his face.

At that moment the telephone shrilled in the hall. He heard Dave pick up the receiver and say, 'Hello.' Then he heard the receiver drop on to the hall table. Dave stood in the doorway, his face white. 'It's the police,' he said. 'It's the bloody coppers!'

Louise wrenched away the wooden lid and stood up. 'The police! *C'est impossible*!' She turned back to Philip and said in a hard voice, 'What have you been saying?'

As she did so a bar of shadow seemed to cross her, as though a cloud had raced across the sun; only there wasn't any sun. And then Philip saw that the drawstring of the travelling bag inside the crate had been loosened, probably when she had pulled off the lid, and that the shadow seemed to be coming from the bag. The three of them saw it at the same time, as it drew back its head to strike. Louise screamed.

Dick Howard was letting himself in the front door when he heard the scream. He thought, God, it's Phil! and ran up the stairs two at a time, oblivious of the tearing pain at his gut. He burst into Philip's room. The three of them were still in the middle of the menagerie. Louise was holding her arm and blood was seeping from two holes on the inner side of her left forearm.

'She's been bitten by a bloody snake,' Dave yelled.

Another man came in behind Howard. For a moment everything was confusion. 'I tell you, she was bitten by a bloody great black snake.' There was hysteria in Dave's voice.

'There's nothing to worry about,' Howard shouted. 'It's harmless. Where is it?'

They looked round the room.

But the snake had vanished.

Part II

Friday 6.12 p.m. – 7.22 p.m.

'It's a house snake,' Howard said. 'In Africa they keep them to eat rats and mice like we keep cats. D'you think I'd have ordered the boy a venomous snake! It's shock. That's all.'

He tried to recapture the fleeting seconds. He had come into the room after she had been bitten and had not seen the snake. But there was no venom in a house snake and it was her own bloody fault for interfering. And who the hell was this Frenchman? Boyfriend probably. Just like bloody servants, the moment the boss was away they took advantage.

Louise had been helped into a chair in the Great Ngorongoro Crater Menagerie; her face was chalky white and her lips were blue. She stared at them in terror, unable to speak.

'Did you see the snake?' Jacmel said.

Howard shook his head. 'Gone by the time I got here. Heard her scream though.'

'It was big?' Jacmel said.

'Huge,' Dave said. 'Bloody great monster.' His face was puffy with fright.

It would be a bloody python next, Howard thought. Thirty … forty … fifty feet. Bigger than the room … bigger than the house … You could never trust a layman to give you an accurate description of anything in the bush, especially if he was frightened. He remembered clients from his days in Kenya: buffalo the size of cathedrals with horns into the middle of next week, and lions as big as eland. Yet when you saw them they were creatures you knew, often smaller than average. It was the adrenalin talking.

'Black,' Jacmel said.

'Like a shadow,' Dave said.

'Tell me again.'

'She'd pulled off the top of this box —' Dave began.

'Travelling crate,' Philip said. He had been standing at the door between the two rooms while they spoke. When the snake had emerged from the bag he'd felt as though his chest was going to burst, the excitement had been so intense, and then events had moved so rapidly he had not time to think of his breathing. Miraculously, when the snake had disappeared and he could collect his thoughts, he found he was still breathing smoothly.

Dave turned on him. 'Why don't you shut your mouth —'

'You wouldn't say that if Mrs Blanchet was here,' Howard began.

'Well, it's true. It's his fault. Keeping snakes isn't natural.'

'Enough.' The word came from Jacmel, not loudly but carrying an imperative.

Dave looked at him defiantly. 'Well ...' he said, to have the last word.

Howard glanced thoughtfully at Jacmel and turned to Dave. 'Did you see what happened?'

'He didn't,' Philip said. 'I was the only one in the room. She took the top off the travelling crate. It caught the string on the bag and pulled it loose.'

Howard said gently, 'Did she know what was inside?' Philip shrugged, seeing which way the conversation was moving. 'I don't know.'

'You didn't tell her?'

'No.'

'Why didn't you stop her, Phil? You knew what was inside.'

'How was I to know she was going to open the bag? Anyway, I couldn't breathe.'

'Remember our pact,' Howard said. 'We said we weren't going to mention it the whole weekend.'

'Well, it's true.' The tone was sullen.

'All right, Phil, no one's blaming you.' The boy turned and went into his own room.

'I am dying,' Louise said.

'Nonsense,' Howard said. 'I keep telling you it's a harmless snake.'

'I am dying.'

'*C'est pas vrai, chérie, il y ...*'

'It's shock,' Howard said. 'But I think we should get some help.'

'Help?' Dave said. 'What do you mean, help?'

Howard ignored the chauffeur and moved past him to the telephone in the hall outside.

The receiver was on the table. He picked it up. 'Hello?' he said, but there was no response. He replaced it and checked the doctor's number on the list Ruth had given him. He began to dial.

'What are you up to?' Dave said. He was standing behind Howard.

Again Howard ignored him. 'I said, what are you doing?' Dave moved forward and grabbed the receiver, trying to wrench it from his hand. The two men struggled for a moment then Dave released the phone and, bending swiftly, dragged the wire from the wall breaking it at the junction box.

'You little twerp!' Howard said. Then Dave hit him; he was slightly off-balance so the blow was not as hard as it might have been but it landed in Howard's stomach, where the claws had churned, where the stitches had been, and it felt as though someone had directed an open flame to his muscles. He cried out and fell against the wall, both hands covering his abdomen. He looked down expecting blood to flow over the top of his trousers, but none appeared. He felt a tug at his arm and saw, in a kind of pain-filled haze, the figure of Philip.

'Dick, are you all right?'

He tried to speak but could only gasp.

'He's hurt!' Philip shouted. 'You've hurt him!'

'What is wrong?' Jacmel had left Louise to come out on to the landing. 'What has happened?'

'He hit him,' Philip said angrily. 'He hit Dick!'

Howard began to move along the wall, not knowing where he was going, but moving, sliding, trying to find in movement a panacea for the pain. He was giddy and his face was wet with sweat. He knew it had to stop. He also knew he could not take much more without fainting. The pain came in burning waves, each one threatening to engulf him.

Then he felt Philip's hand under his arm and he followed blindly. They moved back into the boy's bedroom and he felt himself being guided on to the bed. He lay back, closing his eyes, and Philip pushed the pillow under his head. In a few moments he began to feel better. Seemingly the pressure on his stomach had been relieved and the pain receded. He opened his eyes and saw Philip above him. The boy's face was drawn and white and he seemed to be breathing badly. Howard was about to say, 'Something's wrong, Phil,' when he realized this would be the worst thing. So he began to form a sentence which would have implied the opposite until he realized how absurd that would sound. There *was* something wrong; very badly wrong. He knew it; Philip knew it; and they, the others, knew that he and Phil knew it.

'In, out,' he gasped. 'One, two, one, two. Regular. Regular.' Talking made the pain come back but he went on. 'That's the boy. One, two, one, two.' He found he was whispering. 'In, out, in, out.' His stomach was suddenly gripped by heated pincers and he fainted. He could not have been unconscious for more than a minute or two but when he awoke the pain had slackened and he looked up into Philip's face. The boy had been bending over him and his hand was against Howard's cheek. Then Howard noticed that his breathing was becoming more regular. Thank God for that, anyway. There were two aerosol inhalers in the house but sometimes even they did not work. His mind was already making adjustments to the future. People don't pull telephones out of walls for fun. It had to be a robbery. Louise, Jacmel and Dave, all in it together. So Barbot was simply a fake. Jacmel, of course. Jacmel was Barbot. And they had wanted him out of the house for half an hour or so. It was all the time they needed. A few paintings, Ruth's jewellery in the wall safe in her bedroom, the silver, her gold lighter, bits and pieces; half an hour, no more, and when he came back Louise and Dave and Philip tied up, perhaps, locked in a room, and months later the share-out.

There was a sudden shout from the room next door and Howard turned so he could see through the door. Jacmel was standing in front of Dave and though he was a shade shorter he seemed taller and bigger. 'Muscles!' Jacmel was saying. Howard saw him make a muscle in his arm. 'In your head,' he said brutally. 'That is where your muscles are.'

'What you expect me to do?' Dave said angrily. 'Please, Mr 'Oward —' He mimicked Jacmel. 'Please don't use the telephone.'

'There is a time for muscle,' Jacmel said. His voice had dropped in pitch and Howard thought it sounded more menacing than when he shouted. 'What do you know of it? Nothing. Strong with old men!' He paused. 'I will tell you when to use your muscles. You understand that?'

The voice had dropped even farther and it sounded to Howard as though it was coming from far back in his throat, the way a lion sounds when it is angry. 'I will tell you when,' he went on. 'I will tell you what to do and what to say and how to act. You understand that? I will tell you when to breathe!'

Dave's voice, the aggression gone: 'You've got no right to talk to me like that.'

Jacmel said something that Howard could not hear. Then Dave's voice again: 'You mean we go on? But ...'

'Don't think; I will think. Go down to the front door and watch. We must go in five minutes, no later.'

Dave left the room. Five minutes. That meant they'd already stripped the house. Five minutes. What could he do? Stop them? How? He moved and the pain came back, not so badly this time, but enough to make him gasp. There wasn't anything he *could* do, not the way he was now. Even if he were fit, what about the boy? If he were to try something they'd get the boy. What would Ruth rather have: her jewels or her son? That's what it amounted to. He looked up at Philip and smiled.

'I'll look after you,' Philip said.

It surprised Howard, for it was much what he had been going to say to Phil. He observed the boy. His breathing was rapid but regular and a little colour had returned to his cheeks. Howard realized that looking after someone else took his mind off himself, and said softly, 'I know you will, old son.'

He looked past Philip and saw Jacmel and Louise in the menagerie. Jacmel had helped her to her feet and was walking her up and down the carpet. He spoke all the time. Howard's French was average but he was speaking too softly for him to hear all that was being said. As far as he could make out, he was encouraging Louise to walk. Telling her there was nothing wrong. That the shock would pass off. That they had to leave soon. This he said in different ways over and over as though to impress it on her mind.

Then she began to cry; it was a pathetic, low-keyed weeping, without passion but full of despair. Jacmel continued encouraging her, his tones those of a lover. Abruptly she said, loudly and clearly, so that Howard understood every word, 'My left leg is numb. I cannot feel it.'

'Sit,' Jacmel said. 'I will rub it for you. It is nothing. It is all part of the shock.'

She said, 'What do we do?'

'As we planned.'

'Where is Dave?'

'He watches the door.'

'Oh, God, it is all over with me.'

'No, *chérie*, it is nothing. Everything will be as before.'

She began to weep again and even Howard felt pity. Then he thought: when they go, what will they do to us? His mind began to look for a way out, even for the boy alone, but Jacmel was facing into the bedroom. Phil wouldn't stand a chance. He thought of the guns on their rack in his sitting-room. The shotguns; the rifles. What wouldn't he have given for the feel of one in his hands? And he wanted a drink very badly.

*

Howard was not the only one to remember the guns. Dave had seen them several times; once, when Howard had been out and the house deserted, he had even gone into the room and taken down one of the shotguns. It was a Purdey. He had heard of them but had never seen one. They were supposed to be expensive but he could not tell the difference between this one and the old shotgun of his dad's. He had aimed it at a pigeon in the square and in his imagination had blown its head off. He had shot it sitting, of course, only fools waited until they rose in the air. Now, on his way to take up his position at the front door, he recalled the guns. The Frog had said no guns, but he had one himself. Anyway, things were different now. He tried Howard's door. It was open. The guns were in their place on the rack and he lifted down the Purdey, broke it, and looked through the barrels. Clean. The gun seemed to give him back his confidence. He had been very frightened. He had been frightened when the telephone had rung and the police had been on the line; frightened when the snake had attacked Louise, and even with the gun, he was still frightened. Things had gone wrong too quickly. Every instinct told him to split: open the door, get in the car and drive like hell. And yet, what if things stopped going wrong? What if Jacmel was right? The police *couldn't* know, for the simple reason that nothing had happened yet for them to know.

He lifted the gun to his shoulder, fast, smooth, imitating his dad, who had taught him to shoot in the woods up past Bell Hanger. They were supposed to kill only wood-pigeons, grey squirrels or crows, for his father had no land of his own but scratched a living off thirty rented acres in Hampshire. But when they got a chance they took a pheasant or a partridge, even a roe deer if they felt safe enough. He thought of the farm: a few cows, a few pigs; ducks, geese, bantams; always underfoot, always in and out of the house crapping on the lino. Christ, what a life. Dirt. Cold. His mother pregnant every bleedin' year. Five brothers and three sisters and he, Dave, the youngest — by seven months. *Seven.* Not twelve or eleven, not even bloody nine; seven. No one had ever mentioned *that* to him. When he was twelve years old he had to take his birth certificate to school. That's when he had seen the date of birth, five months earlier than he had always thought. Which meant he was seven months younger than his brother Charlie, not a year like they'd told him. So if his mother was carrying

Charlie when he, Dave, was born, then who the hell *was* his mother? The answer to that had not taken long. His dad never went anywhere and even if he had, his dirty broken teeth and his smell would have turned the guts of the oldest tart in Pompey. No, it had to be nearer home; *at* home.

His mother had died when Dave was two and the young kids had been looked after by his eldest sister, Mary. She was a big, dim girl in her early twenties with a mental age of nine or ten. When he'd asked her, just put it straight to her, she'd said yes, that was right, that she'd often taken the old man on when their mum was carrying. Still took him on occasionally.

So therefore, he said, she must be his ... he must be her ...

Yes, she said in her dim but kindly way, that's exactly what he was.

He'd gone away then, walked up to Bell Hanger and sat down under one of the beech trees and after a while he had walked down into the town and nicked a bike. He'd been caught, taken to juvenile court and let off with a warning. The following day he had smashed in a shop window with one of his dad's crowbars, but all he'd got for that was probation. It was when he had started shoplifting that the law lost patience and sent him to a borstal. Once inside he relaxed. It was what he'd wanted in the first place. He had never gone home again, never, not even when the old man was dying.

He became an 'institution kid', being passed from one Welfare State institution to the next and by the time he was eighteen he had all the hallmarks: he was self-absorbed, secretive, emotionally stunted, ill-educated, but with a veneer of sophistication and good manners. Of all the lessons he had learnt, two were more important than the rest: look after number one and do anything you like but don't get caught. And one ambition: never, never be poor again.

He was helped into the big world outside. First he became an assistant storeman at a factory whose liberal management employed ex-convicts and young offenders. He took his driving test and became a van driver. He earned good wages and on top of that, pilfering brought in the extra to buy luxuries. From van driving he joined a private hire firm in London and from there he became a private chauffeur — moving always to where the money was. One day, he knew, something would happen and he'd be rich. One day ...

But so far he had never been in the right place at the right time. Again he thought: what if Jacmel was right, that they could still get away with it? Five minutes, that's all, another five minutes and they'd have the boy out of the house. Home and dry. Mrs Blanchet would never go to the police, *never*. He knew that as well as he knew his own name. Every time the boy sneezed she rushed for a doctor; she was never going to involve the police in something like this. That was the basis of the whole thing. And the clever part was that they were asking for an amount which the Blanchets could afford. Sometimes he wondered if they shouldn't have planned for more, these people were rolling in the stuff, but three hundred thousand, Jacmel had said, and to tell the truth it seemed right. It split right too.

He walked over to Howard's desk and began opening drawers. In the bottom drawer on the right hand side he found what he was looking for, a box on which was printed, 'Eley Grand Prix Waterproof Cartridges. High Velocity. No. 6'. He took half a dozen, slipped them into his pocket, then put two into the gun itself, closed it and let himself out of Howard's flat. He stood at the bottom of the stairs, the gun in his hands, listening to the mutter of Jacmel's words and the slow movement of Louise across the floor, backwards and forwards, backwards and forwards; you'd think he was trying to sober her up. He didn't trust either of them. He didn't trust Jacmel because, well, he just didn't. And Louise ... no, not really. She was good crumpet, he had to admit that, even though she was a bit saggy. But sometimes he'd had a feeling that her heart wasn't in it. They'd first done it three months back. That had been a bloody lark: right on Ruth's bed one day when she was out and the boy was at school. It had come as a bit of a surprise; not that he didn't think he was attractive to women, that was a cast-iron certainty. But she'd never given him a clue she was that way inclined. One day she'd given him his lunch and opened a bottle of wine and they had drunk it, and then another, and they'd drunk that, too, and somehow he had found himself in Ruth's bed with Louise all over him. For days afterwards, whenever he saw Ruth he smiled to himself thinking of what they'd done between her sheets. One of the things he remembered most about Louise was the tufts of hair under her arms. He'd found it sexy. Funny, that. And the way she'd put Mrs Blanehet's jewellery on. Stark naked wearing rings and ear-rings and necklaces. She'd looked like a bloody savage.

He stood at the bottom of the staircase flicking the gun's safety catch on and off, listening to the rumble of French from the room where the boy kept his stupid animals.

In the following weeks they'd done it all over the house; in old Blanehet's bed and on the couch in the drawing-room and in Louise's room and in his room and even under the shower and in the huge onyx bath. And then she had started talking about the boy and how much he'd be worth and things like that, just hinting like, at first, but the idea seemed to grow and he began thinking how easy it would be and she said she knew a man who knew about such things, a Frenchman; she said there was no one better because the French were experts at this sort of game and the British weren't. Before he knew it they were planning, really planning, not just lying on a bed spending money they didn't have. Then this Frenchman came over for a recce and after that something happened. She wouldn't do it any more; said she had a bloody cyst in her twat. Like hell ... no, he didn't trust her farther than he could kick her. Well, he had a gun too, now.

He began to pace up and down the hall. They should have gone by now; home and dry. If it hadn't been for that bloody snake. He shivered. God, he hated creepy crawly things: spiders, snakes, centipedes, didn't even like earwigs. Real country boy. Even though the snake was harmless he was glad he was getting out. He looked at his watch. Five minutes, the Frog had said. Come on, he thought, come bloody on!

*

The snake lay in the dark beneath Philip's bed, tense with aggression and fear, its tongue flicking out into the unfamiliar air, registering the vibrations of voices and footfalls and even the tiny vibrations of cars passing up and down outside. It lay ready, waiting, alert either for attack or flight, or attack in flight. Its venom sacs, depleted only partially by the amount which had entered Louise, were in the process of refilling themselves, but there was enough left for any eventuality.

The snake's name was *Dendroaspis Polylepis*, but to the Zulus from whose far-away country it had come, it was known as *iMamba emnyama*, the black mamba. It was a female in its fourth year of growth and had reached a length of nearly eight feet, not massive by mamba standards but big enough to be distinguished from the black house snake in whose place it had been mistakenly labelled.

She was a good example of the species. She had been born three and a half years earlier on a cattle farm near the village of Dannhauser in Natal, South Africa. When she had first broken through the shell of her egg she was not more than an inch or two in length and her colour was greyish olive, which changed as she put on length to a dark olive and olive brown and then to an almost purplish black on top, with a grey-white belly. She had grown very quickly as do all mambas, reaching a length of five feet at the end of eighteen months; but long before that she had been killing her own food, for her venom was highly potent shortly after birth. When she was only a foot long she had possessed enough venom to kill a rat in an hour. At that time she had a fine 'bloom' on her skin like that on the skin of ripe black grapes.

The countryside around Dannhauser is typical savannah; rolling grassland broken up by small hills and kloofs, a sea of grass, acacia and wattle, that rises from east to west until it is checked by the austere spurs of the Drakensberg Mountains; it is good country for black mambas for they are less arboreal than their cousins the green mambas which prefer the bushy coastal plains; black mambas like a mixture of woody country and open spaces where they can bask in the warm upland sun. Man has not spoilt the landscape much. There are collieries at Newcastle and Dundee but their influence on so large an area is relatively small and the wildlife is not in retreat. So the early life of *Dendroaspis Polylepis* was secure and peaceful and it was not until she was nearly two years old that she felt threatened for the first time and killed her first human being.

It happened this way. She had mated with an adult male nearly twice her size and had laid her first clutch of eggs in an ant-bear hole. She never travelled far from the hole, but when she did venture out she liked to lie on a small open patch of red earth on the side of a hillock where the early morning sun seemed to strike the warmest. Here she would sleep. She was then at her most vulnerable for like all snakes she was deaf and 'heard' vibrations instead of sounds. But she was safe enough for there were no cattle paths nearby nor any used by humans. One morning in early summer, soon after she had laid her eggs, she took up her position on the bare patch of red earth, but instead of sleeping remained alert, so that when an African labourer called George Nuxmalo, on his way to a wedding party at a neighbouring farm, took a short cut past her basking area, her sensitive organs relayed the vibrations of his footfalls to her brain. Unfortunately for the labourer, he had chosen a route that took him between the snake and her hole. He came down the hillside ignorant of the train of events he was already setting in motion. He sang quietly to himself, his mind on the pot of maize beer he would soon be lifting to his lips. He did not see the snake uncoil herself, nor did he see her move swiftly to a near-by tree and rest her head on a low branch while she watched him. He came on steadily until he was in a direct line between the mamba and her hole. She left the tree and came forward, head up, two-thirds of her body off the ground, at a speed faster than the ordinary human being can run. George Nuxmalo was aware of a swishing noise. He turned, saw something that he first thought was the shining black lash of a stockwhip, then he felt a burning sensation on the back of his right thigh. It was all over in a second and the snake had flashed on into the grass and down the ant-bear hole. Nuxmalo was more than three miles from his own group of huts and nearly four from those of the farm to which he was travelling. In his terror he turned and began to run back the way he had come. Half way home he began to feel giddy and numb and he sat down to rest. He knew he should do something about the bite on his thigh but he had neither knife to scarify it nor could he reach it with his mouth to suck at the poison. He tore a piece of cloth from his shirt-tail and tied it above the bite, twisting a stick into the material to make it tighter. He had left it too late. Thirty minutes later, when his pace had slowed to a halting stumble, he found he could no longer breathe and he choked to death on the hillside in the summer sun with no one to witness his convulsions. The snake stayed with her eggs all that day and most of the next.

George Nuxmalo's death resulted in a search for the snake but, since he had died nearly two miles away, she felt very few vibrations near her hole and she remained unmolested. Her young were born and disappeared into the bush to live their own lives. She returned to the patch of warm red earth and it was here, while asleep, that she was taken.

She was caught by a white man called Frans Opperman who spent his annual two-week summer vacation roaming the countryside, catching snakes for profit. To him, it was a purely routine affair. On the day he caught the mamba he had already found and captured two puff-adders, a mole snake and a black house snake. He came upon the mamba where he expected to find one and, approaching silently, had the long catching tongs fastened at the back of her head before she was fully awake. In less than a minute she was in a musty black bag inside a carrying crate; later this was placed in the rear of his station-wagon.

Opperman did not catch snakes like mambas without help. His assistant on this occasion was an African cook called Humphrey. Humphrey knew little about snakes and cared less. He was frightened of them and what he did he did for the money and so it was with a sense of relief that he climbed into the rear seat of the station-wagon at the end of the day. The boxes containing the snakes were behind him. Before setting off for Durban with his load Opperman wrote out the labels for the last two snakes he had caught, the house snake and the mamba, and gave them to

Humphrey to tie on to the travelling crates. The labels were printed in red. CAUTION. DANGEROUS REPTILES. And in the space under the printing on one he had written in heavy black marking ink, 'Black House Snake', and on the other, 'Black Mamba'.

'Tie these on,' he said, passing them back to Humphrey. He started the engine and began the long drive back to Durban. It was then that the mistake occurred: a simple human error. Humphrey had seen two black snakes placed in separate bags; the only difference was size and he thought they were both the same species. Since he could only read and write his own name, the heavy red printing followed by the thick black of the marking pencil meant nothing to him; and so when he tied the labels on the boxes he mistakenly transposed them.

Opperman reached Durban a little after midnight, went to his home and slept till eight, then took his specimens to the premises of Messrs Mowat Bros near the Indian market. They had been dealing with each other for several years and the transaction was simple and swift. The snakes were unloaded and carried into the darkened rear of the building to take their places with dozens of other travelling crates containing yellow cobras, spitting cobras, Egyptian cobras, night adders, horned vipers, green mambas, African pythons, mole snakes, file snakes, coral snakes, gaboon vipers and *boomslangs*, all ready to be shipped to different parts of the world, either to zoos, or to medical foundations for research into poisons, or to have their venom milked and made into anti-venom.

Messrs Mowat Bros had never had a complaint against Opperman, who knew his snakes as well as they did, nor did they ever unpack black mambas once they had been bagged and crated for travelling, for they considered the snakes far too dangerous. On this particular day a consignment of fresh snakes was being sent to Loewenthal's of London, with whom Messrs Mowat Bros had been dealing for nearly fifteen years. In their last letter Loewenthal had ordered, apart from several other items, one black mamba and one black house snake. The crates were simply attached to the order and taken out to Durban airport just after lunch where they caught the midafternoon 727 to Johannesburg, from which they were transferred that evening to a British Airways London-bound Jumbo. By midmorning the following day the snakes were in the customs building at Heathrow Airport. Again no one opened the bags containing the snakes, for customs officials are no braver than other folk nor do they have facilities for handling angry and venomous reptiles. The following day the black mamba and the black house snake and several other crates were picked up at the cargo terminal by Loewenthal's van and taken to Camden Town.

In all that time the snake had not been removed from the bag nor had the bag been removed from the wooden travelling crate; nor indeed had the snake moved much from the coiled position she had taken soon after being captured. In fact, had anyone been able to see, it would have appeared that she was either dead or dying. This had happened because of the changes in air temperature. She had been warm enough in a South African summer but once placed aboard the Jumbo the cold had affected her like a drug and she had remained almost immobile for the entire flight. London Airport in February was no place for a tropical snake and she had remained in a partial coma until she had reached the comparative warmth of Loewenthal's shop. It was not until she experienced the heat of the taxi that she had begun to revive. Then had come the warmth of the house; the kind of warmth she had been born into. Now, as she lay coiled under Philip's bed, she began to feel the chill that exists in all houses at floor level in winter, no matter how high the thermostats are set. Cold air entering from outside crept over the rugs and carpets and found its way even under beds. She felt it acutely but her finely-tuned sensors also picked up a flow of warm air near by. She began to move towards it. It grew stronger until it was like a warm river flowing into the room.

The warm air was being generated by a boiler deep inside the house and carried by fans through a complex system of pipes leading to each room. It was the system which Philip's mother had argued for and finally won, of ducted warm air containing a controlled percentage of moisture. It had been specifically installed for Philip's lungs; on a February evening in London it was nirvana to a cold-blooded reptile. The snake moved up the flow of air until she reached the point at which it emerged from the wall. Because the system had only recently been installed and was still being tested, the airduct covers had not been screwed into place and the ducts were open. The one in Philip's room was hidden by his armchair. The snake paused for a moment, testing the air for danger, but there was no danger, not at least from the duct, while from the other room behind her dangerous vibrations still entered her brain. The duct offered security and warmth and there was a familiar shape and size to it; it was like the ant-bear hole which had been her home near Dannhauser in Natal. She entered the duct, her scales gripping the rough metal, and moved upward and to the right, slowly, testing each foot, until she had left the room behind her and was resting at full length where the warm air flowed over her like balm.

She lay there for a few moments, then began to move again, and soon she had reached a point where pipes flowed away from her in every direction carrying warmed air to the various rooms; she was in a kind of junction from which she could reach almost any part of the house. She lay quite still enjoying the warm air as she had once enjoyed the sunlight on her patch of red earth; but she did not sleep — her surroundings were too unfamiliar for that — and soon she would begin to move again.

*

'Where is he, then?' Alec Nash said into the telephone. 'No, of course he hasn't. He'd never ring me, not here. Look, I told him. Six-thirty. Well, I'm sorry, but you'll just have to tell Mr Arkwright. Have you tried the Rose and Crown? And the …' He tried to visualize the pubs in that part of the Fulham Road. There were three within fifty yards of each other and Jim seldom went elsewhere. '… The Magpie,' he said at last. 'No? Well, I'll go there first. On the way home. Yes, now. I would have left twenty minutes ago but something's come up. No, no. Just routine. Five … ten minutes at the most. Well, explain. Give him a cup of tea or a gin. Talk to him. He'll want to hear from you anyway.' He paused as she spoke then he took out his pen and drew his pad towards him and began to write: 'Milk, spuds, bread, coffee …' He wrote just above another note which read, '412 Eaton Square.' He put a ring around that.

'All right,' he said. 'There's a supermarket open in South Ken. It's on my way. Are you sure we've got some gin? Tonic? See you in half an hour …'

He put down the telephone and stared unseeing at the list. Jim had sworn blind he'd be at home tonight. Now he'd have to comb the bloody pubs for him. Christ, what a bloody shambles.

Then he remembered the telephone call he had made to Eaton Square. Someone had answered and had then put the receiver down without hanging up. Nash had waited and waited and finally after much clicking of the bar, had given up. There had been some sort of noise in the background but he had not been able to make it out. He had put down his own receiver to dial again when, in that moment, Mary's call had come through and he had heard the distress in her voice.

Nash caught up his dark blue issue topcoat booked out a police Hillman and drove cautiously through the freezing misty night towards Elizabeth

Street. First Eaton Square and get that done and then to the supermarket in South Kensington. As he thought of that he remembered the list. It still lay on his desk next to the telephone. He braked, then drove ahead. He could see the paper with the writing on it in his mind's eye. The address. Then the food. Milk. Spuds. Bread and something else. What the hell was it? Butter? No. Tea? No. Coffee. Yes. Coffee, that was it. Milk. Spuds. Bread and coffee. He turned left into Elizabeth Street and headed for Eaton Square.

*

'Get up,' Jacmel said.

'What for?' Howard said.

'We go now.'

'Go? Where?'

'Get up.'

'Look here,' Howard began. 'You'll never get away with this. If you leave things as they are you've got a chance. I promise I'll —'

Jacmel moved his right hand and Howard saw he had a gun in it. 'Get up.'

Howard pushed himself off the bed. The pain came again but not as fiercely as it had at first. He stood weakly, letting Phil take his weight. 'What do you want us for? We'll be nothing more than a hindrance.'

'Downstairs.' Louise was holding herself up against the door and Jacmel put his left arm around her waist.

'Don't you understand? The boy's sick. What d'you want a sick boy on your hands for? Only slow you down. You've got enough trouble with her.'

'We go now.'

'Where are we going, Dick?'

'It's all right, Phil. They don't want us. They've got what they came for.'

Jacmel motioned with the gun again and Howard and Philip moved from the room on to the landing. 'They only want us for cover,' Howard whispered. 'Just to make it look good in the street. They'll let us go then.'

'But why, Dick? What've they done?'

'Probably taken the paintings and your mother's jewels.'

'Look.' They were passing the drawing-room door and Philip pointed into the room where the paintings still hung under their small showlights.

Howard stopped. Something began to chip away at his mind. He turned and looked at Jacmel. 'Aren't you taking the paintings?' he said fatuously.

Jacmel and Louise came on slowly. She looked terrible. 'Move,' Jacmel said.

'They're worth a few quid,' Howard said, stumbling as he stepped backwards.

'She took the jewels with her,' Philip said.

'What?'

'My mother. The best ones. I saw her pack them.'

Howard turned and faced down the stairs. He saw Dave with the shotgun. It wasn't robbery then. And if it wasn't robbery it could only mean — Christ, he thought, it's the boy. They want Phil. His hand on the bannister-rail was sticky with sweat. Phil. All along. Never the paintings. Never the jewels. Only the boy.

He pretended to trip, held himself on the bannister and said, 'Give me your shoulder, Phil.' He put his arm round the boy's shoulder and leant on him, bringing their heads close together. He could feel Philip trembling. 'When they open the door you run,' he whispered. 'Doesn't matter where. Just run. Understand? I'll try and stop them. You run. Fast as you can. Understand?'

He felt Phil shiver and fight for breath. 'Easy now. One, two, one, two. In, out. In, out. You run. Flat out. Got it?'

He felt the boy nod. Good, he thought. At least he's understood. They'd never shoot him. Not the boy. A split second. Just as the door opened. Then out into the dark and away. But what could he do in that split second. How could he hold them? Stop them? Distract them?

They came down slowly, two couples, their arms about each other. Howard heard Louise give a small cry and Jacmel said something to comfort her. Could he grab her, Howard thought? Would that be distraction enough? He felt himself cringe inwardly. If he did, what would they do to him? Shoot him? Bludgeon him to death with their guns, with *his* gun? If only he were stronger he would not have hesitated. But he wasn't strong. He tried to block a thought that had been hammering at his mind, but could not: Blanchet had said that day in the hospital in Nairobi, *I need a brave man* ...

Dave met them at the bottom of the stairs.

'Okay?' Jacmel said.

'I must rest,' Louise said. 'I feel ...'

'Not now. In a little while. Hold on, *chérie*.'

'I cannot feel my leg.'

'Soon you can lie down. Every — What is that?'

A sudden silence.

'What?' Dave said.

'A car,' Jacmel said. 'A car door.'

'I didn't hear,' Dave said. He held the shotgun more tightly. Jacmel seemed to notice it for the first time.

'Leave it,' he said.

'You've got one.'

'Leave it here! How can you walk into the street with that? You …' he said to Howard. 'You take Louise. You go first. Understand? Take her to the Citroen.'

'Look here, there's no need —'

'Enough! Take her. You,' he pointed to Dave, 'unlock the door. Put the gun away. Now!'

Dave turned the key in the lock and stepped back. He held the shotgun tightly as though it were a spar in a lonely sea. 'Take her,' Jacmel said. Howard came back across the carpet to put his arm around Louise when the front doorbell rang. It was like a sudden flash of lightning. Its peal rang through the silent house, screaming its urgency. For a second everyone was stunned, then Howard opened his mouth and yelled 'Help!' at the top of his lungs.

On the other side of the door Inspector Alec Nash heard the cry. He put his hand on the door-handle and pushed and, surprisingly, the door flew open, throwing him into the threshold off balance. In the brief seconds he remained there his impression was of a group of people assembled at the bottom of the stairs, suspended in time. Together they resembled marble statuary in a city park. Then he saw the gun in the hand of one of them. He was unarmed. He began to turn away. He saw the other gun, the shotgun. And as he saw it he heard the terrible noise of the exploding cartridges. The No. 6 shot, excellent for pheasant or grouse, was expelled from the breeches of both barrels at a distance of almost exactly three metres. The pellets, having no room to spread over such a short distance, travelled in two closely-packed swarms and entered Nash's body as though they were dum-dums, smashing in the right side of his chest and blowing away part of his right lung and also blowing him off the top step and sending him sprawling back towards the pavement.

*

'Oh, God,' he said out loud as he lay crumpled at the bottom of the steps. 'Oh, God.' Then, like some territorial animal, he began to crawl instinctively to the car. His right arm was useless. Blood was soaking into his uniform and as he pulled himself along he left a wide rusty swathe on the dirty pavement. He reached the car and began to struggle upwards to grab the handle of the door. He was tasting blood now, warm and slightly brackish. Instinct had brought him to the car; training and discipline took him into the next phase. He managed to kneel, opened the door and groped for the radio. With his left hand he pulled the microphone down. It lay on the dusty carpeting in front of the passenger's seat and he bent towards it.

'M.P.,' he said. 'From Alpha Six … Urgent message.'

The crisp voice of the operator in the information room at Scotland Yard said, 'All cars wait. Go ahead, Alpha Six.'

Nash was barely alive. 'I've been shot,' he whispered. 'I've been shot.'

'Your signals are unreadable Alpha Six. Repeat.'

'Shot,' he whispered. 'Shot.'

The microphone began to grow and slowly started to spin.

'Alpha Six give location.'

His mind responded to the authority in the voice. 'Four twelve,' he said. 'Four twelve …' He began to slip away.

'Alpha Six give location. Repeat, give location. Give location.'

'Four Twelve Eaton … Eaton …' Then he said, 'Shot', and 'Oh, God', and 'Help me'.

Inside the house the noise of the explosion still seemed to echo around the walls and up and down the stairs. The group had remained like statues for several seconds after Dave had fired. Then Jacmel had burst forward, slamming the door and wrenching the gun from the chauffeur's hands. 'Imbecile!' he yelled, and hurled the gun down.

'What d'you expect?' Dave shouted, his voice high-pitched with hysteria. 'He was a bloody copper!'

'He knew nothing,' Jacmel said. 'Nothing.'

'Let's go! If it hadn't been for her we'd have been out long ago. Come on!'

'Look from the window. He may have had a companion.'

Dave went into an adjoining room and came back in a few seconds. 'Only the one. He's lying by the car. Won't do us any harm.'

'Quickly, then.'

At that moment Howard, who was standing a little in front of Louise, heard her give a choking cough. He turned, but was too late to hold her. She fell back on the staircase. Jacmel ran to her. 'Please, *chérie*,' he said in a French so heavily accented that Howard could hardly understand it. 'We must go —'

She lay, trying to drag air into her lungs, her body jerking and bending, and Howard watched in horror as her backbone arched until he thought it must snap. She was dying. She was dying right there in front of him.

'What is happening to her?' Jacmel said. 'Cannot you do something? Is there no possibility of helping?'

The convulsions came one after another, like an epileptic fit, her legs kicking out, her skirt half-way up to her waist. She began to froth at the mouth and she caught at her throat as though to force air down into her desperate lungs.

'Help her!' Jacmel shouted.

'She can't breathe,' Howard said. 'She's dying.'

In her extremity, she tore at her dress ripping both it and her bra from her chest. Everyone stood transfixed. Covering her left breast and side was a huge purple mark as though she had been bruised by a gigantic fist. Another purple mark covered the left side of her neck and a third her upper arm surrounding the marks of the snake's fangs. It was then that Howard guessed what had really happened. But there was no time to pursue the thought for unless something was done Louise would die. Jacmel had knelt beside her and placed his lips on hers, breathing in and out, blowing down into her lungs, giving her all the breath he could expel from his own.

'What's happening to her?' Philip said.

Howard crossed quickly to him, his own hurt forgotten.

'She's having a fit,' he said, preparing the boy for something much worse. 'It's the snakebite. It does that to you sometimes.'

'You said it was a harmless snake.'

'No snakes are really harmless,' he said, lying again.

Jacmel turned. His broad face was grey. 'What can we do?' he said.

Howard shook his head. 'Nothing.' He put his arm round Philip and began moving him slowly towards the door. Dave had turned away and was looking at Louise. So was Jacmel. Howard bent to Philip. 'When I say go, run, got it?' Again he felt the boy tremble. The door was unlocked, if there was a moment it was now. 'You can do it. Run like hell.' They reached the door and Howard tried to make his hand go out to open it. It stayed by his side, held there by his own fear. Louise was in the last stage of her life, choking and gasping. Jacmel was breathing his own life into her. Dave was walking across the hall with his back to them. *Now*, Howard thought. *Now*. But his arm seemed paralysed. As though in a dream he watched Dave pick up the shotgun and put two more cartridges into it, then he closed the gun and eased off the safety. It was too late. Too late. Dave would shoot. A sense of despair mingled with relief flooded through him. It was too late.

Dave held the gun pointing loosely towards them, his face was chalky and corrugated with emotion. 'Leave her!' he yelled suddenly. 'Can't you see she's had it? Leave her. Let's go.'

Jacmel pulled his mouth away from Louise's. 'Get a rug,' he said. 'We will take her to the car.'

'Let him get it,' Dave said, indicating Howard. 'I don't trust him.'

Jacmel hesitated then said to Howard, 'You fetch it. Get the boy away from the door.'

Dave said, 'He's not going anywhere.'

Howard went into his own room and pulled a blanket from his bed. The guns were in the sitting-room. Perhaps he could take one down under cover of the rug. He turned and saw Dave in the doorway and knewr, again with a sense of relief, that he could do nothing without being seen.

'Faster,' Dave said.

There was no way out for the boy, no way he, Howard, could grab a gun, no way he could dominate what was happening. He must slow things down. The longer they remained in the house the more chance they had. He knew the house, Phil knew the house, it was their territory, and animals always had more chance in their own territory. Once they were away from the house they would be in Jacmel's territory. He began to walk slowly back into the hall carrying the rug.

'Move!' Dave said.

Howard pointed to his stomach. 'I can't,' he said. 'You've bloody nearly finished me.'

He limped forward holding out the rug to Jacmel who raised Louise's legs and wrapped her body in it. 'All right,' Jacmel said. 'You and Dave, pick her up.'

'There is something,' Howard said.

'What?'

'I've got some anti-venom in my room.'

'You said the snake was not poisonous.'

'Mistakes can be made. I didn't see it.'

Jacmel paused and Howard could see he was fighting a battle within himself.

'He's lying,' Dave said. 'Can't you see what he's doing? He's wasting bloody time.'

Howard turned on him. 'She's dying. There's a chance this might save her.'

'Why the hell didn't you think of it sooner then?' Dave said.

'I hadn't seen the black marks.'

'You think it poison?' Jacmel said.

Howard nodded. 'I've seen it before.'

Jacmel stared at Louise. Then he made up his mind. 'Quickly. Fetch it.'

Howard went into his rooms followed by Dave. The snakebite outfit he had used in Africa was in his desk drawer underneath the cartridge boxes. It had been manufactured in South Africa and was one that could be bought in most parts of the continent south of the Sahara. He had not used the syringe for years and on that occasion — like this one, if he was right — it had been used too late.

There was only one ampule of poly-valent anti-venom left and he filled the syringe, his hands trembling so badly he could hardly fit the needle into the top of the little bottle. His left hand obscured the label on which it clearly stated that the serum should be used before June 1974. It didn't make any difference now, he thought, she was too far gone for anything. He drew the anti-venom up into the syringe. Take your time, he told himself, someone *must* have heard the shot. Someone must see the body lying on the pavement.

'Come on,' Dave said, pushing the gun at him.

'The needle could break.'

'I don't give a fuck.'

He filled the syringe as slowly as he dared and limped back to Louise. *Someone* must have heard. How long was it since the policeman had been shot? Five minutes? Ten? More like six. He lifted Louise's bitten arm from under the rug and was about to plunge the needle into the soft blackened area in the elbow joint when she gave a convulsive jerk that knocked the syringe from his hand. It fell on the floor and shattered, the serum making a viscous blob against the dark tiles. She was arched like a bow. Then abruptly she collapsed. 'She's dead,' Howard said.

As he spoke the house was filled with the wee-waa-wee-waa of a police siren. They heard the shriek of brakes then the slamming of doors. Dave ran to the window of the room opposite Howard's flat. The others followed. Jacmel took his gun from his trouser belt and looked at the cylinders. Howard watched him. It was methodical, professional. Jacmel turned: 'I say this once, no more: if you doing anything — anything at all — we shoot the boy. Then we shoot you. You understand this?' It was said calmly, deliberately, just as the examination of the gun had been, and Howard was reminded of a soldier, a commando perhaps, going into battle.

'I understand,' he said.

'Lock the front door and give me the key.'

Howard did so and watched him put the key into his jacket pocket. Only then did Jacmel walk to the window and look out into the street. Howard tried to follow with Philip but Dave held the shotgun on them. The room was dark and net curtains hid them from view; Howard could just see the pavement. One police car had pulled up outside the house, a second was blocking the cul-de-sac that led to the square.

Dave turned to Jacmel, 'Christ,' he said, and his voice was thick with fear. 'What do we do now?'

A big man had got out of the second car and was walking along the pavement. In the street lights Howard could see him clearly without making out his face. Bald head, massive shoulders, made bigger by the heavy sheepskin coat he was wearing. A man came up to him from the first car and said a few words. Then a second. They backed the first car to the end of the street. The big man came on. It was obvious he was in charge. He stopped at the bottom of the steps and knelt by Inspector Nash's side, placing his head on the dead man's chest. Then he rose again. It would have been easy enough to shoot him from where they watched yet his very presence defied them. It was as though he was offering himself as a target. He stood looking up at the house for a few long moments, and turned away. He picked up Nash as though he weighed no more than a child and carried him along the pavement. An ambulance appeared and stopped. The big man passed Nash to the two attendants and the ambulance drove off. Slowly he returned along the pavement to the front of the house.

'What are we going to do?' Dave said. 'They've got the bloody place covered. Look, there's coppers at the end of the street even. And that's another car.'

Jacmel looked at him briefly. 'Now it is your test,' he said. 'What bloody test?'

'To see if you are a man or a little boy to run to his mother.'

'Look, you may be bloody great over there in France with your French police but over here —'

'Don't talk so much. Don't talk. Don't think.'

Jacmel was talking to Dave but it was apparent that he was preoccupied with the figure on the pavement. The big man stood there in the misty street outlined by a street lamp. Huge.

Immovable. Implacable. And inside the house, Jacmel square, short, tough, calm now in the face of arrangements that had gone badly awry. Howard could almost feel the antipathy that each man had for the other. That they did not know each other, that at any other time they might have made common ground, have found common thoughts and emotion, was irrevelant in the circumstances. It was something he understood: the hunter and the hunted. The seconds ticked away and turned into minutes and still the big man stood there; still Jacmel said nothing, did nothing.

'For God's sake,' Dave said. 'There's another bloody carload.'

Jacmel did not appear to hear him, so intense was his concentration on the policeman.

At last he moved. He slid the double-glazed window partly open. It moved without any noise.

'Can you hear me?' he said, not loudly but with a carrying voice.

The big man made no move, although he must have heard.

'Can you hear me?' This time slightly louder but still not audible much beyond the man on the pavement. Slowly he raised his head and they could see a heavy, rather brutal face. It seemed to Howard that there was a slight smile on the lips, though he could not be sure. Perhaps it was his imagination, but as the silence had deepened the feeling had grown in him that it was somehow the silence itself that was the first stage in a war between the two men and that Jacmel had lost a round in speaking first.

'I can hear you.' The voice matched the man, heavy and rich in timbre with an overlay of a Scottish accent diluted by living in a Southern society.

'We have a boy in here,' Jacmel said.

'Yes?'

'Yes. A boy. Philippe Blanchet. Ten years.'

'Send him out, then.'

'That is impossible.'

The policeman made no reply, hunching down again in his sheepskin. After a moment Jacmel said, 'There are certain things we wish.'
'Yes?'
'I talk to you?'
'If you like.'
'Have you the ... authority?'
'Depends what you want.'
'A car. Money. Time.'
The policeman gave a short laugh. 'You must be joking.'
'It is no joke. We have the boy.'
'We have a dead policeman.'
'That is regrettable. We wish to leave soon. Please fetch your superior. Someone who has authority.'

The policeman stood for a moment, hunched against the cold, then turned and began to walk slowly back along the pavement to the knot of policemen and cars. Howard watched him until his figure became blurred by the mist. Then Philip said, as though voicing all their thoughts, 'He's gone. He's left us alone.'

But they weren't alone, Howard thought, for somewhere in the house was a snake that was not the snake he had thought it was. He recalled the convulsions which Louise had suffered before she died, the difficulty in breathing, the dark blotches on her body. More than two metres long, Jacmel had said. Black. Fast. Like a shadow, Dave had said. Rearing up, most of its body off the floor, Philip had said. There was only one snake which fitted that description.

Part III

Friday 7.23 p.m. — 9.50 p.m.

Detective Chief Superintendent William Bulloch of the Murder Squad walked unhurriedly back to his police Rover at the end of the cul-de-sac. He was aware that someone in the house — as yet he did not know how many there were — might take a shot at him but it was a calculated risk. Dirt. Bloody dirt. His whole attitude, careless, contemptuous, dared them to shoot him. As he had stood outside the house he had felt the anger build up in him as it always did. His shield. His buckler. And now as he walked away from the front of the house it was still with him. Dirt, he thought. Bloody dirt.

Detective Sergeant Harold Glaister and Detective Constable Edward Rich waited at Bulloch's car, where they had been ordered to wait, and watched their chief come back through the mist, a huge, shambling, bear-like figure which even the kindly blurring of the night could not soften. Their own car was parked some yards away from the others, of which there were now nearly half-a-dozen surrounded by plain-clothed and uniformed policemen. Glaister and Rich waited silently as he came up with them, waited for him to say something, anything, but instead he opened the back of the car and climbed heavily in. Without looking he reached back on to the window sill and tapped his fingers along it, finding nothing. He wound down the window and said, 'Rich, where's my coffee?'

Rich reached into the front and took a vacuum flask from the shelf, unscrewed the top, poured the steaming liquid into the plastic cup and passed it back to Bulloch, who accepted it without thanks. A strong smell of black coffee and rum filled the back of the car. Then he said, 'Got a cigarette?' Rich gave him one and lit it. Again Bulloch accepted it in silence. He sat puffing and brooding in the back of the car while his two younger officers got into the front seat. Detective Constable Rich, fresh-faced and looking young enough to be still at school, turned round in the seat and said, 'What's the score, sir?'

Glaister looked swiftly at him, apprehension on his face, which cleared almost instantly. You didn't ask the Boss what the score was, he told you if he felt like it; not unless you were Rich, that is, and Glaister had never really understood how it was that Rich had not been expelled to some far-off division, some Siberia of the Metropolitan Police, at Bulloch's instigation. Glaister, who had been in the force for more than ten years — three times as long as Rich — only knew that he, Glaister, would not have asked Bulloch what the score was, would not have asked him anything, would have been content to await what information and orders he liked to direct.

The relationship between Bulloch and Rich was too complex for Sergeant Glaister, who was running to fat now and content to be a sergeant, to keep his nose clean, to live out his career in the same job to the best of his ability and find a pension at the end of the road. Until two years before he had worked for Jefferson at Savile Row and Bulloch had only been a name. He'd heard the stories, of course, like the time Bulloch had drunk too much at the Christmas party in 1968 and he and some of his lads had gone out to the Shanghai Moon across the river in Lambeth for a chicken chop suey and how one of the waiters had asked them to leave when they started making a din and how Bulloch raided the place the next day and found a hundred grams of uncut heroin taped to the back of a lavatory cistern. That had been the end of the Shanghai Moon and the end of the waiter and the waiter's father who owned the place. Like the time he had brought a black woman to a cocktail party at Scotland Yard to welcome the new Deputy Commissioner. It wouldn't have been so bad, it was said at the time, if she had been unknown, but she had been picked up a few days before in a massage parlour in Brixton, and Bulloch was said to have spotted her in court the day after when he was there on his own affairs. Some even said he had paid her fine. Anyway, she'd been released and he had brought her to the cocktail party. What made things worse — as far as the other wives were concerned — was that she wasn't more than eighteen and as beautiful as an ebony statuette. Like the fact that they said he dyed what was left of his gingerish hair, that he was a queer, that he was a stud, that he'd never married, that he'd had two wives, that he'd beaten up several prisoners, that he'd killed a man once in Edinburgh, that the only person he'd ever really loved was his mother ... There were many stories about William Bulloch, some he knew, some he didn't, he neither confirmed nor denied them; people who wanted to know could go and fuck themselves as far as he was concerned — and that applied to the Commissioner as well. It was not surprising therefore that Bulloch at fifty-two had everything behind him. All he was heading for was retirement and the betting was that he wasn't going to make it. If he was worried, no one knew that either.

No one knew very much about him at all except Rich and it was a mixture of some fact — and some guesswork or intuition or whatever one called it. And one did not call it by either name in front of Bulloch for there was one thing he despised and that was guesswork. Not that he was a detective in the Holmesian sense, he did not spend much time gathering clues, he achieved whatever successes he had achieved as a bull achieves coitus, with passion and a great deal of effort. He tended, Rich thought, to confront things head on and sometimes it worked and sometimes it didn't.

Rich watched him now in the dim light of the car's interior and saw the sweat on his neck and remembered seeing it on other occasions.

'What's the score, sir?' he said again.

'There's no bloody score, Rich. What d'you think this is, Rangers and Celtic? Give us another drop of that coffee.' Rich filled the cup again.

Suddenly Bulloch said, 'They've got a boy in there. At least that's what they say.'

'How many are there, sir?'

'Two, maybe more. One's a foreigner. Sounded French.'

'And the other?'

'Didn't talk. Didn't even see him properly. Just a shape at the right of the window.' Abruptly he turned to Glaister who jumped slightly. 'You sure about the back?'

'There's no way, sir. Houses on either side face the other way. No. 412 backs on to ...' He consulted his notebook, straining his eyes in the poor light, '... on to Sloane Mews, sir. Rear wall abuts on to dressmaking establishment.'

'But you've got two men there just in case.'

'Sampson and Hodges, sir.'

There was a tap on Bulloch's window and he opened it half way. 'What?'

A policeman lowered his head to speak. 'Marksmen just arriving, sir.'

'How many?'

'Two, sir.'

'All right.' He wound up the window and said to Glaister. 'You know where they go?'

'Houses on either side. We've got permission to use the upstairs windows. They give a good field of crossfire, sir.'

'That control vehicle arrived yet? I don't want this thing,' he pointed to the radio in the car, 'squawking on and off all night.'

Glaister looked out and saw a large dark blue caravan which served as a mobile office in cases like this, pull into the kerb. 'There it is now, sir.'

'You know what to do then.' Glaister nodded and climbed out of the car. 'And Glaister,' Bulloch shouted after him, 'tell those forensic people and the photographers not to come any nearer. No one's to go anywhere near the front of the house or I'll have him. Got it?'

Bulloch knew most of the details, which he had checked with Glaister, but he liked things clear and now he went over in his mind everything from the moment he had taken the call on the car radio as he was coming over Chelsea Bridge. By the time he had reached the house in the cul-de-sac he knew everything Nash had known before he died — except why he had gone there in the first place. He knew Nash had been shot and he knew it was with a shotgun, but that was something he would have known whether Nash had said so or not. He had only to turn him over. You couldn't mistake a shotgun at close range unless it was a bloody howitzer. The *why* might be answered soon if Glaister did his bit on the radio in the control vehicle. And the *who*? That too. Who owned the house? Who the boy was? Once they knew the *who* they might know the *why*, and when they knew the why they might have some idea of who the dirt was. All they could do now was wait until Scotland Yard turned up some of the answers and while they were waiting keep those in the house in the house. The art of the thing was in the waiting; who could wait longest, us or them.

The position of No. 412 worked in his favour: the fact that it was the only house fronting into the small street, that it backed on to another building, that it was joined at the sides by two houses facing the other way — all meant that you went in one way and you came out the same way, either by the front door or by the door in the basement area just below the front steps. Anyone going into or coming out of No. 412 had to be visible to Bulloch — and that was just fine.

'Got a fag, Rich?'

Rich did not smoke but ever since the first day he had been on Bulloch's team and had been put out of the car at 3.30 a.m. in the Queenstown Road with an injunction to 'bloody well find some, then', he had always kept a packet in his pocket. Now he gave one to Bulloch and lit it for him. Again he saw the sweat lying like shining threads in the wrinkles of his neck. They said that Bulloch didn't know the meaning of fear, but Rich knew different. He had been with him on the Sutherland Street siege when two Irish gunmen had barricaded themselves into an upstairs flat belonging to a seventy-two year old widow and he'd been with him when the Turkish Airlines office was held by four Greek-Cypriots, and both times he had seen the sweat lying in the furrows of his neck. Not surprising in view of the way he had run the sieges. There were two ways, he had said; *their* way, meaning the soft approach, getting on friendly terms, talking, talking, talking, the fashionable way. Then there was *his* way, Bulloch's way, the freeze, the deliberate cutting off of all external stimuli like telephones, lights, warmth, noise, speech. He liked to clear everything away, to unclutter the stage, and to place himself there as the only actor. Rich had been appalled by the chances Bulloch took; the needless exposure, the arrogant baiting of the gunmen with his own body, the way he used his own personality like a club to beat them with. And his method had worked. The other method, the softly-softly, catchee-monkey method might have worked too, but that was no argument; there was no gainsaying that he had twice been in siege conditions and twice broken the sieges. The Sutherland Street siege had lasted a fortnight and the fact that the elderly widow had died in hospital three days after her release was, in Bulloch's opinion, irrelevant to the breaking of the siege and the capturing of the dirt. That's what his job was all about, capturing the dirt; it was hard luck on the old woman.

Rich knew that there was certain support for Bulloch's one-man methods in the Yard itself especially after the Macaroni House siege of 1974 when there had been more Deputy Commissioners and Assistant Commissioners getting into the act than ordinary coppers. And when the siege was over and the officer in charge of the criminal case was preparing court evidence and had asked these senior officers for verbatim notes of the dialogues they'd had with the terrorists, it turned out there weren't any notes. The senior officers were so senior they'd forgotten to take notes, forgotten basic police procedures. So the one-man show was back in favour and Bulloch was the man. Two sieges, two successes. Rich knew that in the police, as everywhere else, there was nothing like success. So at least in the early stages, none of Bulloch's superiors at the Yard was going to bother him.

After he'd broken the Sutherland Street siege and the one in the Turkish Airlines office, Bulloch's fellow officers had begun calling him Bismarck, but the name hadn't stuck. In the early days people had called him Willy and Bill, but they hadn't stuck either. You called him Mr Bulloch, or William, or Sir, depending on your own status. No one ever called him Bull.

But he was not the iron man, not through and through, as Rich well knew. After the Sutherland Street siege, the second he had conducted in less than a month, Rich had been privy to an incident which gave him more insight into Bulloch's character than both sieges put together.

Sutherland Street had been a bad business, perhaps because it had come so soon after the Turkish Airlines operation and they were short of sleep or perhaps, in hindsight, because the old woman had died, or perhaps because Rich had never really believed that the Greek-Cypriots would use their guns on the British police while he had no such feeling about the Irish gunmen who had taken over the top floor of the house in Sutherland Street. It had lasted nearly a fortnight and Rich could only remember cat-napping in the car, though he must have gone home to sleep at some stage. Not so Bulloch; he had stayed there day after day, night after night, sleeping in the car in bitter weather, not so very different from the cold they were experiencing now, only then there had been no mist.

It had turned into a war of attrition between Bulloch and the two gunmen. At certain times each day, and in the early hours of every morning, he had gone to stand outside the house. At first Rich had thought him mad, for they knew the gunmen were well-armed — as it turned out later they had an Armalite rifle, an FN rifle, a machine-pistol and half a dozen hand grenades — and Bulloch seemed to be offering himself as a target. Except for the big man the street had been entirely empty. Parked cars had been towed away, road blocks set up at the Lupus Street end and at Ebury Bridge. It had always seemed to Rich like an empty stage on which Bulloch made his appearances. He didn't talk, didn't even move much, just stood, hunched in his sheepskin, implacable, angry; the anger seeming to grow as the siege continued.

It had worked. At the end of a fortnight the gunmen had given themselves up. One of them, according to the old woman, had been crying a lot. Rich was later told that prisoners in solitary often cried. The gunmen gave themselves up at seven o'clock on the thirteenth morning and Rich could only recall the rest of the day in snatches. After the formalities of the arrest had been finished, and the TV interviews, Bulloch had started to drink. He had taken Rich from one club to another, dark basements tarted up with red plush wallpaper, stained with drink and substances Rich did not wish to analyse. He was never able to recall what they talked about during that lost day. There were long periods of silence interspersed by slurred monologues. He remembered that Bulloch had spoken about his mother, he could not recall what had been said but remembered the tenderness in the big man's voice because it had come as such a surprise. And then a jumble of other subjects. Golf, he thought, had been one, though why he couldn't say. And Edinburgh. That was logical enough for that's where Bulloch came from. About midnight he took Bulloch home, if 'home' was a word that could be used in such circumstances. Bulloch's home was a bachelor flat in a mean street near the Battersea heliport. He had turned it into a lair, a kind of foetid burrow. It comprised one large room off which led a kitchen and a bathroom. The room contained an unmade double bed, with sheets that had once been white but were now a brownish colour, and pillows in their original ticking. By the dirty window stood a formica-topped table on which was the remains of a breakfast eaten before the siege had started. Mould had attacked a loaf of bread and the open pot of apricot jam and had grown an island in what was left of a cup of coffee. Rich had been reluctant to touch anything, even to sit down.

But Bulloch had swept a pair of stained pyjamas from an easy chair and pointed to it and Rich had sat. Then the big man had rummaged in the kitchen and come back with a bottle of whisky and two glasses. They had sat there drinking for the better part of an hour before Rich began to notice what was happening to Bulloch. He saw it first when Bulloch had had to use both hands to hold his whisky glass. He clamped the fingers of his left hand around his right wrist but still he could not stop the shaking. Rich saw the sweat on his neck and on his brow even though the room was freezing. He was shaking all over, jerking and twitching so much that the whisky began to slop out of his glass. He lurched to his feet and the glass slipped to the floor. He turned away from Rich and gripped the table with both hands, trying to control his shaking.

Frightened, Rich stood up and carefully put down his own glass. He was very new and very unsure of himself and he did not know how to cope; what he did know, instinctively, was that Bulloch might never forgive him for being a witness to his trauma. He began to tiptoe to the door when Bulloch said, in a shaking voice, 'Don't leave me, lad. Don't go.'

Rich had stayed the night. He had held Bulloch's head while he vomited into the lavatory and had then made him a cup of Nescafé and put him to bed. Bulloch had lain awake for a long time staring at the ceiling until finally the trembling had stopped and he slept. Only then had Rich left.

He did not see Bulloch for a week, for both men were given leave, but all those seven days he worried at the thought of what Bulloch's reaction would be when they met again. He could have saved himself the distress, for Bulloch never referred to it, never by a single action let Rich know that he recalled what had happened. It was part of the paradoxical nature of Bulloch that where Rich might have expected anger there was none; anger would establish that it *had* happened whereas clearly Bulloch had decided that it had not. But Rich knew it had and he knew the fear that lay deep down in Bulloch and he knew that Bulloch's anger at the dirt was some kind of armour, but he never knew why.

*

At that moment the radio went in the car and Glaister took it. He listened for some minutes and wrote quickly in his notebook before replacing the receiver then turned to Bulloch. 'House belongs to a Frenchman called Blanchet, sir. Owns a chain of hotels in …' he consulted his notebook, '… Africa and the Far East. The Yard have been on to his number two here, sir, and it seems he's away.'

'Where?'

'Singapore, sir. But should be in Vienna later tonight.'

'Is there a wife?'

'Yes, sir. Ruth Blanchet. The office here says they booked her into a hotel in Vienna. Also got her a ticket for a flight that left this afternoon.'

'What time?'

'Wasn't sure, sir, but thought about four or five.'

Bulloch looked at his watch. It showed a little after eight. She'd be there by now.

'Have they tried her?'

'Yes, sir. She's not there. Hotel says that the Vienna airport is fog-bound, sir.'

'Tell them to keep trying. What about family?'

'One boy, sir. Wasn't sure about age but he thought around ten.'

'Name?'

Glaister looked at his notebook again. 'Philip. Father calls him Philippe. He's actually the stepfather.'

'Staff?'

'There's a maid, sir. He thinks she's French, sir. And a chauffeur. English.'

'That all?'

'They've found something on Nash's desk, sir. A note. They're sending it round.'

A French maid, Bulloch thought. The man who had spoken to him had had a French accent. And a chauffeur, English.

He heaved himself out of the rear seat into the cold night and fastened the sheepskin more securely around his heavy body.

'Didn't he know the names?' he said, leaning towards the front window.

'Who, sir?' Glaister said.

'Blanchet's number two. Didn't he know the names of the staff?'

'He didn't say, sir.'

'Get them to find out. Wages may have been paid by the firm. Could be on the books.' He turned to Rich. 'Keep your eyes open,' he said, and then began to walk back towards the house.

*

'Move,' Jacmel said, indicating with the gun that Howard should climb the staircase. Dave had the boy now and Jacmel no longer seemed troubled by the shotgun, perhaps he realized it was the one thing that kept Dave from edging over into hysteria, perhaps because conditions had changed.

'You couldn't ask anyone to go into those rooms,' Howard said. His mouth was dry and he could feel his skin crawling.

'We cannot stay here. We must go up,' Jacmel said for the second time. The sitting-room on the first floor had tall windows overlooking the street, giving anyone in the house fire-control over the entire area. But somewhere on the first floor was the snake. Or was it? Perhaps it was down here on the ground floor. No one knew. In the flurry of panic that had surrounded the attack on Louise no one had seen where the snake had taken cover.

'Look,' Howard said. 'This is a mamba; a bloody black mamba. For God's sake let me take the shotgun.'

'Ask yourself,' Jacmel said. 'How can I give you the shotgun?'

'Please!'

'There is no possibility.' Although his voice was low there was a quality of grey granite about his face and eyes.

'You don't understand,' Howard said. 'They're like lightning. I wouldn't stand a chance.'

'Then we'd know where it is,' Dave said. 'That's something.'

Howard turned and saw Philip. The boy was looking like a ghost. But Howard was too occupied with his own problem.

'I understand too well,' Jacmel said. 'I see what happened to Louise. Come, you are wasting time.'

'At least let me take a stick,' Howard said desperately.

'Move.'

Howard stepped past Louise's body over which Jacmel had thrown a coat, and began to climb the stairs. The snake could be anywhere, behind a chair, in a dark corner, under the sofa. There was a fireplace. A display cabinet. The television set. As his mind recalled each piece of furniture, everyday things gathered menace.

He stopped. He hated himself but could not check the plea. 'Couldn't he come?' he said, pointing to Dave. 'Shotgun's the only weapon against a mamba.'

'You shut your bloody mouth,' Dave shouted. 'You get moving, you hear!' His eyes had widened in fright.

Howard turned to Jacmel. 'What about it?'

Jacmel's mouth turned down in distaste and he shook his head.

'Look,' Howard said, 'why don't we stay down here. We're pretty sure the damn thing isn't in that room.' He pointed to the room they had just left.

Jacmel seemed about to lose his temper but he took a grip on himself and walked up behind Howard. 'Move,' he said.

The sitting-room was dark except for where the light from the landing shone into it. Howard stood at the open door. In front of him was a shadow world, familiar yet unfamiliar, substantial yet insubstantial, a place entered in nightmares. Jacmel stood beside him, then reached through the door and felt for the light switch. The room flooded with light. Howard felt a hand in the small of his back pushing him forward and then he heard the door swish behind him, as Jacmel almost closed it; he was alone in the room. He stood blinking into the light unable to move, waiting for the first blurred movement on the edge of his cone of vision. He was rooted, fixed.

'You want the boy to be hurt?' Jacmel's voice sounded like a thunderclap and Howard looked from side to side in terror until he realized he was being foolish, that the snake was deaf.

'No.'

'Dave would hurt him.'

Slowly, as though his legs were made of some heavy inert substance, Howard moved into the room. He had been in it a hundred times yet now he looked at it as though he had never seen it before. It was about twelve metres long and six metres wide. Opposite him were heavily-curtained long windows that opened out over the street and looked to the square beyond. To his right was a Provençal fireplace set with rustic gas-logs.

On either side of the fireplace were two heavy floor lamps made from glass carboys. The hearthrug was white Himalayan goatskin over a thick gold Wilton carpet. A three-piece suite in brown-and-white tweed was arranged around the fireplace. The remainder of the room was given over to displays of one kind or another; good pieces of Victoriana; an eighteenth-century globe of the world which dominated one corner; a cabinet with a collection of Meissen.

On either side of the chimney-breast were books bought by the yard from a shop in Pimlico Square: Dickens, Scott, Thackeray, Macaulay, Lamb, a set of Grove, the political novels of Trollope, all in their leather bindings, never opened, shadowy. Space there for a long black body that would never be seen until one placed a hand on the shelf. And the curtains. Heavy dark green velvet. Was it there?

He needed protection, anything; but what? The long-handled brass tongs. Antique. Bought but never used. He moved towards the fireplace. It, too, was dark from old fires. Shadows. Black against black would be invisible. He stepped forward again, this time reaching the sofa. Then suddenly without conscious thought he stamped his foot hard on the floor, sending vibrations around the room, causing the chandeliers to tinkle. Would that make it move? A small movement was all he needed for his bush-trained eyes. Nothing big, God, nothing big. But there was no movement. The room was as still as a vacuum. He leaned towards the sofa and stared at the cushions. Nothing. His hand went out and he picked up the largest and dragged it towards him, holding it to his chest as though it were some valuable artefact.

Now the tongs, the only things in the room that looked like a weapon. He began to move sideways towards the fireplace. Log basket, billets of pine. Was there anything else? He strained his eyes. The mamba could be deep down amidst the logs, coiled, waiting. The heat in the room was intense. He could feel the drip of sweat running down his collar and forming on the inside of his legs.

The tongs were in his hands and he stepped back violently from the dark fireplace. Surely if it had been there it would have moved. He held the tongs in his right hand, the cushion in his left; the tongs became a sword, the cushion a shield. He stepped into the centre of the room.

'The corners,' Jacmel said from the door. 'Search there.'

Each piece of furniture was an object of terror. A chair was not a chair but a thing that occupied space and which had underneath it an area of darkness; each table cast a shadow; he went out to each as though to an unknown land, returning always to the centre of the gold carpet for there, like a bull in a ring, he had instinctively made his *querencia*, his territory, the only place in the room where he felt safe.

'The corners,' Jacmel said again.

He searched each corner. The wall cabinet sat flush, there was no place for a snake to hide behind it or underneath it. The globe, on its four legs, cast a deep shadow. Nothing there.

'The curtains,' Jacmel said.

The curtains he had kept for last. They hung in their rich dark folds, covering the sides of the windows, bunched, dangerous. Standing as far back as he could, he touched the first with the tongs, making it shake. Nothing. Carefully he lifted the bottom. They were heavy. Too heavy. God, he thought, was it there, wrapped in the velvet. Then he remembered the weights in the hem. Nothing.

One curtain. Then another. He moved to the second window. First curtain, nothing. A feeling of huge relief began to spread through his body. He stepped to the last curtain. Touched it with the tip of the tongs. Nothing. He leant forward and lifted it — and there it was. Shining. Black. Lying across the floor. He gave a cry and fell backwards against the sofa, covering himself with the pillow, hiding his head as a child might, waiting for the vicious hiss of escaping steam and the burning needles as the fangs entered his body. But there was nothing. He moved the pillow, scrambling back on the sofa and dropping behind it. No movement. He looked over the sofa. It was still there. Dead. Inert. And then he saw what he had not seen in his terror. It was too thin. He looked closely and discovered that it was the television aerial cable coming in from the window. He bent his head and felt a sob of relief rise into his throat. It was some moments before he raised himself and turned to the door. 'There's nothing here,' he said.

He did not hear the others come into the room until the door clicked shut. Then he was aware that the two chandeliers went out and one of the floor lamps near the fireplace was switched on and a cushion cover placed over the shade, giving the dimmest of lights. Only then did Jacmel open the curtains. Howard stood by the sofa hearing his heart hammering and feeling the sliminess of the sweat that had built up in his groin.

'Are you all right, Dick?'

The voice was a whisper and Howard pushed himself away from the support of the sofa and took the small hand. 'Yes.'

'We'll be all right, won't we?'

'Yes. As long as we do as they say.'

Jacmel was at the window, hidden from the outside by the folds of the curtains.

'What do you want us to do?' Howard said.

'Sit.' He indicated the sofa. 'Sit and be quiet.'

When he turned away from his inspection of the road he said to Howard, 'After that you wish a drink?'

Howard had not been unaware of the basket of liquor on the antique games table. Gin. Whisky. Vodka. Punte Mes, Pernod, Dubonnet ... the inside of his mouth gathered saliva as he yearned for something to quiet his raw nerves, but at the same time he was aware of the boy's stare.

'I need one,' Dave said and his voice cut Howard like a razor. It had a sharp edge to it, brittle and fine, and Howard turned and saw him standing in the middle of the floor, his knees slightly bent, his arms drawn up almost as though he were about to spring. Howard registered an aura as familiar as an old friend: fear. Dave was as fearful as he, perhaps even more so. He saw the pasty, chalk-white face, the body tensed and the eyes that flitted constantly round the room, probing, seeking. He's not sure, Howard thought; he's terrified it might still be here. And he tucked away the knowledge as a prisoner might hide a weapon.

Jacmel was still looking at Howard. 'You can have something,' he said.

'I've got a thirst like a horse,' Dave said loudly and began to move towards the table which held the liquor. He did so slowly, testing each footstep as someone might who crosses a bog.

'What?' Jacmel said, still looking at Howard.

'Mine's Scotch,' Dave said again loudly and Howard recognized the bravado. It was like someone talking to himself in a dark room.

Slowly Howard shook his head and the effort of will brought out the sweat on him again. He loosened his tie. 'It's a *jour sans*,' he said.

Jacmel looked at him oddly, and shrugged. Dave was at the table pouring himself a whisky.

'That is too much,' Jacmel said, seeing the half-filled tumbler.

'I can take it.'

'I don't know you.'

'Believe me.'

'It is too much,' Jacmel said again and he took the glass and tried to pour some of the whisky back into the bottle. 'For Christ's sake!' Dave said and made a grab for the glass. The whisky slopped on to the table leaving a small measure behind and this Jacmel handed back to him.

'That is enough,' he said.

They stared at each other, hostile, natural enemies, yet brought together by circumstances into an unnatural alliance.

'Watch the window,' Jacmel said. He poured himself a shot of vodka and threw it into the back of his throat.

After a moment Dave said, 'What do we do now?'

'We wait.'

'I don't like it.'

'We wait. We have the boy. No one will shoot the boy. We are not in South America.'

They waited. Time in that quiet room seemed to come to a halt: Dave at the window; Howard and the boy on the sofa; Jacmel pacing the floor, sometimes at the window, sometimes at the far side of the room, sometimes in Howard's vision, sometimes behind him. There was danger all around but in a sense they were on an island of safety within the danger. The snake was not in this room.

Abruptly Jacmel came to a stop in front of Howard. 'Why do you say a mamba?' he said.

'Oh, Jesus —' Dave began.

'Why?'

Because I know, Howard thought, because I have seen it happen before.

'They are few, no?'

In Eaton Square, Howard thought, but not in Africa; there, if you used the bush as he had, they were never far from your thoughts. You tended to discount other snakes, you knew they'd move away, afraid of you. But you could never tell with a mamba. 'No,' he said. 'They're not rare. You find them all over east and south-east Africa.'

'They are very bad,' Jacmel said. It was half-statement, half rhetorical question.

'Very bad,' Howard said. 'You saw what happened to Louise.'

'Jesus, can't you belt up!' Dave said from the window.

In his mind's eye Howard saw Harry Marshall, joking and smiling, thinking they'd got rid of the poison, and all the time he was dying. 'It happened to a friend of mine,' he said, and watched Dave under his eyelids.

Jacmel, who had walked to the window, now turned and came back. 'The same that happened to Louise?'

'Yes.'

'Can't you stop bloody talking about it?' Dave said.

'Where was this?' Jacmel said.

'Zambesi Valley.'

'When?'

'Some years after the war.'

Howard was aware that Dave had turned completely away as though trying not to hear and had begun to whistle softly through his teeth.

'With a mamba?'

He was forcing Jacmel to drag the details from him.

'Black mamba. About the same size as this one. You said it was more than two metres, didn't you?'

'Nearly three,' Philip said.

Howard did not want to look at Philip in case what he saw made him stop. It was a choice between what might happen to Philip and what might happen to Dave and he chose the latter.

'What happened?' Jacmel said.

'Why are we talking about this?' Dave said. 'What the hell's the matter? Talk. Talk. Talk.'

'What?' Jacmel repeated.

'I was a District Officer,' Howard said. 'Place called Chirundu.' He felt Philip's fingers tighten on his hand and remembered that Chirundu was where the incident with the lion and the terrier had occurred. 'It was Christmas,' he said and the memories came crowding back; heat, loneliness, heat; a tin of Crosse & Blackwell's Christmas pudding, which he had been saving and a box of crackers he'd bought on his last leave in Salisbury; a razor from his mother; a pipe he had bought himself, socks, hankies, the usual things. And just like a kid he had wanted to open the parcels when they arrived but he knew that if he did Christmas Day would be a disaster; he knew he'd get drunk at ten in the morning and stay that way until Boxing Day wiped out the feeling of loneliness. So he'd got one of his servants to cut a tree and he'd put it in the living-room of the small house in the middle of the *boma* and he had got out the presents and hung them amidst the broad, shiny, unChristmassy leaves. But even as he did so he knew that the holiday was only going to be possible if he had enough whisky inside him. It was his first Christmas alone in the bush and he was dreading it.

And then, on Christmas Eve, Harry Marshall had come marching in from the neighbouring administrative post nearly fifty miles away. He had half a dozen bearers with him and they were carrying all kinds of things, wine, cake, nuts, a tinned ham, tinned butter, even brandy. '*God Jul*,' Harry had said as he marched into the *boma*. 'I've come to keep the feast with you.'

Howard thought he had never been so pleased to see anyone. That night they'd sat up drinking whisky and swapping stories about the District Commissioner's wife.

Somewhere around midnight Howard had confessed that if Harry had not arrived when he had he, Howard, would have been drunk by now and would have stayed that way for a week and Harry had said that habits were the most dangerous things for a lonely bachelor. 'If you get into the *habit* of boozing by yourself, you're done for,' he said. 'I try not to drink every day. *Jour sans. Jour avec.* That sort of system.' It was a system that Howard had followed from then on, except for a while in Kenya.

The following morning they had decided to go out with the guns for a few hours' sport while their combined staffs put together a meal worthy of the festival.

Howard remembered the morning vividly. An early mist on the river which had been burnt away by eight o'clock and then the wet heat of the valley closing in on them. They had taken shotguns to see if they could get a couple of duck or guinea fowl for the larder, for Marshall was staying for at least a week.

*

Howard did not tell the story in this detail, instead he filtered out the personal memories, hardening the facts, telling it briefly as it happened.

'We never saw a guinea fowl,' he said, 'but I remember Marshall shot a couple of francolin.'

'Francolin?' Jacmel was squatting down in front of the sofa, his head cocked on one side.

'Red-legged partridge.'

'What then?'

They had been a good way from the river when Harry had shot the birds, more open, less bush, and they were coming home when he was bitten. He had either tramped on the snake or very near it; it had probably been asleep at the edge of the path. Anyway, it had hit Harry in the left calf, just a smack, as though someone had softly clapped his hand; then the shining whiplash through the grass and it was gone.

'We tied ligatures above and below the wound,' Howard said, 'and I cut it and sucked it and let it bleed. We weren't more than half a mile from home and I had serum there and I gave him a shot and I also rubbed permanganate of potash into the cuts. I put on two more ligatures, one above the knee and one at the top of the thigh. Then I put him to bed and wrapped him in blankets.'

Neither of them had been unduly apprehensive, Howard thought. They had done everything: anti-venene, potash crystals, four ligatures which he released every few minutes so the limb wouldn't die from lack of blood. All they could.

'He wanted brandy. I tried to talk him out of it because alcohol's not too good for snakebite but I remember him saying it was Christmas and he had walked fifty miles for a drink with me and that's what he was going to have.

'He'd been bitten around ten o'clock and for the first hour he was somewhat excited, talking a lot and laughing, I thought it was the reaction to the fright. Then he seemed to calm down and was perfectly normal except he had a touch of diarrhoea. He also said that the muscles in his mouth and tongue were twitching a bit.'

Howard had sat by the bedside as the hot noon hours came and went. Christmas lunch was announced but Harry had said he didn't feel like it and had asked if it could be kept until evening. He was sure he'd be ready for it then. They chatted, rather like two people in a convalescent home where the patient is almost whole again.

'About four o'clock in the afternoon he became less talkative,' Howard said. 'I noticed that his eyelids were getting puffy. He seemed rather tired. Then at five o'clock, without any warning, he grabbed at his throat and jumped out of bed. He tried to hold out his hands to me but couldn't leave his own throat. I think he was trying to force air down it. He shouted my name once, then fell down and was dead in five minutes.'

There was a complete silence in the room as Howard paused. Then Jacmel said, 'Were there black marks, you know, like Louise?'

'For Christ's sake!' Dave shouted. 'Leave it alone!'

Howard nodded. 'When I laid him out I noticed that the left side of his body was stiff and rigid, the right side quite relaxed. When I took off his clothes I saw a dark purple line —'

'Stop it!' Dave shouted and swung the shotgun. 'Stop your fucking mouth or I'll shoot you, you bastard!'

Howard dropped his eyes. He doubted very much that Dave would use the gun with Jacmel in the room. '— a dark purple line,' he went on, 'about two inches wide running up the left side from the bite, over the left shoulder, up behind the ear to the base of the skull.'

Again he paused. 'How old was he, your friend?' Jacmel said.

'Same as me, early twenties.'

'What did you do?'

What was there to do, Howard thought? He'd sat with Marshall all that night and into the next morning. He hadn't wanted to bury him on Christmas Day; he'd not known why, just that the feeling was strong. He had drunk the rest of the brandy and almost a bottle of whisky and had become maudlin with loneliness and shock and found himself crying like a child. Later, when dawn came, they had carried the body to the far side of the *boma* and dug a grave. 'I buried him,' he said, 'just as someone has to bury Louise.'

Jacmel shrugged and resumed his pacing. Dave turned and looked out of the window again. Silence crept back. Howard and the boy sat holding each other's hands on the sofa. All was as it had been before except that Dave had developed a nervous habit of drying the palm of his right hand on the side of his trouser leg. It was a movement that Jacmel missed, but Howard did not.

Jacmel reminded him of an animal in a small enclosure, the sort they had put the leopards into at the safari park hotel. It had been about the size of a tennis court, big enough one would have thought, for a couple of leopards, but the male had never got used to it. He had paced up and down the side of the wire until he had worn out the grass and formed a wide dirt path. Like the leopard, Jacmel did not pace through nervousness but restriction.

After a few moments he went and stood at the other window, hidden from anyone in the street by the curtains.

Howard could not make him out. With Louise he had seemed almost gentle, now he could shrug off her death as though it had not happened or did not really matter. There was something very hard about him, Howard thought, which made Dave's tough-boy bravado seem childlike by comparison. He wondered what his background was. Marseilles? Paris? Corsica? His accent was thick enough to be almost incomprehensible. It was said that the French were experts at kidnapping, that it was a French crime, but apart from that Howard knew very little about the French underworld except what he had gained from movies and books. But he knew one thing: France was one of the few countries in the West that retained the death penalty, the guillotine tried and true, and there had to be good reasons for retaining it. There was a streak of brutality in the French, he thought, which had come out in Indo-China and Algeria and he knew that if he had eventually to face either man in the room he would rather it was not Jacmel.

He looked over at Dave and thought he was the kind of person who could not stand silence. He was reminded of several of his safari clients: big men in their own fields, from Germany and America, tycoons — you had to be a tycoon these days to afford to shoot big game in Africa — people you'd have thought might have welcomed the solitude and quiet of the African bush. But some had brought cassette recorders and others fancy Japanese radios and one or two even radio telephones that would keep them in touch with their nearest office. They couldn't keep still, talked all the time, nervous, brittle talk; always fiddling with the radios or the recorders or trying to get in touch with Cable & Wireless in Nairobi.

Perhaps it was fear. The biggest talkers were the most afraid, that was an equation Howard had solved early on. They were the ones who wanted to shoot from the Land Rover or sleep in the back of the truck away from the creepy crawlies or the hyenas that might come into camp and snatch off a toe from a sleeping body with their powerful jaws. They were the ones who drank too much, who called him Dick in the first five minutes. Dick this ... and Dick that ... Whose voices were a shade too loud, who couldn't sit still, who were most like Dave. Was that where it had begun for him, he wondered? Was fear something you could pass on, not just for a moment, but for ever; did one get it, like leprosy, from being so often in contact with it, or had it started for him long before he became a white hunter, when he was still a young man in the Colonial Service watching Marshall die of mamba bite.

If Dave was like many of his clients, Jacmel was like very few. Perhaps more like Blanchet than most. Which was odd because the French were supposed to be emotional and highly-strung and one could not possibly say that about Jacmel or Blanchet.

Blanchet had come to him about ten years before with one simple demand: he wanted an elephant. Nothing else. Didn't matter about lions or any of the buck, didn't want a buffalo, just an elephant; which was like saying you wanted Marilyn Monroe and no one else would do. It was not possible to get a licence to shoot an elephant at that time. The Game Department had made a count the year before and they had found that stocks were down by nearly twenty-five per cent because of an increase in poaching.

Blanchet had come to see him in his office in Nairobi one burning hot afternoon when the blinds were down and Howard was hungover from a too-hectic night in the Stanley the night before.

'Can't be done,' he had said. 'Could get you a lion. Buffalo. Kudu. Tommie, of course. Pig.' The little Frenchman had stood on the other side of the littered desk and shaken his head.

'I will give you five hundred American dollars above your price.'

'Could probably get you a zebra; oryx too.'

'I will give you a thousand American dollars.'

Christ, Howard thought, anger rising to make his hangover worse, you bloody little turd. Slowly he picked up Blanchet's business card from the top of his desk and flicked it over so he could see the name. It was a gesture filled with angry contempt.

Why the hell did these little turds always want to shoot the biggest bloody things on Earth?

'Look, Blanchet,' he said, enunciating his words with care, 'I said it can't be done. No can do. It's not bloody on, old sport. Absolument pas. Comprendo?'

'I understand but ...'

'Not for five hundred. Not for fifty thousand bloody American dollars.' His voice had been steadily rising.

Blanchet seemed unaffected by his emotion. 'Not here, perhaps.'

'Where then?'

'Mozambique.'

'Mozambique! That's on the other side of Tanzania.'
'I know.'
'It'd cost you a fortune.'
'I know.'
'Well, why not go *there* and hire yourself a white hunter?'
'Because I want you.'
'But I haven't a licence to operate there.'
'We go as two friends, two hunters. Cannot we do that?'
'I suppose so. But, look, it'd be a hell of a lot cheaper …'
'I am not worried about the money.'
'You just want an elephant, is that right? Nothing else. All that way just for one elephant. And when you drop it, we come home? Have I got it straight?'
'That is correct.'
Howard shrugged. 'It's your funeral.'
For the first time Blanchet smiled, it was thin and rather wintry. 'That is not a good joke, M Howard. It is to avoid the funeral that I wish you to come.'
So they had gone down south of the Rovuma River and Blanchet had shot his elephant, or rather Howard had shot it for him, a female carrying less than thirty pounds of ivory a side. But it turned out that the elephant was only one of Blanchet's ambitions, he also wanted to bag a big game hunter. They hadn't been together more than a day or two, when Howard found himself being carefully scrutinized and judged, and it was towards the end of the two-week trip that Blanchet had begun to talk about his concept of a safari hotel, rather like the famous Tree Tops, except that guests would not only have a night view over a waterhole but during the day they would be conducted through a small game park owned by the hotel where a certain number of animal sightings was guaranteed and where the feeding of the big cats in the open would be the centrepiece of the entertainment. He wanted Howard to take over the running of the park.
On the last evening in camp before returning to Nairobi, Blanchet was sitting upright in his canvas safari chair drinking a whisky, neat and dapper even in the bush, and Howard said, 'You knew there was a moratorium on shooting elephants in Kenya.' The Frenchman had nodded. 'So the business of the five hundred and the thousand dollars was just so much blah.'
'Perhaps.'

'And if I'd said all right, I'll take your money, you'd have disappeared into the hills, wouldn't you?'

Blanchet had looked surprised. 'Why?' he said.

'Because it was a bribe.'

'But I have no objection,' Blanchet said. 'Why should you?' Howard had not pursued it; the French were a strange, impenetrable people.

At the end of a year the Gametrails Safari Hotel had been built eighty miles from Nairobi and Howard was its first Park Director, making more money than he had ever made as a white hunter and having some of it paid into an account in Basle which Blanchet had suggested he open on his first European leave. That alone made the job worthwhile, for Kenya's exchange control regulations were ferocious and ever since he had been forced to sell his farm at a loss after independence he had begun to plan for the time when he would leave Kenya. The problem had always been — until Blanchet came along — finding a way to get money out.

The irony was that Blanchet had been grateful. Whether it was for the elephant or for his decision to join him, Howard had never known, but Blanchet had made his gratitude felt in the only way he knew and that was by giving Howard a salary far in excess of anything he might have expected. The *real* irony was that Blanchet could have had him for half the money. He was ready and willing to pack in the white hunter bit. He knew his nerves had gone, frayed by years of living in the bush, starting perhaps when Marshall had been bitten by the mamba. Of late he had been drinking too much. No *jours sans*, all *avec*. That was a classic symptom. Luckily he had been given the opportunity in time. A few months more and Blanchet would have heard the bar stories and he would not have come to Howard.

He'd never been so happy in his life as he was in the hotel. He knew where every meal was coming from, didn't have to prepare it himself, didn't.have to wrorry about his laundry, or his clothes, or his quarters; all the boring details taken care of and a whopping salary on top of it. It was like boarding school all over again; he'd loved school. And the animal side was easy to someone with his experience. The park was about twenty thousand acres with the hotel built at the side of the main waterhole. The rest of the land was light bush, low hills, scrub. He'd created a series of camps cut off from each other by high game fences and he had brought in wildebeeste and eland, impala, kongoni, sable, puku, roan and oryx and separated them from the cats, lions, leopards and cheetahs which had a camp to themselves. He had managed to lay his hands on a pair of giraffes, and a fewr crocodiles for the waterhole. Hippos were already there and George Biddle, an old friend of his and now Director of National Parks, had heard of a baby rhino being bottle-fed at Tsavo after her mother had been killed by poachers. Howard had taken the truck and fetched her and they'd called her Rosie, given her a small enclosure to herself and she'd been a star turn.

No, there had been no danger there. No one was shooting at anything except with telephoto lenses and the animals soon got used to the powerful arc lights that lit them up at night when they came down to the waterhole to drink, and soon got used to the convoys of cars led either by Howard or one of his black game rangers that drove through the camps — eland became so accustomed to them that they would poke their heads through the windows whenever the cars stopped. The only real danger was the hotel guests. The rules were that no car windows were to be opened and no one was to get out to take pictures. In the ten years that Howard was at the hotel they had several accidents. In one case a baboon playing on the roof of a car had bitten a woman's hand to the bone when she opened the window and offered it a banana. In another a Japanese guest had gone down to the waterhole late at night to try and photograph a Greater Kudu and had nearly been undone by one of the crocs which had stalked him round the water's edge and had been frightened away just in time by a second guest who had seen what was happening and thrown an ice-bucket at it.

They'd been lucky. *He'd* been lucky. Until that last day.

*

The picture reared itself in his mind and this time did not go away at his command. It was an Englishman named Prentiss who had started it. Howard could remember him clearly: fat, pink-fleshed from sunbathing in the unfamiliar heat, stripped to a pair of blue linen slacks, his hairy gut spilling over the waistband, two wobbly tits. Bald, but wearing a sun-visor. Expensive Japanese single-lens reflex with telephoto slung around his neck and a pair of Zeiss binoculars. He had spoken with the flat accents of the Midlands where he'd made his money selling ballbearings. Howard had had a drink with him the evening before and all he'd talked about was his bloody Jaguar and the beat he had on the Spey and the grouse he shot over on the hills of Strathdearn. Very nasty. He'd got drunk the first night at the hotel and abused one of the black waiters for imagined insolence to his wife, who had ordered a whisky-mac and had got something else because the bartender had never heard of it.

He remembered the wife, too. Her body shape was almost the twin of her husband's but she exaggerated it by wearing shorts. She had an arse on her like a Bushman woman Howard had once seen down in Bechuanaland; stuck out like the haunch of a mare held up by corrugated naked thighs. Ghastly sight. She'd had a conversation trick that the other guests had quickly discovered and had become a kind of hotel joke for a couple of days. Each time her husband said something, she confirmed it.

They'd been talking about wild animals and Prentiss had been telling Howard about lions. 'No different here from what they are at Longleat,' he'd said. 'Told Lord Bath as much when I visited the place.'

'He did, you know,' said Mrs Prentiss earnestly.

'I said to his Lordship, what's the bloody point of going all the way to Africa when you've got what we want to see right here in England.'

'That's true,' said Mrs Prentiss. 'He said that.'

'We went to the Windsor Safari Park last year,' Prentiss said. 'Lions all round the car. Tame as anything. Gave one of 'em a bar of choclate.'

'... a bar of chocolate,' echoed Mrs Prentiss.

'I wouldn't try that here if I were you,' Howard had said, disengaging himself.

At noon each day Howard took a group to see the lions being fed. This was done in a ten-acre enclosure with high fences all round. He'd get the guests there about five minutes to twelve, just before the meat arrived. Usually there were half a dozen cars and the two hotel kombis, between twenty and thirty people all told. The vehicles would go into the enclosure and draw up in a semi-circle near the middle where they bristled with telephoto lenses.

It was always a nervous time for the lions. There were fourteen of them including cubs and at this time of day they were very hungry. Howard had built several platforms eight to ten feet high of rough logs and some lions would lie watchfully on the platforms while others would pace up and down, tails moving from side to side; hungry expectant, and on a knife-edge of tension.

On this day the cars and minibuses had drawn up in their places some minutes before the meat was due and he and his black game-ranger had seen everyone settled down and quiet. Then the Ford truck protected by heavy wire netting all around it had come into the enclosure, the gates had been shut and the truck driven to the centre of the area. The lions had come bounding down from their platforms and, with the others, had run after the truck. Great gobbets of donkey and goat meat were flung on to the ground in the middle of the enclosure and the lions fell upon them, growling and snarling. At this point the fat Englishman, Prentiss, followed by his wife, got out of his car and began to walk towards the lions, taking photographs. Howard had not seen him at first because he was hidden by the other kombi. Then he heard his game-ranger shout and saw the incredible sight of the English couple ambling along, the man taking photographs, the wife holding a second camera.

'Get back!' Howard shouted. 'Get back to your car!'

They either did not hear or did not take notice. He saw the game-ranger get out of his own kombi and go after them.

Fourteen hungry lions, lionesses and cubs, all after a share of food make an atavistic sight as they tear whole joints from each other and it was this that the hotel guests had come to see. Always, at the beginning of their meal the lions were nervous and there was a great deal of snarling and posturing, as the hierarchy sorted itself out. It was towards this complex and dangerous behavioural melée that Prentiss and his wife were moving.

'GET BACK!' Howard shouted again. 'YOU ARE IN DANGER!' But the couple who had visited the lions of Longleat in Wiltshire and the Windsor Safari Park near London were not to be deterred. Howard scooped up his .375 Magnum and shouted to his startled passengers, 'Nobody move out of here!' Then he was running towards the couple, with the ranger converging on them from the far side of the cars.

'For Christ's sake!' he yelled at Prentiss when he reached him. 'Are you bloody mad? Get back to your car!' He put out a hand to grab Prentiss by the arm and turn him physically in the direction he wished him to go. What happened next took only a matter of seconds. A young lion with a short mane had only a moment before been relieved of a piece of meat by a bigger and stronger male, had then taken a small piece from one of the cubs and must have felt threatened by the presence of humans, for it dropped the meat and charged at the group now made up of Prentiss, his wife, Howard and the ranger.

They saw the lion together. Mrs Prentiss screamed. Prentiss threw his arms up in front of his face and Howard ... something, some message or impulse went astray in his head, for instead of his brain telling his arms to bring up the gun, it told his legs to run. He turned in terror, blindly, the gun slipping from his hand, but Prentiss was in the way and he tried to fling him aside. In that moment the lion crashed into him, spinning him over on to his back and churning at his stomach with its back claws, trying to disembowel him. He had a flashing memory of teeth above him, of the foetid stink of the animal's breath, of its weight, of the roar of the ranger's gun, then merciful darkness. It had been some weeks before he came back to real consciousness in his hospital room. By then he was a hero. What the watchers in their cars had seen, because it was what they had *wanted* to see, was Howard flinging himself in front of Prentiss and in so doing losing his rifle. Shortly afterwards Michel Blanchet had come to see him and given him the chance of coming to London. Howard was, as he had said, a brave man and he could always use brave men.

*

He fought his way back to the present, back to the room in the house just off Eaton Square, which was horrible enough, yet at that moment seemed preferable to his memories.

'We can't just bloody sit here,' Dave was saying, rubbing the palm of his right hand up and down his thigh.

'Be cool,' Jacmel said.

'Cool! I like that. That's nice, that is. Half the coppers in London down there at the end of the street and you say be cool.'

'Not only in the street,' Jacmel said. 'Up there and up there ...' He pointed to the dark windows that overlooked the front of the house.

'What's up there?' Dave said. Then his eyes widened as he understood. 'You mean up *there*?'

'They are not fools.'

'Jesus,' Dave stepped farther away from the window. 'And you do *nothing*!'

'It makes no difference,' Jacmel said. 'We have the boy. It makes no difference if they have all the English police. All the English army —'

'You keep on bloody saying that but what about us in here with that ... that ...'

'It is not here in this room.'

'We can't stay here *all* the time, I mean ...'

'If you want to piss, then piss,' Jacmel said.

'It's not that,' Dave said, curiously embarrassed. 'It's just that ... look, why not make them give us some of that serum stuff. We could tell them that if they didn't we would cut off one of his ears. Like they did to that kid in Italy.'

Jacmel shook his head. 'Let me tell you something,' he said. 'It is a war, this; between him and me.'

'Who?'

'The big man, the policeman. He wants us to stay, no? The longer he can keep us in here the better for him. This is what they do. They keep you in one place for days, for weeks. They have everything, you have nothing; they have the world around them, you have silence. Yes? That is what we have to fight and anything that makes us weaker helps *them*. If he knows we have a poisonous reptile here in the house with us he must know we are afraid. But until now he knows nothing. Not even how many we are, nor who we are. Everything he does not know makes it stronger for us. You understand?'

Dave said nothing. He was unconvinced. 'Don't worry,' Jacmel said. 'When you wish to piss *he* will go first.' He pointed his thumb at Howard.

'Here he comes!' Dave said in a harsh whisper as though his voice might carry down to the big man shambling through the mist towards the house.

*

Bulloch came on past the Citroen and the yellow Cortina, the only two cars in the cul-de-sac, and as he passed the Citroen he bent and looked in the windows. That was careless, he thought, the key was still in the ignition. He opened the door and pulled it out. Then he looked at the Cortina. The key was gone. All right, he thought, we'll deal with that one later. Not now. Now it was time to show the flag, make the dirt sweat a bit. He came on, heavy-footed, until he reached the pavement in front of the house, where he stopped. He hunched down in his sheepskin coat and looked at the house from underneath his eyebrows. Nothing at the downstairs windows. No tell-tale movement of curtains. Well, they'd have been bloody fools to stay there. First floor. Two good big windows, long, rather like French windows, opening on to tiny wrought-iron balconies. There Was something different about the windows on the first floor compared with the others in the house; they were not like dead eyes; there was the faintest life there. Warmth. That's where they were then. Must have a light on somewhere; probably covered with a towel, almost impossible to see it in the orange glow of the street lamps. Who were they trying to fool anyway? Then he realized they had probably done it because they had guessed there were marksmen in the adjoining houses. They weren't such fools. Still, anyone could have thought of that. It wasn't particularly clever. All it did was show the dirt were thinking.

How many, he wondered? Two for sure. Could be more. French. Political? Hadn't sounded political. They usually shot their mouths off in the first minute with their demands. What were the French mixed up in? Algeria was over, so was Indo-China; there were some former French colonies in Africa but there'd been no excitement there. Blacks had simply taken over and shot their opposition or put them in jail, as far as he could tell — or care. Owner of the house was a wealthy Frenchman. Voice from the house was French. They had the boy. Straight kidnapping? French crime. Remember the Peugeot kid.

Nash must have got on to them. But how? Anyway, you didn't handle something like this on your own. Whole bloody force would have known about it. You don't just go and knock at the door and say I'm a copper and you'd better stop kidnapping that boy. Or if you did you got the shotgun treatment and you bloody deserved it. What the hell *had* Nash been doing there? If he knew that he'd know a lot.

He thought he saw just the smallest movement of one of the curtains in the upstairs room. Good, he thought, they're watching. He turned slowly so that his back was to the house. Let them have his arse, he thought. Of course they could put a bullet through his head as soon as wink. They'd shot Nash. They weren't shy about it. He felt the protective anger build up like a carapace shielding his back and his nerves. Bloody dirt.

The minutes ticked by. Ten … fifteen … twenty … His feet began to freeze and the cold slowly crept up from his toes through his feet to his ankles like damp rising in a rotten wall. This was the worst part, he thought, but he would not move. No stamping up and down. No blowing on the hands. No exercises to keep warm. That was part of everyday life; that's what normal people would be doing. He gets cold just like us, they'd think, looking at him. He wasn't like them; not like the dirt. And he'd show them he wasn't and sooner or later something inside them would recognize that and they would cringe a little and that would be the beginning of the end. What did the kids call it these days? You *psyched* someone; you did it on the tennis court or on the battlefield. Psyched. That was it. Well, this was his battlefield and he didn't need stupid long-haired words to explain what he was doing. Christ, the way they used words these days. Only pure English spoken in these islands was north of the border. Any Scot could teach these bastards about words.

Stamping was a weakness. Blowing on hands was a weakness. Walking up and down a weakness. They mightn't recognize this at the beginning but his presence, his strength would wear on them in the end. The end ... would they shoot the boy in the end? Would they strangle him? Hit him from behind? In spite of himself, Bulloch shivered. Not his problem. Don't think about it. If you think about it your resolve goes. Hard. That's how it had to be played; hard. The old woman in Sutherland Street. She'd only lived a few days after they broke that siege. People had said he'd been too rough. That a little of the gently-bentley treatment might have got her out sooner. You couldn't tell ... But a boy. Christ ... What was he, ten? Well, where the hell were his parents? You didn't fuck off half way round the world and leave your ten-year-old in charge of some poncy chauffeur and a French maid, then ask him, Bulloch, to pick up the pieces. It would never have happened when he was a kid. Never ... Don't think about the boy. Think about something else. Think about the cold that was numbing his calf muscles.

Cold. Real cold. He'd known real cold. This was pansy stuff. Edinburgh on a February day. An east wind howling in off the Firth. Binns corner, waiting in the terrible cold for his mother to finish work in the packing room. Too frightened to go home by himself in case his father was already there. That had been cold. When you were hungry the cold always felt worse.

And in the school holidays, the winter holidays, getting up at six to look for golf balls on the Braid Hills or Craig-lockhart or even out at Gullane: Dunlop 65s, Warwicks, Penfolds. Like bloody diamonds because during the war you couldn't get them. Hands and knees in the grass where the duffers sliced. Beating through the whinns in a northerly gale, nose streaming, eyes weeping, knuckles orangey-blue. That had been cold. And then when you had found a few balls, round to the clubhouse and a knock at the shop door and the secretary would come out and see what you had to sell. Dunlop 65s ninepence, all the rest sixpence, less if they were badly cut, and he knew the bloody secretary sold them at nearly twice what he paid him. Then home with the money and sometimes his mother would buy a couple of baps and have something warm herself if his father wasn't there; and sometimes he wasn't. Sometimes he'd get a few weeks for petty thieving, sometimes a couple of days for drunk and disorderly. Often he wished they'd cart him off to Barlinnie Gaol and throw away the key. That's where he'd first come across the dirt: his father.

Bulloch stood there in front of the house staring into the heavy mist, unmoving, gross, smelling the smell of his childhood, the smell of coal fires, heavy now on the London air, unable to escape because of the low cloud layer. The smell caught him at the back of the nose: Edinburgh winters, the whole Gothic skyline belching smoke.

They'd lived up a stair on the Royal Mile between the Castle and Holyrood House. The Royal Mile! The Stinking Mile more like it. Full of bloody tourists gawping at the tartan shops and the trinkets. The Happy Haggis. The Frying Scotsman. Jesus bloody save us from winsome Scots. What the tourists didn't do was poke their snouts into the wynds and smell the smell of urine and vomit. Who could blame them? They'd come to Scotland to look for Rob Roy and Bonnie Prince Charlie and buy up kilts and sporrans to wear at Caledonian Society meetings back home in Woolloomooloo and Bloemfontein. They hadn't come to see Hamish Bulloch, Esq, sleeping it off by the dirtbins in the pale sun.

That was a time he just might have made something of himself. As a kid his mother had given him an old set of his grandfather's golf clubs, hickory shafted, still called by the old names, mashie and niblick and cleek, and when he was looking for lost balls he'd play as many holes as he could — out of sight of the clubhouse of course, for he couldn't afford the green fees — and the old men who sat on the benches in the August wind would say they hadn't seen a better swing since Harry Vardon. Once a pro told him he had the makings of a champion. He *had*; he knew he had. But there was never the time to practise and he'd gone into the Army the day he had left school and they'd shipped him out to Burma and by the time the war was over the world was a different place and there wasn't much time for hickory-shafted golf clubs.

His mother was dying when he came back and if his father had been at home when he got there he'd have killed him with his own hands for what he'd brought her to. Daughter of a school-master in Dundee. That's what she'd been. And married Hamish Bulloch, Esq, self-employed builder. Jesus. He'd never been able to keep out of prison long enough to dig a set of foundations. He tried to recall his mother's face but could only bring back a hazy figure, short, plump — dumpy she would have been called. But lovely silky brown hair that she wore in a plait. It was she who had fought to keep him at school when their family circumstances cried out for him to find work; it was she who heard him his lessons, who gave him a love of words and reading. How she'd ever married his father he could not think. Had there been some chemistry there in the early days or was his the only proposal? He didn't know and never would now, for she died six months after VJ Day.

Bulloch only saw his father once more after that. It was on an evening in early May and he was coming down the Lothian Road near Toll Cross and he'd looked over a wall into a derelict building site where a group of meths drinkers were huddled round a fire of old door-frames and one of them had looked up. The face was covered in stubble and there were sores at the corners of his mouth. He had recognized Hamish Bulloch, Esq, self-employed builder, but there was no corresponding recognition in the blank drugged eyes that looked up at him. They simply looked up and looked away and Bulloch walked on down towards Prince's Street. A week later he left Edinburgh for London, he was in his early twenties and had been to war, but all he had so far gained from life was a store of hatred. At first it centred solely on his father but then shifted to embrace those like his father. Once, when he was twelve, he had heard a neighbour talking about his father. She and another neighbour had been gossiping on the stairs and they had not known he was listening. They'd talked about his mother, too, saying how much better she was than his father. Then one had described him as dirt. Bulloch had often read of children flying to the defence of their parents when they heard them criticized. But he had simply stood there listening and then had crept away. He agreed with them. His father *was* dirt. And there were thousands like him.

In London he joined the Metropolitan Police and for twenty-five years he had been looking for the dirt and been paid for it. In a strange way he was a happy man. His own man, too. There'd been Muriel, of course, and the flat in Notting Hill Gate (Kensington, she'd insisted) but that was a long time ago. Seventeen or eighteen years. Couldn't even remember what she looked like. How long had the marriage lasted? Eighteen months? Two years? Could hardly call it a marriage. They'd wanted different things. She'd wanted a Chesterfield suite and doilies. He'd wanted six pints of a Sunday lunchtime and a chance to get the dirty water off his chest. He doubted she'd ever seen a naked man before they were married and was quite sure she'd never had one on top of her. Doilies and butter-knives and coasters under the glasses and don't touch me there I don't like it.

Well, he still touched them now and then when he got the chance — and he did get his chances; payment for favours received you might say, but as often as not he passed them by. Fifty-two years old, and a lot of whisky and fags and something had to go. Age. Old Age. He'd never see sixty-five, thank God. There'd be no geriatric ward for him. If nothing else got him this bloody cold would. He had an impulse to stamp his right foot. Fought it. Won. And then turned slowly back to look at the house. As he did so he saw a window open.

*

From the house the two men watched him. During the past thirty minutes as Bulloch had stood in the freezing mist, tension had built up in the room. It had begun as an edginess, a layer on top of the tension that existed already. It had been the contemptuous way in which Bulloch had turned his back on them that had worked it up and up.

'Bloody old git,' Dave had said. 'What the hell's he think he's up to?'

Bulloch might have been made of stone, for there was no movement whatsoever. Jacmel and Dave were waiting, although they did not realize it, for him to turn back again. That was how the tension arose. Subconsciously they knew he had to turn round, the unknown factor was *when*. It was like an unresolved phrase in music, the notes hanging in the air without the resolution to give them shape. Bulloch had performed half the musical phrase by turning away but they knew he had to turn back because until he did, whatever was going to happen next could not happen.

From the sofa Richard Howard could not see what was happening but he could gauge the effect on Dave. His hands seemed to be sweating continuously and when he removed them from the gun to wipe them on his pants Howard could see damp patches on the barrel and stock. During most of the half hour in which Bulloch had his back to the house Jacmel hardly moved, but Dave began to display a nervous pattern of movements starting with the hand-wiping. Then he would raise his hand and use his sleeve cuff to wipe his forehead as though sweat was gathering there. He did this regularly once every three or four minutes until Howard could almost time him. Then, abruptly, he broke the pattern. His hand had gone down to wipe itself dry when suddenly it shot forward, grabbed the window and flung it open. It was at this moment that Bulloch turned to face the house once more.

'Don't you turn your back!' Dave shouted wildly. 'You turn your back on me once more and I'll fucking shoot you!'

Jacmel took one step, slammed Dave against the wall and beat him with the side of his left hand. Dave held on to the curtain, blood trickling from a cut on his lower lip.

'Can you hear me?' Bulloch's voice came through the partly opened window.

'I can hear you,' Jacmel said.

'You ready to send the boy out yet?'

'Where is your superior?'

'Superior?'

'Yes, your superior,' Jacmel said and for the first time Howard heard a slight note of anger. It was very slight, almost imperceptible, but it was there, like a faint pulse. Again he thought Bulloch had made a small gain.

'What for?' Bulloch said.

'You went to get ...' Jacmel paused as though sensing where the next question might lead him.

But Bulloch was not going to let him off. 'Oh, you mean just now. No, no. I went to have a pee and a cup of coffee. You can talk to me all right. By the way, if we're going to talk we'd better know who we are. What's your name?'

'My name is immaterial.'

'I see. What about the other lad? He's the chauffeur, is he? You're English, laddie. Bit out of your depth in this one, aren't you?'

The two men at the window remained silent and after a while Bulloch said, 'Well, no matter. We'll know in a wee while. By the by, my name's Bulloch.'

Dave swung towards Jacmel. 'He's the copper who —'

'Be silent!'

'For Christ's sake,' Dave hissed. 'He's the bloke who broke the Sutherland Street siege. It was all in the papers. I tell you he *never* gives in.'

'He will give way in this one,' Jacmel said. He turned to the window again. 'Hey, policeman!'

'I hear you.'

'Good. Then listen well. We want money. A car. And one hour.'

'How much?' Bulloch said and Howard saw Jacmel turn to Dave and smile. 'How much d'you think a copper's life's worth?'

'We want a hundred thousand pounds, but not all in English.'

'And?'

'A car. The yellow one down there. The Ford.'

'And?'

'When we bring the boy out the road is clear. And we have one hour before the police begin anything. Otherwise —' Jacmel turned into the room and took Philip by the shoulder, forcing him to the open window. 'Can you see him?'

'Yes,' Bulloch said, and Howard heard a sudden change in tone as though some of the confidence had gone. 'Yes, I see him.'

At that moment the lights of one of the cars at the end of the cul-de-sac flicked on and off twice. Jacmel and Dave saw it, as did Bulloch, and for a second the lights lit up the figure of Philip standing on the balcony. Then Jacmel pulled him backwards and returned him to the sofa.

Dave said, 'He's going back. It's some sort of bloody signal!' He turned on Jacmel. 'You don't understand,' he shouted. 'He's a bloody killer, that copper.'

'Calm yourself,' Jacmel said, and Howard could see he was making an effort with Dave. 'Be calm. Remember we have the boy.'

'Yes, but what can we do? Where can we go? What the hell can we do in an hour, where can we hide?'

'But we already have a place,' Jacmel said. 'You have seen it yourself. We can be there in five minutes. There is food, drink, everything. The rent is paid. We do not have to move for a month if we do not wish. By that time who will be looking for us? A few police, that is all. The next crime and the next and the next will have happened. We will be stale.'

It took some seconds for this to sink in, then Dave seemed to relax. 'Yeah,' he said at last. 'That's true. Shakespeare Close.'

Jacmel had been about to stop him, but was too late. Howard was watching the Frenchman's face. It seemed suddenly to become resigned. 'Yes,' he said. 'Shakespeare Close.'

That was the part he should never have heard, Howard told himself. Never. Never. Never.

*

'What the bloody hell is it?' Bulloch said to Rich as he shambled back to the end of the street. 'I thought I told you —'

'I wouldn't have called you if it wasn't important, sir,' Rich said, unabashed.

'It bloody better be.' He was fuming, anger spurting in all directions, much angrier than he had any need to be. Rich wondered why.

'What is it?' Bulloch said. He could still feel himself shaking with rage. It had swept over him the moment they had brought the boy on to the balcony. Then the headlights coming on as though it had all been rehearsed. Flick. And there he was, lit up like someone in an opera or play. White. Ghostly. A kid. Ten years old.

'Glaister's taken a call, sir.'

'Well?'

'It's some woman, sir. About Inspector Nash, and something about a snake, sir.'

'A what?'

'A snake, sir.'

'What the hell's the use of you and Glaister if you can't stop these cranks?'

'Didn't sound like a crank according to Glaister, sir. She's a doctor, sir.'

'I'm bloody impressed! Anyone can say they're a doctor. How the hell does she know anything about Nash? I mean how the hell did she know it was Nash who was shot? We haven't released his name, have we?'

'No, sir.'

'Well, how then?'

'She phoned Gerald Road. Wanted to speak to him. Said she'd spoken to him earlier.'

'This makes less and less sense. She spoke to him about a snake, is that it?'

'As far as we can make out.'

Bulloch's anger began to wane. 'All right. Get her here.'

'We've sent a car, sir. She should be here any time. That's why we called you.'

'Bloody marvellous. Got a cigarette?'

Rich found him one and lit it.

Then he said, 'They've brought round the note from Nash's desk.'

He passed it to Bulloch who held it close to the car's interior light. 'Coffee,' he read aloud. 'Tea. Spuds. What the hell's all this, Rich?'

'Here, sir,' Rich said, pointing farther down the paper. 'It's this address, sir. Four-twelve.'

'So what? We know the address. We're here, outside the bloody place.'

'And there,' Rich said, pointing again.

'What's it say?'

'Mambo, sir.'

'Mambo? What the hell's "mambo"?'

'Dance, sir. Your era.'

'Don't talk balls, Rich. What's he writing down a dance for?'

'Don't know, just thought you'd like to see it, sir.'

Bulloch stared at it for a long moment then put it in his pocket. 'What about Blanchet's London man?'

'He's on his way.'

'And Blanchet?'

'Vienna's still fogbound. We phoned Schwechat and —'

'Who's he?'

'Vienna airport. They say all flights have been diverted to Rome.'

'And the mother?'

'British Airways say her flight has been diverted to Paris. We could try the airport there, sir.'

Bulloch considered for a moment. He still didn't know who was in the house. Not the names. She'd know a couple. Perhaps more. Couldn't be sure. One thing was certain though, she'd be hysterical and what he didn't need now was an hysterical mother. Anyway Blanchet's London director might know. Try him first. 'No,' he said. 'Leave her. Nothing she can do.'

'It's her child, sir.'

Bulloch felt rage boil up inside him. 'I know it's her bloody child! We all know that!' He felt Rich's eyes on him and knew what he was thinking. But she was a complication and he didn't want complications. Everything simple. Just himself outside and the dirt inside. Like the Sutherland Street siege. Like the Turkish Airlines siege. Two gunmen in the airlines office. Two gunmen in the old woman's flat. Two gunmen now as far as he could make out. The pattern was the same. Why change things? Pressure. That's what did it. You put the pressure on and held it on. Under pressure people became desperate and desperate people did stupid things.

'Did you see the boy, sir?' Rich said.

'Yes. Yes. Yes. I saw the boy.'

'The doctor says she thinks there's a snake in the house, sir. A poisonous one. Inside, sir.'

'You'll believe anything, Rich.' But in spite of himself Bulloch felt a stab of unease which even his protective anger could not entirely blanket. He had only ever seen one snake in his whole life, in Burma, deep in the jungle, right at the end of the war. It was after the morning brew-up and he had gone out a hundred yards or so from the camp to relieve his bowels. He remembered the morning clearly, dappled sunlight and shade. A feeling of security because the Japs were known to be miles away. Hadn't even got a gun, just a few squares of paper torn from an old magazine. The snake had been in the middle of the path. Huge, ten or twelve feet long, about four feet of its body off the ground and a great flattened hood. Hamadryad they'd told him afterwards when he described it. The King Cobra of Asia. The bloody thing had sat there looking at him, hissing like a steam pump. Everyone said snakes were more afraid of you than you of them. Balls. This one hadn't moved. Just waited for him to come on. Ready for him. He'd got the fright of his life. Nothing had ever scared him as much before or since. He had stopped dead. The snake had raised itself even more, threatening to come forward and attack. Bulloch had retreated backwards down the path until he'd felt safe enough to turn; then he'd run like a buck into camp. He'd been so frightened he'd been constipated for days.

But that was in Burma. In the jungle. He'd never heard of a snake in Eaton Square.

*

In the dark cloacal depths of the house the snake began to move. She had moved several times since she had taken refuge in the warm-air system, compelled to go deeper and deeper into the maze of pipes by impulses coming from her brain. These were triggered by the vibrations that regularly rippled through the house. To a human being they would have been imperceptible, but to a waking reptile whose survival depended upon an alarm system able to pick up the faintest scratchings of a rat in the midst of a field of sugar cane, these vibrations were severe enough to cause fear, and fear produced the need for safety. All these were unconscious needs, for her brain, in the evolutionary pattern of brains, was very small and very primitive. Her behaviour was limited to bio-chemical reactions which in turn started neurological processes. In simple terms they were like equations: vibrations caused unease, unease could only be alleviated by safety, therefore search for safety. But still other mechanisms in her brain were telling her that these air ducts, warm, dark, familiar in the sense that her earlier homes had been in warm dark places, were safe. Yet the vibrations continued. Earlier she had moved yards at a time when the vibrations began; now, though still uneasy, she had got used to them and moved less. Also the vibrations were becoming less frequent.

The vibrations were caused by Circle line tube trains travelling from Victoria to Sloane Square. They passed near the house, thirty feet below street level, causing a series of small vibrations just perceptible enough to keep the snake uneasily alert and to cause her to move from time to time along rivers of warm air.

*

Dr Marion Stowe had never been in a police car before. Like millions of others she had seen them in the street, part of the urban furniture, and on television in a dozen police series. As a child she had seen movies in which they burst along London streets, bells clanging; now they made different sounds which she vaguely associated with France. Had she been asked she might have answered that police cars did not have to observe traffic regulations as did everyone else, but the one she was in, driven by a young man whose neck seemed to grow out of his shoulders like the trunk of a sycamore, stopped at red lights, kept on the correct side of the road, did not sound its siren as they did in TV thrillers. It was only when he cut away from the main thoroughfares and took a series of one-way streets towards Marble Arch that she saw how fast they were travelling.

'Would you like to sit back in your seat, madam,' the young driver said. 'You'll be more comfortable that way.'

She had not realized it, but she was perched on the edge of the rear seat, tense and strung-up. She leant back and felt her muscles relax. What he had meant was, sit back for your own safety.

She huddled in one corner and stared out at the swiftly-passing buildings. They were in a series of small streets just north of Upper Berkeley Street and the shops had no interest for her. The sense of unease which had begun with the realization at the Institute that a mistake had been made returned more strongly and she wished, not for the first time that evening, that she had someone to talk to about it. No, not someone, Tim.

Unease. That was the understatement of the year. Fright. Apprehension. Those might be better words.

Her mind went back over the evening. She had phoned Nash early, say six-ish or perhaps six-thirty, somewhere about then. Afterwards she'd gone home and she and Susan had had scrambled eggs and bacon because after tracking down Mrs Loewenthal she had forgotten about the Chinese food. They had eaten early and by eight-thirty Susan had been asleep. It was always the same on a Friday night, the child was dead tired after a full week's school and went out like a light. And often Marion followed her to bed herself feeling the need for all the energy and enthusiasm she could muster on the two days of the weekend, the only two days she had Susan to herself.

She had not been able to settle. She had switched on the TV but, although her eyes followed the pictures, her mind did not absorb the content. She tried to read but concentration was even more difficult. Finally, about nine o'clock, she found herself staring at the wall, tense and anxious, waiting for Nash's call. He had *promised* to phone back. But no call. Well, she had told him to get in touch with Mr Beale at the London Zoo, told him they had procedures for snake-bite, told him that in all probability Mr Beale would alert St George's hospital. What more could she do?

At nine o'clock she switched on the BBC news and stared numbly at the screen. She could not recall clearly what the main item of news had been, something about North Sea oil, and she had a blank about most of the other items. It was near the end that the newscaster had said, 'Reports are coming in of a shooting in Eaton Square. We have no details yet but hope to have further information in our late night news ...'

That had been all. Eaton Square. It was such an unlikely place. Brixton, Southall, the East End, these were the territories one associated with shootings. But Eaton Square was too rich and too elegant. It was then that she had wanted Tim so badly. He'd always been able to take the tension out of things. He'd been cool and soft-voiced. That had had a lot to do with it psychologically, she had always thought, the soft voice. Things took on a different aspect when discussed softly. By nature she was an erupter, a shouter; which is why Tim had been so good for her. She saw him now, tall, slightly stooping, an expression of faint amusement at the corners of his eyes. Hard to imagine that three years had slipped by since he'd gone. Three years, almost to the day, since they'd phoned her from the hospital to say he was dead. At first she couldn't believe them, wouldn't believe them, for she had seen him off to work that morning.

He'd had his own little kingdom then with his own laboratory at University College Hospital where he was doing research on tissue rejection by cold-blooded animals, and often they would both be able to get back to the flat at lunchtime — for sex and a sandwich as he had called it. Everything had been going just fine. And then they'd telephoned. Cerebral haemorrhage. No chance at all.

That was three years ago, yet whenever she felt a crisis coming on she half-expected to be able to go into the next room and talk to him. Perhaps it was the suddenness of his death that made it seem as though he was so close; there had been no time to get used to the thought of his dying. One moment he was there, the next gone. For God's sake, she told herself, *I must stop thinking about it*. She had picked up the telephone, dialled Gerald Road police station again and asked for Inspector Nash. It had been like setting off a train of gunpowder.

She had spoken to the Duty Officer who had asked her all sorts of questions and then she had been put through to a Sergeant ... Glazer was it? She had told him substantially what she had told Inspector Nash, then she'd had to hang on and finally he had told her he was sending a police car for her and when she asked specifically about the snake and about Inspector Nash he had said he had no information. No information! Then there had been all the business of coaxing Mrs Lloyd from the flat next door to come and babysit and then the young police car driver who also didn't have any information. 'Routine' had been *his* word. How many movies hadn't she seen, with smoking guns, and corpses littering the set, and the bland Scotland Yard man saying everything was purely routine? It made her extremely angry to be treated this way. It *couldn't* be routine. Something must have happened to Nash. Something must have happened with the snake. Could it have been an accident? Had the police gone in with guns to shoot the snake and shot one of themselves?

That meant the snake was loose, why else would they be calling on her? Briefly her fingers felt along the seat until they touched a small leather satchel containing the anti-venene. She placed it on her lap. It had been Tim's and she could still see the scratch on the leather where it had fallen on that trip to the Hex River Mountains sixty miles from Cape Town. They had gone out to South Africa in the long winter vacation supposedly on a catching trip — Tim had wanted to study the yellow cobra — but instead they'd spent most of the time in a double sleeping-bag.

They had met at Cambridge. She was studying medicine, Tim was doing research on the isolation of protein poisons of certain snakes, and she had made the switch away from medicine to work with him. She had made her decision after that trip to the mountains and it had not had much to do with science but a lot to do with Tim.

He was a South African, a PhD at the University of Cape Town, so in reality he had been going home. She had never been south of the Equator and having left London in grey December, the heat and sunshine of southern Africa had come as a shock of pleasure. They had spent a few days with his parents in a Cape Town suburb and had then hired a Volkswagen camper and driven out into the mountains where they had stayed for nearly a month. It was the best time she had ever had in her life. As a youth Tim had been a trout fisherman and knew all the rivers of the Western Cape Province including several small streams that only he and a few other fishermen had ever penetrated. They went up one such stream. Sometimes high grey cliffs came down to the river's edge making it impossible to walk upstream and then they swam through the deep dark water pushing their supplies ahead of them on inflated inner tubes; at others the stream opened out and they could splash through the shallow golden water pulling the tubes behind them. At each bend a new vista opened before them, wild grey mountain slopes reminiscent of the Scottish Highlands, and the river bubbling over white stones and sand spits. They'd slept in the open, swimming naked, making love, eating, in what seemed a never-ending cycle. By the time the holiday was over they had seen one yellow cobra and she was pregnant; it had been that sort of time.

Now, sitting in the police car as it sped round Hyde Park Corner and made for Belgrave Square, she felt a sense of desperate longing, of a need to put the clock back, for a second chance. Why had it had to be Tim?

She was still held by the web of memory when the car came to a halt. There were half a dozen other cars near the opening of a short cul-de-sac. She could see a TV camera, a sound truck and a group of people, some with cameras, others with notebooks, being kept back by a couple of constables. There was an air of tension and purpose. Farther on, at the beginning of the street itself, was a rope barrier on the other side of which was the misty figure of a man, big, almost gross, standing with his back to the police, sipping a cup of coffee. As she left the car another young man — were they all so much younger than she? — this time fresh-faced and looking like a schoolboy, held the door for her. He was wearing a fur-lined parka with the hood hanging back. 'My name's Rich,' he said. 'Thank you for coming.'

'What's happened?' she said. 'And don't say routine to me.'

He smiled briefly. 'No, it's not routine. But I'd best leave it to Detective Chief Superintendent Bulloch to tell you.'

The name touched some chord in her mind but what she did not know. Then she said, 'It's about Inspector Nash, isn't it?'

'Yes, it's Inspector Nash.'

'I *knew* it. What ha —'

There was a commotion behind them and a police Land-Rover edged slowly past. It had a towing hook and a cable on the back. She watched as it went slowly up to the single house at the end of the street, turned and one of the men fixed the hook to the front of a parked yellow Ford. A second policeman got into a Citroen and started the engine.

*

In the house the two men, Dave and Jacmel, watched from the window. At first Dave was speechless, then he blurted, 'They're taking the fucking cars away. Look! They're towing them away!'

Jacmel nodded. 'He is a hard one, your Mr Bulloch. But we have the boy.'

Howard was still sitting on the sofa, Philip was asleep, leaning on his shoulder. For the first time Howard heard a note of indecision in Jacmel's voice. He did not know whether to be glad or sorry.

'There's always him,' Dave said, pointing at Howard. 'Him as well. That's two of 'em.'

'Yes,' Jacmel said dryly. 'There's is M 'Oward. But no wife. No mother. No family. Who would bargain for M 'Oward? Not the police, I think.'

No, Howard thought, not the police, nor the British Government, nor the Kenya Government, nor Blanchet. He suddenly realized that there was no one to bid on him, that his body, his whole being, was worth nothing in the only market where modern man was given a valuation. Zero. They would kill him, he knew, because he had heard the words 'Shakespeare Close'. And they would not feel a thing, nor would anyone else. He was already a blank.

Part IV

Friday 9.50 p.m – Saturday 2.45 a.m.

'I've said all this twice — no, three times — already!' Dr Stowe was saying.

Bulloch stood over her, dwarfing her, sipping loudly at his coffee. 'Well, tell me again,' he said. 'You say a mistake was made. That the boy got the wrong snake. Is that right?'

'Yes. Yes. Yes.'

They went over it, Bulloch probing, Marion telling it as it might have been told to a child. And while they talked they judged each other. Bulloch saw a physically attractive woman who had the misfortune to be English and who spoke with an educated accent. He wouldn't mind brutalizing her, he thought. She saw a figure bending towards her, with a huge head and heavy shoulders, which reminded her of the friezes at Knossos depicting the Minotauros. Given a chance, she thought, he would bruise her physically and mentally.

They went through her story item by item, starting with the discovery that the Institute had been sent the wrong specimen and ending with his question about the anti-venene shots and whether she had brought the serum.

'Now it's your turn,' she said.

'My turn?'

'Yes, your turn. I've been fobbed off by words like routine!' She waved her arm in the direction of the police cars and the media and said, 'If this is supposed to be routine for Eaton Square at ten o'clock at night … !'

He stared at her over the top of the plastic cup and wondered if she liked doilies and Chesterfield suites and magic-glow electric fires. She was putting on a little weight, he thought, just how he liked them. A good grip on the cheeks of the arse. He'd like to … what? But all he could think of was watching her undress. Jesus, he thought, if that's all, I'm over the top.

'I'm waiting,' she said.

It was the tone of her voice, not so much what she said, that got to him. He hadn't been spoken to like that, he thought, for a long time. Not even by the Deputy Commissioner. He shrugged. 'All right.' And he outlined what he knew.

When he'd finished she said, 'And that's all? You mean he didn't tell anyone. Not the Reptile House at the Zoo? Not St George's Hospital? Not even his colleagues? I find that astonishing.'

'D'you know how many calls a day we get telling us there's a bomb in the Houses of Parliament or under a bench in Hyde Park? Or that there's a body in the Kingsway underpass or a cat up a tree in Surbiton? Christ, woman, we get hundreds of calls like that every day; ninety-nine per cent of them cranks.'

'And mine was just one of them?'

'That's right.'

'The fact that I represent a government institute has nothing to do with it, I suppose.'

'Sometimes they ring us up and say they're the Archbishop of bloody Canterbury. We don't necessarily believe them.' She swallowed her anger. 'Inspector Nash said he was writing it down. Why didn't he leave a note?'

He felt in his pocket and brought out a crumpled piece of paper, showing it to her. 'Hardly a note,' he said.

'Yes, I see, there's not much to go on,' she said.

'Not unless you wanted coffee and tea and spuds.'

'But there's the word —'

'We read it as mambo. My constable tells me it's some sort of dance. Now you tell us it's *mamba*. It's easy when you know, Doctor. What do you want, Rich?'

'Thought Dr Stowe might like a cup of coffee, sir.'

'That's very kind of you,' she said.

'That's very kind of you, Rich,' Bulloch said, deliberately parodying her.

Rich tried to hide his distaste, then said, 'Sampson and Hodges in the mews behind have been inside the dressmaking place, and they've found a door.'

'A what?'

'It was papered over. Leads into the house, sir.'

'Who told them to go in.'

'I did.'

'On whose authority?'

'Yours, sir.'

'Warrant?'

'No.'

'You're learning, Rich. What about the door?'

'Well, sir, the dressmaking place must be in what were the old mews stables. It was natural to have a door between the house and the stables — save the owners walking round to the end of the mews. Like a door between a garage and a house.'

Bulloch stared past Rich. He should have thought of that. A door. Christ, of course there must have been something. If he'd thought he'd probably have assumed it was bricked up. But he'd never thought and that was bloody bad.

'What d'you think, sir?'

What *did* he think? What Rich was asking was: do we send them in? But the snake might be loose. Well ...

He turned to Dr Stowe and said, 'How's the coffee?' Surprised, she said, 'Very good, thank you.'

'Rich'll make someone a marvellous wife. Tell me about the snake, Doctor. Everything. And give the doctor a cigarette.'

'They come from Africa,' she said. 'South-east mainly. They spend their lives in open grassland but are just as at home in trees. Family *elapidae*. Genus *dendroaspis*.'

'I don't want any bloody long words, doctor. We're not all as educated as yourself.'

She looked up angrily and then realized he had a point. She was not lecturing to a group of students. 'I'm sorry,' she said. 'All right. They come from Africa, they grow to between ten and twelve feet long — that's about average — and they're probably the most aggressive snakes in the world. That's what makes them so awkward.'

'Awkward,' Bulloch said, tasting the word. 'I like that.'

'Drop for drop they're not the most poisonous snakes in the world. The Australian tiger snake or the Cape cobra is more toxic but that's academic since a drop or two of mamba venom can kill. The biggest problem is their aggressiveness and the fact that they rear so high off the ground that when they strike they can cause the wound as far up as the shoulder or neck. This cuts down the victim's chance of survival because the bite is closer to the vital organs.'

'Even with your needle?'

'Without it there's no hope at all. No one's ever been known to recover from a serious mamba bite without antivenom — and even that's not certain. In fact, nothing's certain about snakes. When you're bitten it depends on your state of health, their health, where the bite is located, how much poison was injected, how soon you can be treated, lots of factors. But there is one certainty — this is the worst of all the snakes. It's a neurotoxic poison mainly. Which means it acts on the central nervous system and paralyses the lungs and you die by being unable to breathe. Its venom also contains a *haemorhagin* —'

'What's that?'

'It affects the blood. So if you survived the onslaught on your central nervous system you'd die of a kind of blood poisoning. The first, depending on where you were bitten and how much poison was injected, could kill you in minutes. The second would take hours, perhaps days. But you can forget the blood poison; when you're bitten by a mamba you die of a failure of the nervous system. Is that clear?'

Bulloch ignored the implied insult. 'And you have an anti whatever it is to counteract it?'

'Anti-venom. Or anti-venene. Same thing. Yes.' She tapped the satchel. 'South African poly ...'

'Polly?'

'Polyvalent. In other words wide-spectrum. It's specific against both or either.'

'So as long as you've got your wee needles we haven't too much to worry about?'

Irritated, she said, 'You haven't been listening. I'll go over it once —'

'Oh, for Christ's sake save your lectures,' he said brutally. 'I'm fighting a bloody war, don't you see! And I want to know how many fronts I'm fighting on. Do we have to fight the dirt *and* the snake? That's what I want you to tell me. If you say you can control the snake then I can think of letting my men in the back —'

'You want *me* to decide for you. And if something goes wrong you'll say, well, Dr Stowe's the expert and she said so.' Bulloch took a step towards her.

'More coffee, doctor?' Rich said. 'Another cigarette?'

She took one without thinking and by the time he had lit it for her the tension had diminished. 'Look,' she said. 'There's nothing certain about snakes. There are cases where people have been bitten by mambas and got anti-venom shots within a minute or two and still died. Just because I've brought along some anti-venom doesn't mean you can risk your men.

Anyway, some people are allergic to the anti-venom: it's dangerous stuff and we only use it because snake venom is *more* dangerous.'

'All right,' Bulloch said. 'All right.'

'And surely you're overlooking one thing. We don't know for sure that the snake's loose. Often they're kept in their travelling crates for days until they settle down after a journey.'

'I hadn't forgotten it,' Bulloch said.

'We could ask them,' Rich said.

'Oh, for God's sake, Rich —'

'Not ask,' Marion Stowe said. 'Tell them.'

'What the hell for? If it's loose it's working on our side.'

'I thought you said there was a child in there,' she said bitterly.

'You could tell them,' Rich said. 'And then —'

'Rich, I'll —'

'You've *got* to,' she said.

Bulloch moved from foot to foot as though about to put down his head and charge. 'You think they'd believe that!'

'They may already know,' she said. 'I mean, there seem to be several alternatives. A, the snake may be loose in the house and they may know that. B, it may be loose and they may *not* know. C, it may still be in its box. But whatever the alternative is *they still think it's a harmless African house snake*!'

All three paused for a moment as the truth of her statement sank in.

'You've got to let them know, sir, whether they believe you or not,' Rich said.

Bulloch turned to Dr Stowe. 'They might believe you,' he said.

She felt a touch of fear. 'What do you want me to do?'

'Go to the front of the house,' Bulloch said. 'Talk to 'em.'

'They could ...' Rich began and then stopped, but Marion read his thoughts. So did Bulloch.

'They haven't shot at me,' Bulloch said. 'There's no reason to shoot at her. I'll go with you,' he said.

What would Tim have done, she thought? And then: but I'm not Tim.

She felt the eyes of both men on her. Then Bulloch said, almost gently for him, 'I've stood outside for ah hour or more, talked to 'em and they've done nothing. Haven't even shown themselves.'

'But they shot Inspector Nash,' she found herself saying.

'That's true. But he went to the door. Must have surprised them. And he was in uniform.'

'It's the boy,' Rich said.

'Yes, the boy,' she said, and saw a picture of Susan's sleeping face. What if it were her child and someone else was wasting time? 'All right,' she said.

'Come on then,' Bulloch said and they began to walk slowly through the mist, that was lit by the street lamps, to the house, which was dark.

Half way there she faltered and turned to Bulloch. 'You really want an expert,' she said.

He looked down at her. '*You* are an expert.'

'Yes,' she said after a moment.

'There's no time to get anyone else,' he said, and his mind was saying: You don't want any more experts. You don't want any more people. Keep it simple. Uncomplicated.

'Yes, I suppose so,' she said and they went on.

They stopped outside the house in the position that Bulloch had made his own and he said softly, 'Let me talk.' Her mouth was dry and she nodded.

'Can you hear me?' he said.

After a few seconds they heard the double-glazed window being slid to one side. 'Yes,' the now-familiar voice said in its heavily-accented English. 'I hear you. I do not wish to talk further unless you have an agreement —'

'Listen, there's something you should know.'

'*You* listen. In one hour from now we send you a present. One hour. You understand? We do not wish to talk. You think you can frighten us by taking away the voi — the motors. But you bring pain for the boy. You understand me?'

'Yes, I understand you. But there is something you don't know. This lady —'

Marion stepped in front of them and said in a voice she hardly recognized as her own. 'Can you hear me?'

'Yes. Of course.'

'What I am about to say you will think is a trick,' she said and realized she was talking as though he were a child. 'I'm not a police woman,' she said. And then thought: *get on with it.*

'My name is Dr Marion Stowe,' she said to the blank face of the house. 'I work at an Institute which studies snake poisons. I have come to warn you that there may be a poisonous snake loose in the house.' She had caught her breath but her voice still sounded high. There was no reply from the window.

'This afternoon the little boy Philip went to fetch a pet snake in Camden Town. He was given the wrong one. Instead of a pet snake he was given a black mamba by mistake. He brought it back in a travelling crate. Please do not for any reason open the crate … Her voice tailed off. 'The police asked me to tell you this …' She hesitated. 'And so I've … well, I've told you …'

'Tell them about the anti-venom,' Bulloch whispered.

'Oh, yes,' she said. 'I've brought an antidote in case anyone is bitten. But that won't happen if the snake is still in the crate. That is all I have to say.' She turned and was about to walk away. Her legs felt weak and trembly.

Suddenly the voice at the window said, 'The snake is not in the crate.'

She turned back, a feeling of relief surging through her body. 'You mean the crate was empty all the time!'

'The snake is not in the crate. He is loose in the house.'

Inside the house Howard heard what Jacmel said with a sense of shock. He had been sitting still, trying to keep his arm from moving and waking the boy, thankful that Philip had been asleep when Jacmel had given the ultimatum, unwilling to imagine that such a thing could happen, much less be spoken of, but finding little reassurance in the fact that they were in London and not back in the Mau Mau emergency in Kenya. After what had happened to the policeman he had no doubt that if Jacmel made a threat he would carry it out.

Whatever Jacmel said they had been affected by the removal of the cars. It had shown that Bulloch was made of pretty strong stuff. Dave was afraid, that was obvious. And Jacmel? Afraid was putting it too strongly. But less confident, surely. Or was Howard fooling himself? And did he *want* Bulloch to be made of strong stuff? When the big jets were hi-jacked and the demands were made you wanted governments to be strong, like Israel; no bargains with terrorists. Hard luck on the hostages, but that's life. Give in now and you have to give in again … and again … etc. But what about when *you* were a hostage? Then you weren't so keen on the strong stuff; then you wanted people who would give a little.

His mind returned to what Jacmel had said about the snake, that it was loose. He had told Dave that police knowledge of the snake would weaken their position so why had he changed his mind? Howard did not see a reason and nor, if his expression was anything to go by, did Dave. How it would influence them he could not tell.

Jacmel spoke again. 'The snake has attacked someone,' he said.

'I cannot hear you.' Her voice rose clearly on the bitter air that was seeping into the room through the partially open window, reminding Howard of someone else, but who he could not recall. 'You say the snake is loose in the house; has it bitten anyone?'

'Yes,' Jacmel said. 'It is what I say. It has bitten someone.'

'The boy?'

'Not the boy.'

'Who then?'

There was a pause, then Jacmel said, 'It is the maid, Louise.'

'When was this?'

'Just now. A few minutes ago.'

In the street Bulloch said softly, 'He's lying. Too bloody coincidental. You tell him there's a snake in the house and suddenly he tells you someone's been bitten.'

'If the maid has been bitten, then she's dying,' Marion said.

'Could you tell? From what he says?'

'I think so.'

Jacmel's voice came down to them. 'You have something for the poison. Cannot you use it? We did not know the snake was dangerous. It was the boy's.'

'When was she bitten?' Marion said.

'I told you, a few minutes past.'

'Where?'

'In the left arm. Half way up.'

Bulloch said softly, 'Ask him why she doesn't tell us herself.'

'Why does she not speak to us?' Marion said, falling into the Frenchman's idiom.

'She is in the bedroom. She has ...' They could almost hear him searching through his vocabulary for the English word. '... She has fainted. When she was attacked she fainted. We thought it was from the shock.'

'What is happening to her?'

'There is a black mark on the arm. It goes up to the shoulder. And also there is ... ' He paused again. '... *ordure* ...' He used the French word as though too delicate to speak its English equivalent.

Marion turned to Bulloch. 'Those are two of the symptoms. Especially the loss of bowel control.'

'He could have made it up,' Bulloch said.

She shook her head. 'No. Not the part about the bowels. Only ...'

'What?'

'That part comes later. I mean, he says she's just been bitten. She must have been attacked earlier.'

'Why didn't you tell us sooner?' she called, usurping Bulloch's role for the moment.

'She is of no concern to us,' Jacmel said brutally. 'But if you wish her to live you must use your ... your medicine quick.'

Marion turned to Bulloch. 'He's right. If you want to give her a chance we've got to act fast.'

'All right.' He turned to the house and said, 'We'll leave the ... medicine on the steps. You can get it.'

'No.'

'Why not?'

'You know why not. You have men in the windows.'

'I'll give orders not to fire.'

'No.'

'What then?'

'Let the doctor come in. We will give her free passage.'

'Impossible,' Bulloch said without even consulting her. There was silence for several minutes then Bulloch said, 'Are you there?'

'Where else?'

'We will leave the medicine on the steps. It is in a satchel. It's the best we can do.'

'No.'

'Don't you care about the woman?'

'I told you. She is not our concern.'

'Why won't you?' Marion said, her voice high with urgency. 'Ask yourself, madame doctor. We do not know even if you are a doctor. You say you are, but we cannot know. You say you wish to save this woman but we do not know. You say you have medicine in that bag but it may be a bomb.'

'Please believe me,' she said. 'I am what I say I am. You *must* believe. Otherwise —'

The silence lengthened and the cold crept into their bones. 'You've done all you can,' Bulloch said softly but she disdained to answer. He sounded as though he, like the man in the window, considered the dying woman to be no concern of his, she thought.

Then the Frenchman's voice came down to them again. 'I have seen her,' he said. 'She is very bad. She has strange feelings in her tongue.'

Marion turned to Bulloch. 'That's another symptom! A sort of numbness.' She turned back to the house and shouted, 'You're letting her die!'

'There is one way,' the voice said.

'What's that?'

'We bring her to the steps and you inject her there.'

'I don't like it,' Bulloch said.

'What else can we do?' she said, feeling again the dryness in her mouth. 'He doesn't care whether she lives or dies.'

I don't either, Bulloch thought, angrily. This was another bloody complication. And yet if they didn't make some effort ... If she died and they hadn't tried ... 'It's up to you,' he said. She looked down at the ground unable to answer.

Bulloch turned to the window. 'Bring her down and *I'll* do it,' he said.

The voice said, 'No.'

Marion looked up. 'Bring her down. I'll come.'

'I'll cover you,' Bulloch said. 'We've got marksmen.'

'Oh, for God's sake ...' she said.

'Once you have put her on the steps you will retire inside the house,' Bulloch shouted. 'If there is any movement at the windows or if the front door is opened while Dr Stowe is attending to the maid, my men will fire. Is that understood?'

'Yes. Stay there,' the voice said. 'I will bring her down.'

*

Inside the house Jacmel turned to Howard. 'We go down now. You go first.'

'What the hell's going on?' Dave said.

'Watch the boy,' Jacmel said. 'If there is trouble ...'

'What are you doing?'

'Don't worry. Watch the boy.' He pointed the gun at Howard who was gently disengaging himself from the sleeping child. 'Come.'

Jacmel followed him to the door. 'You go first.' Again Howard moved into a waking nightmare, this time in reverse; the room was now the only safe place in the house because he had searched it and made it safe, everywhere else was a no-man's-land of shadows and corners and places where the eye could not penetrate; the snake could be anywhere. They began to go down the stairs. How long ago, it seemed to Howard, that he had last descended; then he'd had plans, he had been going to do great things. He remembered himself telling the boy to run. It seemed another age, for now he had no plans; he did what he was told to do; fear had filtered out all plans, all other feelings.

They reached the bottom of the stairs and there was the mound that had once been Louise. Jacmel bent and pulled back the rug and Howard flinched as he saw the dead face. The eyes were open and something — he could not tell in the dim light whether it was blood or some other liquid — was oozing from partially open lips. The lips themselves were drawn back exposing her teeth. The big body had stiffened in a sprawling position and the black area of poison was clearly visible where she had torn away her bra exposing her heavy breasts.

'Undress her,' Jacmel said.

Howard knelt at the side of the body and began to unfasten the remaining buttons on the front of her black-and-white maid's dress.

*

In the street Bulloch had moved farther from the house and Marion Stowe had gone to the circle of brilliance cast by a street light. She was very frightened and now she tried to damp down her fear by concentrating on what she was doing. She broke the seals on the plastic cover of a hypodermic and then on the needle and fitted one to the other. Then she selected a small bottle and checked the label. It read: 'Polyvalent anti-venene for snakebite. Batch 745/3655SA 10 ml. Use before 1/1/1979.'

Carefully she inserted the tip of the needle into the bottle and drew up the ten millilitres of anti-venene. She put a second bottle into the pocket of her coat. She had decided that if the maid had been bitten as long ago as she thought then only a massive dose might — might — help. Ten millilitres into the area of the wound, a second shot of ten millilitres into a muscle near by or perhaps under the skin of the abdomen. She should take two needles but she could not take the satchel so she would have to refill the syringe with the contents of the second bottle while she was on the steps. It meant being there longer than she would have liked — and then she thought that was nonsense, any time there would be longer than she liked. She tried not to think about it, to keep her mind clinical, her thoughts on muscles and puncture wounds, poisons and their antidotes, anything but what was happening inside the house or what might happen on the steps. I'll cover you, Bulloch had said. What did he think this was, a shoot-out in a TV western? She didn't want him to cover her. She didn't want anything to do with him. She mistrusted both the man and his motives. She wanted to be home in her flat with her feet up and Susan just along the passage. She held up the syringe to the street light and pressed slightly and a drop of viscous liquid beaded the tip of the needle.

'They're coming out now,' Bulloch called softly.

The front door had opened and two figures were standing in the dark arch. From that distance and with the mist enshrouding the front of the house it was difficult to make them out. They came slowly and she could see the figure of the maid being helped by a man. They walked with great care. The maid was wearing some sort of uniform, no shoes and her feet seemed to drag. She was, in fact, being half carried, for her head and face were partially obscured by the man's shoulder. From what she could make out Marion thought the woman looked very far gone.

Slowly the man helped her down on to the top step, both arms under her shoulders, until she settled and lay there on her back, her face turned towards the door from which she had just emerged.

'All right,' Bulloch called to the man, 'you get back inside and we'll see.'

For a second he hesitated and seemed about to say something. Was this the Frenchman? She tried to see him clearly but the darkness and the mist obscured him.

'What's wrong?' the policeman called.

The man gave a faint shake of his head and then turned and went inside, closing the door behind him.

Bulloch came over to Marion. 'Wait a moment,' he said. He walked half way back to the cars and called Rich. 'Tell the marksmen that if anyone opens the door or moves near the window while the doctor is attending to the maid they're to fire. Understand?'

'Yes, sir.'

Bulloch waited until Rich had carried out his order and made sure that those inside the house had heard before he said to Marion, 'Whenever you're ready.'

She had decided that when the time came she would try to keep her mind blank. She had gone over every possibility while she was filling the syringe: the snake *had* to be loose, no one could have made up those symptoms unless he was an expert in neurotoxic poisons, and that was too coincidental. So why would they want to shoot her or hurt her in any way? No, she had to accept what was happening at its face value.

The woman had been bitten, was at this moment dying and she, Marion Stowe, was the only one who might be able to save her. It was a mission of mercy; no one was going to harm her. So when Bulloch said, 'Whenever you're ready,' she nodded and before giving herself the chance to hesitate or to steel herself, she found her legs moving forward of their own volition.

Like so many other things of which she had been apprehensive in the past, she realized that the initial worry was worse than the event itself, for, once she began to go forward she forgot about what might happen to her and began to concentrate on the victim lying at the top of the steps. What would she find? A woman so far gone that no amount of anti-venene could save her? Someone who would plead for a miracle? Marion had seen snake-bite before; once in the lab, and once on a second field trip to Africa when she had treated an African child. On both occasions the snakes had been venomous but neither as venomous as a black mamba. She had never seen a victim of a mamba bite though she knew the symptoms well enough. And so as she moved forward towards Louise the fear she had felt on her own behalf gave way to apprehension for the poor woman who lay at the top of the steps.

'Good evening,' she said as she began to climb the steps, and thought how fatuous it sounded, but she had said it less as a greeting than as a warning of her approach so that she would not startle Louise. God, what irony, she thought, a Frenchwoman dying on a London pavement from poison put into her by a reptile from Africa.

The woman made no reply but Marion had expected none. The tongue would be numb and movement restricted; she would be like someone who had had a stroke, partial paralysis would have overtaken the mouth.

'I've come to help,' she said as she reached the top of the steps. 'I've got an injection that will help.' Her voice was soothing and low.

Louise was lying partly on her left side facing the house. Her face was in shadow and Marion realized she would have to turn her almost completely over to get at the seat of the wound.

'I'm going to turn you over,' she said. 'It won't hurt.'

She put the syringe down on the step and gently began to move Louise so she could get at the punctures on her left arm.

Louise must have heard her and understood, she thought, for the moment she began to pull her over the maid turned her body to help; she rolled on to her back and Marion looked down into her face. Something dreadful had happened to her. The poison had ravaged her, had hardened the edges and contours. It was hardly female at all. And then the eyes opened and Marion's heart stopped: she was looking into a man's face. A man's face in a woman's body. And in the left hand was a gun which came up slowly and pressed against her stomach.

'Stay still,' Jacmel said. 'Or you will die here.'

She nodded, unable to speak.

'Pick up the syringe,' he said.

She moved her hand and picked it up.

'Now get up on to your knees.'

She got up on her knees and he did the same, facing her, his body so close that they were touching. Then she realized her back was to the street. He was using her as a shield. His right arm came round her and he pulled her against him. She could feel the hardness of the pistol against her abdomen.

'Rise to your feet.'

She rose and he came with her as though they were stuck together. They stood on the top step, a single mass.

'Walk towards the door.'

She walked forwards, he backwards, like some music-hall turn.

'Open,' he called.

The door opened and they were swallowed up by the house. In the street Bulloch had watched what was happening first with astonishment then with a mixture of rage and impotence, for there was nothing anyone could do unless they wished to kill Dr Stowe.

*

As the door closed Jacmel pushed Marion away from him. She stumbled backward in the half dark and would have fallen had two hands not come out and grasped her by the waist and elbow. She turned, terrified again, twisting to try and break the grip, then his voice came. 'Steady,' he said, 'it's all right.'

A feeling of relief swept over her, driving a sob up into her throat. It was Tim's voice. For a second, for one isolated magical moment, Tim spoke to her, not from the grave but here in this house; a Tim with hands and a body, who held her, helping her, steadying her, as he had helped her across the stones of the river bank long ago.

The light came on and she saw he was not Tim at all. This was an older man with a drawn face. He looked frightened, too. Then she saw the body on the floor and she shuddered with this second blow.

Jacmel had stripped off the maid's uniform and had come into the centre of the hall after switching on the light. He pointed at Louise with his gun. 'I was telling the truth,' he said. 'Look.'

Still feeling the protective hand on her elbow, Marion moved towards the body. It was naked except for a pair of pants. She could see the huge black patches where the poison had attacked the blood vessels. The damage was prodigious.

'When was she bitten?' she asked shakily.

'Four hours ago,' Jacmel said.

She turned away from the body, unable to continue looking at it. 'She's dead,' she said, more to herself than to the two men.

'Yes,' Jacmel said, 'she is dead.'

'Why did you want me then?'

'Because you are an expert, Madame doctor. The police have experts, we too must have experts. You are a snake expert. We need such an expert. It is logical.'

She heard a movement at the top of the stairs and a third man came to the landing overlooking the lower hall. She could not see him clearly but his voice was high and brittle.

'What are you playing at?' he shouted. 'What the hell do we want with her?'

Jacmel turned sharply. 'I told you to watch the child,' he said.

'You told me!' Dave mimicked. 'You're always fucking telling me! Except when you go and do something bloody stupid like bringing this woman —'

'Get back!' Jacmel said. 'Get back into the room!' He ran up the stairs towards Dave. At that moment the two men were totally engaged with each other. Jacmel's back was towards Marion. Dave was looking directly down the stairs and not over to the left where Marion, Howard and Louise's body made a small group. For a moment she was sure that she could reach the door. Her muscles flexed. She began to turn, to explode away from the spot on which she was standing, when she felt the hand on her arm again and heard Tim's voice saying, 'He'll kill you.'

In that second Jacmel stopped dead, turned and looked at her. Slowly he put his hand in his pocket and pulled out something and held it out so that she could see it. It was the key to the front door. In a soft voice he said, 'If you try to get out we will hurt the child. You understand?'

She nodded.

'Good. Then you and M 'Oward bring Louise.' He went on up to the landing.

The man with Tim's voice said, 'My name's Dick Howard. I live here.'

'You're not one —'

'No. The Frenchman's Jacmel. The other's Dave. The chauffeur.'

The voices on the upper landing had risen. The two men were arguing fiercely. She turned to Howard and said, 'Thank you for stopping me.'

His reply made little sense to her then, but later she understood. 'It's easy to stop,' he said. 'It's starting that's so difficult. Let's do as he says.'

'The child,' she said. 'Is he ... ?'

'Philip's all right, so far.' He bent down and placed his hands under Louise's arms and as he began to lift, Marion saw a flash of pain cross his face.

The voices on the landing had grown louder and she heard the man called Dave say, 'No! Not me! Things like that turn my stomach!' The argument came to a sudden halt and Jacmel leaned over the bannisters. 'Leave her,' he said. 'Come up.'

Howard lowered the dead woman's torso. 'Who shot the policeman?' Marion asked softly.

'The other one. The chauffeur, Dave. But this one's just as dangerous. More probably. Just do as they say.'

She nodded. And then she asked a question on a subject everyone seemed temporarily to have forgotten. 'Where's the snake?' she said.

'God knows. Could be anywhere.'

The two men at the head of the staircase watched as they came up the stairs; she was aware of their stares, especially the hostility in Dave; she was also aware of how slowly Howard walked. He seemed to be labouring and she began to prepare herself mentally for the fact that he was not going to be of much help. When she had first heard his voice her heart had given a sudden lift; but later he had not sounded so much like Tim, perhaps it was simply the flattened vowels which are common on the eastern flank of

Africa among whites that had made the voices similar. This man was no Tim; this was someone who appeared to be more frightened than she was, who walked like an old man, struggling to keep up with her on the stairs. Yet with an odd gallantry his hand remained under her elbow, helping her, trying to reassure her.

They went into the sitting-room and immediately she froze. It could be anywhere, she thought: behind a chair, in the fire-place, behind the curtains, and in the dim light it would be invisible. She felt a gentle pressure from his fingers and he said, 'It's all right, it's not in here.'

Reassured, she moved forward into the dimness and he guided her to the sofa, his new *querencia*, in the middle of the room, and she saw the child.

Philip woke when they entered the room. He had been dreaming of the Zambesi. In his dream it had been a wide river, not unlike the Thames at Richmond, but where there were buildings at Richmond, *his* river had only trees. The water was all dappled in the African sunshine. In his dream he and Dick were floating on the bosom of the river in the sort of boat he had once seen on the Serpentine in Hyde Park, a kind of rowing boat, but shiny with varnish. They floated down the river in the sunlight, safe, secure and warm. So when he awoke he retained for some moments the relaxed happiness of the dream. Then came reality: Dave and the Frenchman with guns, Dick walking slowly, like an old man, still bent slightly in the middle from the pain where Dave had hit him. And a woman. And Dick's hand on her arm. Who was she? What was she doing here? How did Dick know her?

The relaxation was swept away on a tide of tension; the dream was shattered. And then something happened to Philip that had never happened before: his mind received and translated a flash of insight. It was as though for a brief second he was no longer a little boy, but a grown man. He saw, for the first time in his life, harsh reality shorn of all fantasy. He saw Dick Howard not as a hunter in a dream of Africa, not as something exotic in his drab winter world, but frail and frightened. And seeing him thus made Jacmel and Dave even more menacing. For that brief moment he was gripped by the terror of life — and then it was gone and he was a little boy again with the question still in his mind: Who was the woman?

The legacy of his moment of genuine perceptive fear came swiftly. He turned to Dick, to ask him who she was, when he felt a sudden tightness in his chest and the attack was upon him. In minutes he could hardly breathe. He was aware of the four adults milling about him, aware of their faces looming over him, then Dick was holding the aerosol inhaler in front of his mouth. He fought for breath, wheezing and gasping, trying literally to suck the air down into his lungs. Something else appeared. A spoon. He took it in his mouth, recognizing the taste of the syrupy liquid it carried: Phenergan. They gave it to him when the attacks were bad. Again the spoon was held out. It was a dessert spoon. Before he had only ever had a teaspoon and only one at that. This time the spoon was held by the Frenchman. He felt the cold metal on his teeth. The spoon was forced into his mouth. He swallowed. The minutes passed. How long he did not know. He began to feel muzzy. His breathing became more regular. He heard Dick's voice saying, 'In, out. In, out. One, two. One, two.' The voice became fainter and fainter until he could hear it no longer.

Marion held him in her arms. He lay against her, sleeping heavily, and she moved so his head rested on her lap. 'He needs a doctor,' she said to Howard, who had never seen a real attack before and whose opinion of Philip's 'imaginary' illness was undergoing rapid change.

Jacmel said, 'But you are a doctor.'

'Not of medicine,' she said.

He went to the window to join Dave. 'We must be ready when the policeman returns,' he said.

'Why not let him do it?' Dave said, indicating Howard. Jacmel turned and looked at the sofa and then turned away. 'No,' he said softly, 'it must be done properly. We cannot take a chance. We trust each other, no?'

'Yes.' It was hesitant.

'Well, then?'

'What with?' Dave said.

'This.'

Marion, who had been half following the conversation, heard a snick of metal and saw Jacmel give Dave something but could not be sure what it was.

'What about the ... ?' Dave said.

'But we have just come from there. Nothing.'

'Well ... '

'You want to get out of here? You want the money?'

''Course.'

'To do that we have to make your policeman believe, no?'

''Suppose so.'

'There is no suppose.'

'All right, all right!'

'Good. Do it now.'

Dave walked to the door, hesitated on the threshold and then passed into the lighted landing and they heard him go softly down the stairs.

'How do you *know*?' Marion whispered to Howard.

'Know what?'

'That it's not in here. It could be anywhere. In among the books, anywhere.'

'I looked.'

She glanced around. 'You *looked*? In here?'

He nodded.

'Without protection?'

'Yes.'

'Did they let you have the shotgun?'

'No.'

She paused, then said, 'Alone?'

'Not by choice.'

'Everywhere?'

'Just about. Wherever it could be.'

'Behind the curtains?'

'Yes.'

'In the fireplace?'

'Yes. Don't worry.'

'It's not that,' she said. 'It's just that I can't imagine *anyone* searching for a mamba without some protection.'

He looked away as though not wishing to recall the incident, then said, 'What else besides Dr Stowe?'

'Marion.'

'Didn't know that,' he said. 'Knew it was Dr Stowe because I heard what you said from the street.' He stopped for a moment and then said, 'It took courage to do what you did.'

'It took stupidity.'

'You weren't to know what was in his mind.'

'I looked at you from across the street. I thought you were …' She inclined her head in the direction of Jacmel.

'It was what you were supposed to think.'

'Yes. Was the light on?'

'When?'

'When you looked in here.'

'Yes. They put the light on.'

She nodded. Then she said, 'When I heard your voice I was reminded of someone.'

'Who?'

'My husband.'

'Does he know where you are?'

'He's dead.'

'Oh.'

'It's just the way you spoke. You're from Africa, aren't you?'

'Yes.'

'So was he.'

'Your voice reminded me of someone, too. When you were shouting from the street.'

'Who?'

'I couldn't think at the time. The Queen's. It must have been nerves. You don't sound like that now.'

'What's going to happen?'

'I don't know.' He thought of telling her how tough Bulloch was and then realized that wasn't what she wanted to hear; just the contrary, if anything.

'You'd tell me?'

'I simply don't know. I live in the flat downstairs. I was out, you see. They tricked me, too. When I came back, they were here. Or at least *he* was. The other two worked here. They were in on it from the beginning. Planned the whole thing.'

'He doesn't know that.'

'Who? The policeman?'

She nodded. 'He thinks it's only the two men. He doesn't know about the maid, and he doesn't know she's dead.' She looked at Jacmel but his attention was on the street. She lowered her voice to a whisper. 'They've found a door at the back.'

'What?'

'A door. Papered over. It leads into the mews, into some sort of shop, I think.'

'God,' he said, agitated. 'If they burst in he'll shoot us.'

'They won't,' she said. 'Not with the snake loose.'

'Bulloch broke the Sutherland Street siege and the one in the Turkish Airlines office.'

She tried to recall what had happened. 'Wasn't there an old woman?'

'She died afterwards. There was a lot of criticism. Newspapers said he was unbending. The chauffeur's scared of him.' He bent his head again in the direction of Jacmel who was standing in the shadows of the window, his only movement rolling the television aerial cable backwards and forwards under his right foot. 'Even he's not so sure of himself any more.'

'Why did he want me?'

She must know, Howard thought. The more hostages the more pressure on Bulloch. At first they only had the boy — Howard was realistic enough to accept their valuation of himself at zero — and once the boy was gone, once they'd had to fulfil a threat they would have nothing left. Now they could sacrifice a pawn to save their king; Marion was the pawn and Philip was the king, and he, Howard, had no place on the board.

'In case either of them get bitten,' he said. It was a half truth and would serve

'They've asked for a hundred thousand pounds.'

'And a car and an hour's delay.'

'D'you think they'll get it?'

'Yes,' he said, lying, 'I think they will.'

'And then?'

'And then they'll release us.'

'Do you *really* think so?'

'Of course. We'd only get in the way.'

'It's not as if we *know* anything.'

'That's right.' His mind saw the huge complex of flats known as Shakespeare Close and he switched off the thought like a light, too frightened to let it stay in his skull.

She sensed the change in him, as though he had thought of something that made him more afraid and she wondered if he had been simply trying to reassure her. She didn't want him to be afraid, she wanted him to be strong and capable, to be able to make decisions, she did not want things to be left to her; she felt empty and afraid and she wanted help. She put her hand on his arm and said, 'I feel safer with you here.'

It did not work. He turned away from her without reacting. But she left her hand on his arm for in some childlike way she gained a certain feeling of security just from the contact with another person.

Dave came back into the room, his face whiter than ever, his dank hair lifeless and drooping, and Marion was able to smell the sweat on him from three yards as he crossed the carpet. He said, 'Here,' and passed Jacmel something in a piece of dirty white rag that could once have been a handkerchief. Marion could not see what it was but both she and Howard watched as Jacmel moved closer to the light that glowed near the fireplace.

'What about the ring?' Dave said.

'What about it?'

'Looks good to me — and she can't use it now.'

'Leave it! Is the money not enough that you must steal from the dead?' Jacmel said contemptuously. Dave did not reply and Jacmel pressed home his advantage. 'Find a box.' There was finality in his tone and Dave turned away and saw on a small table immediately behind him a silver cigarette box. He picked it up and handed it to Jacmel who placed the white handkerchief inside it and closed it. For a second they looked at each other then Jacmel shrugged and said, 'Open the window.'

The street was empty. A few moments after Marion Stowe had disappeared into the house Bulloch had gone back to the police Rover hollow with rage. He was still there sitting in the back, smoking and brooding, when the call came from the house. 'Can you hear me?' It was Jacmel's voice.

'Sir,' Rich said after a few moments when Bulloch did not move. 'It's the Frenchman.'

Bulloch had heard. 'Yes?' he growled.

'The Frenchman's calling.'

'So bloody what?'

'Thought you'd like to know.'

'Thought I'd like to know.' He mimicked the educated accent. He shouldn't have had to be called. Not this way. Not when the dirt had taken the woman, for now when they called it couldn't be good, not from his point of view. Jesus, it had been … his mind searched for a word without success. Shock? Outrage? Neither fitted. There had been surprise, shock, rage, frustration, admiration, fear … yes, fear. He had tried to bury it but finally he had to face it. He was afraid because what had happened showed there was a mind in the house at least as ruthless as his own; what he was afraid of was that it might be sharper. For the first time he felt tired, a wave of exhaustion seemed to sweep over him and he slumped in the seat. Rich, staring in through the open door, thought he suddenly looked an old man.

'Well?' Bulloch said harshly.

'D'you want me to go?'

'Yes. Yes. You go.' Rich was surprised. 'Find out what he wants.'

Rich turned and walked towards the house. He had seen Bulloch do it several times during the past few hours and often enough during the siege in Sutherland Street, but he had never done it himself. It was territory which Bulloch jealously guarded. Now he found himself alone in the centre of the stage, aware of the dozens of eyes behind him which belonged to other policemen, to newspaper, TV and radio reporters. He was aware, too, of what those same reporters must have been writing and recording in the past few minutes: that the police had allowed the kidnappers to take a second hostage. On the face of it, it sounded criminally negligent, yet what could they have done? They knew the snake was deadly, and the woman was said to be dying. It was not often Rich felt sorry for Bulloch but he did so now.

'Can you hear me?' Rich called, and heard the quiver in his voice. He stood on the pavement where Bulloch had stood.

'Yes, I can hear you. Where is your *chef*, where is M Bulloch?'

'Back there.'

'Fetch him, please.'

'You can talk to me.' He tried to make his voice sound firm but instead it sounded as though he were asking a favour.

'I do not wish to talk to you.'

'He's having a little nap.'

'Nap? What is that?'

'A sleep. He's a bit tired so he's having a little sleep.' It was the best he could do and he hoped it was what Bulloch would have wanted him to say. Contempt was something Bulloch liked to give; not to receive.

There was a pause. When Jacmel spoke again his voice was angry. 'I will throw something from the window. You show it to your *chef*. It will wake him up. Tell him every half-hour another, until the money comes and the car.'

Something shiny flickered against the dark exterior of the house and fell within ten feet of Rich. He flinched backwards in the dark, thinking it might explode.

Jacmel's voice came again. 'It is not a bomb. Do not be afraid.'

He took half a step towards the object then stopped. He crouched down on his hams and looked carefully. It seemed like a silver box of some sort.

It had fallen and rolled on its side and the force of the fall had half-opened it and something white was visible. He moved slowly towards it. Silver. A cigarette box. He had nothing with him except a ball-point pen and he took this out and gingerly touched the box. It toppled sideways and closed. Couldn't be a bomb, he told himself. You don't chuck bombs about from first floor windows if you don't want them to go off. He picked it up and walked slowly back to the car.

'What is it?' Bulloch said. He was sitting at the door and the roof light of the Rover was on.

'Cigarette box.'

'Let's have a look.'

'I thought I'd let forensic have a go before we opened it.'

'D'you think it's a bomb?'

'It crossed my mind.'

'Don't be bloody silly. What's the prize for blowing up policemen?'

Bulloch took the box, weighing it in his palm. Rich said, 'He told me to tell you we'd better have the cash and the car in a hurry or you'd get another every half-hour.'

'What'd he mean? Another box?'

'I think there's a note inside. I saw something white.' Bulloch wanted to know what was inside the box yet something held him back, something veiled, half-hidden from him, like a nightmare barely recalled.

He felt Rich's eyes on him. 'Let me give it to forensic, sir.'

'Don't bloody ...' He was going to say 'patronize' but he checked himself. It was too self-revealing. His mind went back to the time Rich had stayed with him. During the following days, before he had returned to the office, he had been tempted to telephone Rich several times; he had never felt as lonely in his life. But he hadn't, couldn't; it would have shown a weakness no one had ever seen. So he had erased it, pretended it had never happened, but ever since then he had watched Rich like a hawk; one single wrong step; one flicker of an eyelid; one half-smile; anything that let Bulloch know that Rich remembered and that he knew that Bulloch remembered, and Bulloch would have come down on him like a mountain of slurry and buried him and his career; finished him. So far Rich had trodden lightly as a fire-walker and even now as Bulloch searched his face in the dim light of the car he concluded that he had not meant to patronize him, that Rich was as apprehensive as he was himself.

'All right,' he said. 'Let's bloody open it, stand back.' He pushed up the lid and looked at the small parcel in the dirty white handkerchief. He prodded it. It felt like some sort of tube. Hard but with a slightly soft exterior. A marking pen, perhaps, made of soft plastic. No wires, no ticking, no visible parts of a bomb, nothing to give any hint that it would blow up. It couldn't be a bomb. A bomb wouldn't be logical. Couldn't be one, not if he'd thrown it down. What the hell was it, then?

He lifted out the small white parcel. There was a brownish mark at one end. He sniffed it. There was a faint smell but it was masked by the smell of the handkerchief and he couldn't pin it down. He unrolled the handkerchief and stared down at what had been wrapped inside. 'Oh, Jesus,' he said, feeling the bile come up into his throat. 'Oh, Christ.' He was looking down at the fourth finger of a woman's hand.

Rich stared at it numbly, too shocked to put form to the thoughts that suddenly surged through his head. It was left to Glaister to do that for them. He had come up to the car just as Bulloch unwrapped the bundle and now, as he saw the etiolated finger with the ragged skin at the knuckle joint where it had been severed, he said, 'Oh shit, it's the doctor's.'

For one of the few moments in his life Bulloch felt disgusted, and he was not a man to whom disgust came naturally. The years of childhood and later the years in the police had choked any such embryo feelings, indeed he would have construed them now as weaknesses, and at any other time might have rounded on Glaister for allowing his emotions to come to the surface. Instead he felt the sweat break out on his face and neck. They weren't playing games, that was clear. He wrapped the finger, with its pathetic ring still clinging to the lower segment, in the dirty handkerchief. His mind was trying to form a picture of what might have happened; and the brutality of the scene caused him uncharacteristically to cringe; hazily, before he managed to switch his thoughts to his own role, he saw the softly-rounded body of Dr Stowe, a gag plunged into her mouth, hands holding her arm, the blood spurting from the severed finger; what did they do then? Bandage it? He forced the thoughts away; and like some wonderful release, the anger came again. He could feel it build up inside him from its tiny pilot light that was never allowed to die. The anger brought agitation, the agitation energy. He looked up sharply at Glaister. 'Got anyone there from forensic?' he said, jerking his thumb backwards to indicate the mobile control room.

'Leask, sir. From lab liaison.'

'Let him have a look at it before he takes it to Lambeth. He may be able to tell us something.' Glaister took the bundle gingerly. 'And get Blanchet's London man on the phone, I want to talk to him.'

'That's why I came across, sir. We've just been on to him. You were right. Both names on the company books. Maid's name is ...' He flicked over a page of the notebook he was holding, '... Tillion. Louise Tillion. Came over —'

'Never mind when she came over. What about the chauffeur?'

'David Arthur Jeram, sir.'

'Any form?'

'C.R.O. are ringing back.'

'All right. Get the maid's particulars to Paris and find out who the hell she is.'

'We've already done it.'

Bulloch said, 'Sometimes I have hope for you, Glaister.' It was the nearest thing to a compliment he was ever likely to utter and it had the effect of breaking the tension.

'Thank you, sir.'

'Get cracking.'

After Glaister had disappeared through the police cordon and past the waiting media people in the direction of the mobile control room, Rich waited for Bulloch to say what he had thought he was going to say earlier, what he *had* to say. Instead Bulloch got out of the car and said, 'Any more coffee, Rich?'

Rich shook his head. 'It's finished.' Where the word 'Sir' should have come there was only a vacuum that hung in the air between them and Bulloch was not the man to miss it. He knew what was bothering Rich and he knew he'd have to do something about it soon. No, not soon. Now. But he couldn't bring himself to. It was as though there was some psychological block in his make-up that wouldn't allow it.

Instead he said to Rich, 'Get on to London Zoo. Dr Stowe mentioned someone there called Beale. He's supposed to be the expert on snakes and poisons. Get him here.'

'Sir — '

'And Rich, there's something else. Get me a traffic policeman's uniform. Leggings. Goggles, helmet. The lot. Understand?'

'Sir, there's —'

'Get moving, Rich.'

'You've *got* to get the money!'

'By Christ, you little sod, don't you think I know my own business!' Bulloch went up like a volcano. 'Where the hell do you get off telling me what to do?' And then, because his words had carried to the waiting newsmen, who had fallen silent to listen, he dropped his voice and said, 'You do as I said.'

Rich stood his ground. 'They'll kill her, sir. They're not fooling.'

'D'you think I haven't considered that? D'you think I'd bloody leave her there? You forget there's a boy in there, too.'

'I hadn't forgotten, sir.'

'What's that supposed to mean?'

'Nothing, sir.' He turned to go. Bulloch said, 'And Rich, get someone to draw a revolver from Gerald Road and book it out to me.'

'Yes, sir.'

Bulloch watched him go, felt in his pockets for cigarettes and found none. He didn't know where Rich kept them and savagely pushed his way through the waiting reporters towards the mobile control room oblivious of their questions and of the microphones thrust in his face.

The mobile control room was a dark blue caravan divided into small cubicle offices used for on-the-spot interrogations. It had its own switchboard with a line direct to the incident room which had been set up at Gerald Road. It was a clutter of paper and banging typewriters, of ringing telephones and radio static. Two detectives were watching closed circuit TV screens which showed the back and front of the house. It even had a lavatory. As he entered Bulloch saw Rich at the radio and heard the call go out: 'Any motor cycle unit in the vicinity of Eaton Square please acknowledge.' Then Glaister was handing Bulloch a telephone.

'What's his name?' Bulloch said, taking the receiver. 'Blanchet's office manager? Gent called Prothero, sir.' Bulloch sat down at one of the small tables. This was the part he hated, the time of the first defeat; the time to ask for the money. 'Hello,' he said. 'Detective Chief Superintendent Bulloch here.'

*

A silence had fallen over the house. No one had spoken for some time. It was as though they had been forgotten, Marion thought. Not very long ago she had been out there in the misty cold night with the sounds of traffic and trains, voices, footsteps, telephones, all the night noises that rumble deep down in the throat of a great city. Here there was nothing but the dust settling in the still room. Dave and Jacmel stood at the windows like frozen figures. Howard seemed to have nothing left to communicate. The boy slept, feverish, sick, breathing badly. When would the drug wear off, she wondered? When would they be faced with a crisis that no one could solve without medical help? When would the men make a move? When would the police charge in through the door at the rear? When would the snake show itself? When … ?

'Look!' It was Dave's voice, cracking like a whip in the stillness of the room. 'They're bringing the fucking car back!' Jacmel had seen it even before Dave. The yellow Cortina nosed its way through the barrier at the end of the cul-de-sac and came purring quietly down towards the house. It stopped. A policeman in uniform got out, closed the door, held up the keys so that the watchers in the house could see them, and placed them on the car roof. Then he walked quickly back to the far end of the street.

'We did it!' Dave said, his voice filled with relief and jubilation. 'We bloody did it, mate. They fell for it. You're a bloody genius!'

'He comes, too,' Jacmel said, unresponsive.

Bulloch's massive hunched figure was coming through the mist. They watched while he reached the front of the house and took up his position on the pavement. 'Can you hear me?' he called.

For the first time Jacmel allowed himself the faintest of smiles. He opened the window a foot or two. 'Yes, I can hear you.'

'The money's on its way.' Dave gave a thumbs-up to Jacmel who inclined his head slightly. 'Did you hear that?' Bulloch called.

'We heard.'

'So there's no need to hurt Dr Stowe again. Do you understand that?'

'Small notes. A mixture. Swiss francs. Pound notes. Old ones. None bigger than five. German marks. A mixture.'

'We're working on it.'

Howard couldn't see Bulloch but he could hear him, and his ears, now finely attuned to the war game these two were playing, could recognize the firmness in Jacmel and the lack of it in Bulloch. Their roles were completely reversed. He allowed his head to lie back on the sofa and he closed his eyes. At once he saw the huge sprawling complex of Shakespeare Close, with the river on the far side. They might take him with them, of course. There was just a chance. Or they might not. The point was they had the boy — and the woman now — and he didn't have much value. But would they want to kill him? The answer to that was why not? They had killed a policeman. Another murder couldn't make it worse for them.

'Did you hear?' Marion whispered and he could feel her breath on his cheek. 'They're bringing the money.' Again his ears could pick up waves of emotion: this time of relief and happiness. He felt her hand on his arm again and he looked down at it, seeing the soft white skin, the well-kept nails, the few freckles, the faint bloom of hair. He wanted to take the hand and put it against his mouth and his eyes and his tongue; wanted the tenderness that seemed to lie in the fingers, wanted to hold it on his lap as he had held the hands of girls in the cinemas of his youth. For so long there had been no softness in his life and now, as he yearned for it, he knew it was too late.

'Yes,' he said and put his hand on hers. 'I heard. We'll be all right soon.'

There was something in the tone of his voice that caused her to look quickly at him.

He tried to smile reassuringly. 'We'll be all right. You'll see.'

But she turned away and some of the happiness had gone and there was a frown between her eyes.

*

Ruth Blanchet stood in the arrival section of London Airport's Terminal 2 and watched the luggage go round and round on the carousel. 'That's mine,' she said to the porter, pointing to her expensive hide case. 'The dark brown one. And that.' A smaller matching case hove in sight. The porter picked them up and placed them on a luggage trolley.

'Red or green, love?'

'I haven't been anywhere,' Ruth said bitterly, 'so I've nothing to declare.' He looked at her oddly, shrugged, and led the way to the green exit where a customs official waved them through.

'Going to London?'

'Yes.'

'The bus is this way.'

'Get me a taxi, will you?'

'Cost you a packet, love, and the bus is just as quick.'

'A taxi, please. But first I want to make a phone call.'

'I'll have it waiting.' He pointed. 'Over there, to the right of the doors.'

She saw a line of pay phones and walked towards them, fumbling in her purse for the coins. She was tired and exasperated and angry. Each phone was being used. Well, that figured. In a way she would have been surprised if they weren't. Nothing had gone right since she had left home; why should things start now? She stood there jangling the coins in her free hand, staring at an elderly woman who was feeding the phone with tenpenny pieces and seemed to be renewing an old acquaintanceship. She finally became uneasy under Ruth's stare and turned away, but she still fed the coins into the slot.

Ruth's feet in a pair of new crocodile shoes had begun to ache before she left London; now, with the long walks, first at Le Bourget and then back at London Airport, they were tender and sore. She had had a terrible day.

At first things had seemed to be going well. She had got a window seat on the London-Vienna flight and had allowed her fears for Philip to be eased away by the cosseting she received as a first-class passenger. After take-off she had ordered champagne. She realized it was the time of day when she would normally be having a cup of tea, but she didn't care. Champagne, the hostess had suggested, and champagne she had ordered. Sipping it, she felt herself slowly unwind. After the second glass she began to tell herself that what she was doing was a good thing for both herself and for Philip. Dick Howard could be right after all, perhaps she did mother the boy too much, perhaps it was nothing more than a weak chest. Gradually, as the plane took her farther and farther from London, her thoughts moved with it, switching from the recent past to the immediate future. How long was it since she and Michel had been to bed together, a month, six weeks? Would he want her now, as soon as she arrived, or would they have dinner first, or now and again later? Would he have dinner sent up to the room? She had a momentary vision of herself in a filmy negligee in a huge rococo suite, champagne in an ice-bucket, caviare in a chilled dish, thin fingers of toast, warm, balmy air, a balcony, all Vienna laid out before her; and Michel coming out to her, encircling her, touching her breasts. But Michel was not a great romantic. He always folded his clothes before going to bed — legacy of a thousand nights in a thousand of his hotel rooms — and then he brushed his teeth and gargled with Listerine which made his kisses taste medicinal. And then he went to the lavatory — always — so that it had become an almost Pavlovian situation: the flushing of a cistern and there he was. Shazam!

But she supposed she was lucky. He did not make too many demands on her and when he did she enjoyed them. Admit it. She quite liked the cold clinical approach.

Thinking about it brought a hardening of her breasts and nipples and an unfamiliar warmth on the surface of her skin. 'Could I have another glass,' she said to the stewardess, but the girl said they were crossing the Alps and that there would be turbulence and just then the sign came on telling everyone to fasten their seat-belts. Ten minutes later they had been told that Vienna was closed because of fog and they were turning back to Paris.

Le Bourget was wet and cold under the orange lights but she was glad to get out of the plane. She had managed not to be sick but the effort had cost her a great deal and her face was wan. As soon as the passengers had been brought into the transit lounge she had hurried off to the wash-room and sponged away the sweat that had dried coldly on her forehead, then she had redone her face, and, feeling somewhat better, returned to the lounge.

She took a cup of coffee to a deep armchair and sat sipping and smoking. When she finished she found that all her fellow passengers were lying on sofas or sprawling in chairs and she kicked off her shoes and closed her eyes. But the caffeine in the coffee kept her nervously awake. The romantic vision of Vienna by night was replaced by sudden vivid images of Philip: Philip in bed in Rome with 'flu, Philip in bed in London with asthma, Philip as a baby in his cot with streaming nose and eyes; always Philip in bed. It seemed that he had been in and out of a sick-bed from the start of his life. But that was not really so and she knew it. It had begun one ice-bound day in the Catskills when he was almost four years old. She remembered it clearly. She and Pete had only had the motel a couple of years and things were just beginning to break even — you can't take a derelict motel and hope to make a killing in your first year. It took time and hard work, and they had to put in a lot of both.

It was January and Philip had been going to a play-group three miles down the highway at the home of a neighbour. Normally she picked him up about twelve-thirty, but on that particular day Pete had to go into Roxbury to the dentist and he had offered to fetch Philip up on the way back. It had been bitter weather with heavy snow the night before. The day was clear and very cold.

One o'clock came, then two, without any sign of the car. At two-fifteen, as she was about to telephone the police, a patrol car arrived. There had been an accident. Would she come?

It was worse than anything she could have imagined. The car had come off a bend on a patch of black ice, plunged down a slope and hit a tree where it came to rest. Her husband was standing near the wreck. Dried blood had crusted his cheeks from minor cuts on his forehead but otherwise he was unhurt. He was shaking and crying and hardly recognized her. But her child was still in the car and they were waiting for a mobile crane and oxy-acetylene cutters. It was the waiting, the fact that no one seemed to be doing anything that got to her and in her memory she could hear her voice screaming, 'Help him! Why doesn't someone help him!'

By the time they cut Philip free he was almost frozen. It was a wonder, everyone said, that he had survived at all. From that moment, Ruth had made a pact with herself, that except for unavoidable circumstances she would never leave Philip to the responsibility of others — and that included her husband.

No marriage could survive that, for Pete had soon learned she no longer trusted him with his own son. The marriage collapsed. The motel was sold at a loss. After the divorce she had taken a job as receptionist in a New York hotel. It was there she met Michel. He had been in the States looking for franchises. He had stayed a month, taken her out to dinner four times and asked her to marry him. A fortnight later she and Philip were in London. The nightmare had turned into a wonderful dream.

As she sat in the transit lounge at Le Bourget, becoming more and more enmeshed in memories and anxiety, her ears caught the first announcement of an Air France departure to London and on impulse she checked to see whether there was a vacant seat. In half an hour she wras airborne again, travelling back the way she had come. On the plane she had told herself that what she was doing was the most sensible of all the possible alternatives, for if Schwechat was closed to air traffic from London it would also be closed to aircraft from Singapore and since Michel's flight was due in an hour later than her own it followed that he, too, would be unable to land and might go on anywhere — might even go to London. She had telephoned Sacher's from Le Bourget and left a message for him, and Air France had telexed Schwechat for her and left a message *there*; so now she was going home to her own bed. Home. There was a twinge of disquiet in the word. She had also telephoned the house from Paris and had received an out-of-order tone. But she had told herself that she was phoning from another country and anything could happen to spoil a connection. Living in London she had become inured to bad lines, disconnections, calls that in the words of the Post Office 'Failed to mature', engaged signals before she had finished dialling, out-of-order signals when she knew the telephone was working, in short all the frustrations that telephone users were heir to. But still ... she didn't like it. What if something had gone wrong and there was an imperative need to get through? But nothing had gone wrong. Well, nothing big anyway, except her whole day and half the night. Here she was flying and flying and never getting anywhere except the place she'd left. Hours of wasted time and effort. She was so tired and frustrated, she felt like crying.

The old woman finally stopped feeding the pay phone and Ruth was able to dial the house. Again she received the out-of-order tone. She stood there feeling the frustration build up inside her. She dialled again. And again. Should she get on to 'Faults'? Her will cringed at the thought of all the explaining, all the passing from one section to another she would have to endure. She slammed down the receiver and hurried in the direction of the main doors. The porter was waiting with a taxi. She tipped him less than normal and returned his glare with enough venom to make him flinch, then she was being swept along towards the tunnel and the motorway into London. She noticed that the taxi's meter was not working and knew the driver would try to hit her for ten or fifteen pounds, perhaps even more after hearing her American accent. In a grim way she looked forward to the end of the journey.

But soon her thoughts came back to the house. *Why* was the phone giving the out-of-order tone? Of course it could be a crossed line somewhere. Or snow. Wasn't there supposed to be snow somewhere? Not in London though. Or the receiver might have been left off the hook. But that would have caused an engaged signal. She sat staring at her reflection in the window, seeing two dark holes for eyes and a downward slash of mouth.

Part V

Saturday 2.45 a.m – 5.58 a.m.

The atmosphere in the house had changed, Marion thought, since she had been brought in. Before that Bulloch had been in charge, big, aggressive, dominating the situation, but now Jacmel had taken over. She sat on the sofa with the boy's sleeping weight on her lap and watched Jacmel and Dave at the windows. They, in turn, watched Bulloch shamble back to the cars.

'What about a drink?' Dave said.

'You think we can celebrate now?' Jacmel asked.

'Why bloody not? You heard him. They're getting the money.'

'Easy? Just like that?' He snapped his fingers.

'You were right, mate. We've got the boy. And now the woman. That's what counts.'

Success had brought not only euphoria into Dave's tone but a respect for Jacmel as well. He's like a little child, Marion thought, getting his own way. What would his reaction be if things went wrong? Rage? Panic? Fright? Probably a mixture of all three with a behaviour pattern no one could anticipate. And he had a shotgun in his hands.

'Now we must think,' Jacmel said.

'Think?'

'My friend, no one is going to *give* us money and let us go without ... how do you say it? ... strings.'

'Strings?'

'Ask yourself.' Marion could hear the patience in his voice; he's humouring him, she thought. 'Ask yourself. You have killed a pol ...'

'We. *We*, mate. That's the law here. Conspiracy, they call it. You're as much to blame as me.'

'All right. As you say. A policeman has died. Right? So ... they are just going to give us money and let us go?'

'What can they do? You're the one who says that if we've got the boy they can't touch us.'

'I do not know what they can do. I am not a policeman but I know if I was a policeman I would do something. No one can get us while we stay here in this house. But eventually we will give up. They know that. We know that. It is inevitable. But in a place of our own, where we are not besieged, where no one knows us. Where we can even get out for a while. That, my friend, is different. They know that, too. They are not fools, and it was you who told me that.'

'So what do we do?' The euphoria had gone and in its place Marion heard uncertainty.

'It is now that we must be most careful. When the tiger smiles it is not amusing. That is your English saying, no? There are only two doors are there not, the front door and the door below it from the cellar?'

'That's all.'

'And at the back?'

'I told you. A mews.'

'A couturier, not so?'

'Cou — ?'

'They make dresses.'

'Oh, yes. A dressmaker.'

Jacmel began to pace up and down the room. At last he said, 'Go down. Check it. See that there is no other way in or out.'

'I told you. Blank walls, that's all.'

'There may be a window.'

'I'm not going, mate. That bloody snake could be anywhere. I'm not setting foot outside this room till we go.'

'Don't you understand,' Jacmel said patiently. 'We have no freedom here. We cannot manoeuvre. We must make safe areas where we know the —'

'That's what it's all about, isn't it? You want me to look for the bloody snake. The hell with that, mate. I did what you wanted with the knife but —'

'Dave, listen to me.' His voice had dropped again and Marion began to realize how clever Jacmel was. He knew what sort of person he had for a partner and knew just how far he could push him. One moment he was firm with him. The next soft. One moment he held out safety; the next danger. It was the carrot and the stick. Now he went on to repeat his arguments about the house being a trap, about the shot policeman, about the lack of manoeuverability, about the possibility that there was another way into the house, but equally and more importantly that there might be another way out. It was this he had saved until last and it was this that seemed to reach Dave.

'Not by yourself,' Jacmel said. 'Take him. He will go first. And you have the gun. What can happen to you?'

For some minutes past Howard had been sitting with his head thrown back on the cushions. Now Marion saw it snap upright. He's terrified, she thought. And who could blame him? He had already done it once, in this room. Had cleared it for them. Searched it. Made it safe. By himself. No protective clothing. No gun. Now they were asking him again. It was too much to ask of anyone, she thought angrily. And then suddenly she had the answer. She couldn't think why it had not occurred to her before, unless it was because she'd had a hell of a lot of other things to think about since she had looked down into JacmePs face on the steps of the house.

'You don't have to search for the snake,' she said and her voice dropped into the silence like glass splintering.

Jacmel turned and strode back towards her, to stand over the sofa, square, dark-grey in the sombre light.

'What do you say?'

'You don't have to endanger anyone,' she said. 'If you turn off the heating you'll be safe.'

'What?'

'The central heating. Turn it off and open the windows. The snake won't bother you then. They can't stand cold. It'll go into a sort of coma and then die.'

'Is it true?'

She nodded wearily. 'Yes, it's true.'

Jacmel turned to Howard. 'What do you say?'

'They're cold-blooded,' he said, grasping at the relief. 'That's why they don't come out in winter. Snakes can't stand cold.'

He stood over them, poised; then suddenly he made up his mind. 'Where is the control?'

'Just outside the door.'

'Turn it off.'

Howard went into the passage. The main thermostat which controlled the whole house was set into the wall near Philip's room. It was set at seventy-five degrees and he turned it to the 'Off' position. Somewhere in the depths of the house a pulse, too faint for anyone to feel, had been beating, now it stopped and the fans which blew the hot air through the ducts spun freely on their shafts growing slower and slower until they finally came to rest; in the cellar there was only the ticking of hot metal as the boiler began to cool.

Upstairs Jacmel ordered Howard to go from room to room opening windows. Soon cold air was rushing into the house, flowing first over the carpets then rising up the walls like floodwater until whole rooms were filled with cold air and the walls themselves began to lose their heat. Fifteen minutes after the heating had been switched off and the first floor windows opened, the temperature in the drawing-room, where the largest windows of the house were situated, had plunged from between seventy and eighty degrees Farenheit to less than fifty. Marion felt the freezing air whirl around her feet and rise up her calves and shivered. She had taken off her heavy coat and now she tried to put her arms through the sleeves as gently as possible so as not to shift the child. The operation took some minutes and she was chilled by the time she pulled the coat around herself. She put her hand on Philip's forehead and it was icy. Then she noticed that the pattern of his breathing had changed, he had begun to suck at the air as though he had difficulty in getting enough into his lungs.

'We'll have to close the windows again,' she said to Jacmel.

'We have just opened them.'

'It's the boy. His breathing's getting worse.'

Dave had poured himself a whisky and was sipping it. 'You must be kidding,' he said.

She ignored him, addressing Jacmel. 'If he gets really ill he'll complicate things for you.'

'And if he dies,' Howard said brutally, 'you'll have another body. Bodies can't be explained away. What'll you do? Throw him in the Thames?'

'Shut up!' It was the first time they had seen Jacmel really angry, but when he spoke again he was in control of himself. 'You,' he said softly to Howard, 'you must take great care.'

'Why? My value to you is nil. D'you think I don't know what's going to happen?'

'Why would they harm you?' Marion said. 'The money is coming.'

It was time she knew, he thought, yet something held him back from spelling it out; perhaps he did not want to hear it himself. 'You don't think they're going to take the money and leave us here having breakfast, do you?'

'But you said —'

'I said you'd be all right. You probably will be.'

'Then —' Philip moaned and turned in her lap. She felt him again. 'He's freezing! For God's sake!'

'Get a blanket,' Jacmel said to Howard.

'Why not let him go to his room?' Howard said. 'It could be a couple of hours before they get the money together. Marks, francs, pounds ... it's not that easy. There's an electric heater in his room. At least he'll be warm.'

Jacmel hesitated. Dave said, 'Keep him here where we can see him. Doesn't matter if the little bastard does catch cold.'

'Louise said he had asthma.'

'So what?' Dave said.

'He's not going to wake up for hours,' Howard said. 'Not after a double dose. His windows are locked. Lock his door too if you like. But believe me, if you don't, you're going to have a very sick child on your hands.'

Jacmel nodded. 'All right. But first you ...'

'I know,' Howard said. 'I know.'

He moved towards the fireplace and pointed to the long brass poker. Jacmel nodded again and then said to Dave, 'Go with him. It is time to earn your money.' This was not the friendly tone of camaraderie but that of an officer to a ranker.

Marion watched as Howard moved towards the door. There was sweat on his face in spite of the cold. She wanted to say something to help but could think of nothing. She told herself that Dave had a shot-gun; the moment they saw the faintest shadow of a snake he would kill it. She sat holding the boy very tightly.

The boy's room was where Louise had been bitten — more accurately the dressing-room or, as Phil had named it, the Great Ngorongoro Crater Menagerie. Howard's legs were feeling weak again; he had tried to walk with a straight back from the sitting-room because of Marion Stowe. He did not want her to see how afraid he really was. He told himself that if she knew she might become hysterical and that would complicate things still further, but that was only partially true.

He came to the dark square that was the open door to Philip's room and switched on the light. Dave was some way behind him and quite useless if the snake were to attack. It was the sitting-room all over again, beyond the doorframe lay a nightmare land of shadows.

'Get in,' Dave said. It was no more than a whisper, as though the snake would hear.

Howard moved forward and the door clicked closed behind him. If anything he felt slightly safer. He had no trust in Dave's ability to overcome his own terror in an emergency. He was alone. He had the poker. He could smash the windows and jump for it. The thought died, still-born. What about Philip? What about Marion?

Again he unconsciously formed his territory, this time within a few feet of the door, the only patch of known safety; again he forced his feet forward and fought to control the shaking of his legs. And then in the half darkness of the Great Ngorongoro Crater Menagerie his bush-trained eyes saw something which gave him hope. From the door of Philip's bedroom he could see the guinea-pig and the rabbit and the golden hamster feeding unconcernedly in the front of their cages. The presence of the snake in either the Menagerie or in Philip's bedroom would have caused the terrified animals to huddle deep in their sleeping quarters. He moved forward, strengthened somewhat by his knowledge. He searched and found nothing.

*

Howard carried the boy into the room and placed him on his bed. As he was tucking the blankets over him Philip came drowsily awake.

'It's all right, old chap,' Howard said soothingly.

Thickly, Philip mumbled. 'The name ... haven't got a name ...'

For a moment Howard was confused, then he realized that Philip had been dreaming and had gone back in time to refer to an earlier conversation about naming the snake. 'Don't worry,' he said softly, not wishing to wake Philip further. 'We'll think of one. A really good one.'

'You weren't here,' Philip said drowsily. 'Can't open the box.'

'Tomorrow.'

'When?'

'Tomorrow. We'll open the box tomorrow.'

'You must ... must wake me early.'

'Yes.'

'Promise.'

'I promise. Early.'

Jacmel was testing the double-glazing.

'The clock,' Philip said, sliding away. 'I didn't ... I didn't set the clock.'

Howard picked it up and wound it. 'All done,' he said. 'No need to worry now. Just get some sleep.'

Philip's eyes flickered then closed.

'Come,' Jacmel said.

'Why don't you leave the light on?' Howard said. 'Then he won't be so frightened if he wakes.' Jacmel nodded. 'That's the heater,' Howard said, pointing to a two-kilowatt fan heater. 'Shall I switch it on?'

'Yes.'

He canted it at an angle so the warm air blew upwards across Philip's bed. The vibration of the fan made a slight humming noise.

'All right,' Jacmel said. He motioned Howard to go back to the landing, then he locked Philip's bedroom door and placed the key on the telephone table. They went back to the sitting-room. Marion was huddled on the sofa writh her feet tucked up underneath her. The temperature in the room had dropped into the low forties and the whole house, with the exception of Philip's room, was very cold. As she saw Howard, however, she smiled and shifted her feet, making room.

'Don't move,' he said and began to veer away from the sofa towards an armchair.

'I'd feel better if you sat here,' she said.

He tried to answer with a smile but it was tight on his face. He sat down in the place he had occupied before. 'Is he all right?' she said.

'For a while. He's warm enough, anyway.'

*

The snake was not warm enough. For some time her body temperature had been dropping, with a consequent drop in heartbeat and breathing. She lay where she had lain for the past few hours, at the junction of the hot air ducts. Every now and then, as a Circle line train rumbled along the underground track on its way from Victoria Station to Sloane Square, she would lift her head. Some minutes after the vibrations ended, the head would gradually drop down to a resting position. But the vibrations had now almost ceased, and instead of being alert, a torpor was gradually enveloping her body as cold air moved along the ducts. *Dendroaspis Polylepis* was, like all snakes, highly susceptible to minute changes in temperature. She had been born into a world where summer temperatures varied between seventy and eighty degrees Farenheit and she was able to keep her own body temperature within two degrees of any point within that range. Once, in high summer, she had been caught by a blistering sun at noon on part of a plain on which there were no trees and no ant-hills to give her shade. She had no sweat glands and her body temperature began to climb into the nineties and then over a hundred degrees. She was on the point of death by heatstroke when she had come across the rusted remains of an Anson bomber which had been used as a trainer by the Royal Air Force during the Second World War and which had crashed there in 1943 killing the pilot and navigator. She had slithered up into a patch of shade in what had once been the cockpit and had lain there, barely alive, until nightfall brought coolness.

The reverse had also happened to her. She had been out hunting one warm evening in early autumn when the weather had suddenly changed, and freezing winds had come racing down on to her range from the Drakensberg Mountains, giving the first brutal taste of the upland winter. The temperature had dropped so quickly she had been unable to find shelter and she had simply come to a halt out in the middle of the veld, her body as rigid as an iron bar. During that time any small rodent could have eaten her living flesh, for she had been unable to move. The following day the sun came out and warmed the earth and warmed her, too, and gave new life to her body. Now the temperature in her maze of air ducts was dropping quickly as was the temperature of her body, which she was unable to control or adjust.

But fortunately she was well equipped for survival. She had sophisticated systems at her control even though the functions of each seemed paradoxical. In the air-duct, where no light penetrated and the darkness was as thick as black velvet, she could 'see' with her tongue. Her normal vision, even in conditions of adequate light, was poor and monochromatic. But the perceptions gathered by her tongue were multi-dimensional. It was linked with a mechanism in the roof of her mouth called the Organ of Jacobson which processed the information and passed it on to her brain. Not only did her tongue 'see' it also 'smelt' for her. And while she did not have any external ears the bones of her jaw were able to absorb vibrations and pass these on to her inner ear which in turn routed them to her brain.

So now, in the dark of the middle of the house, her information-gathering sensors were filtering data to her brain which was forming a pattern. Firstly her tongue was getting a strong 'smell' of vegetation, a smell with which she was familiar. Secondly, the nerve endings near the front of her nose were picking up, from the same area, faint traces of heat. Thirdly the Ciicle line had closed down for the night so there were no longer any vibrations to make her afraid. She began to move in the direction which her sense organs dictated.

The smell of vegetation came from a garbage can filled with, among other things, several discarded lettuce leaves, the green tops of carrots and half a stale cabbage. The garbage can stood in the dumb waiter in the basement. It had been sent down earlier in the day from the kitchen two floors above. The warmth came from the boiler. The cooling metal had stopped ticking, but there was a vestigial heat remaining in the walls and also in the flue pipe that rose from the top of the boiler and entered one of the old chimney breasts. *Dendroaspis* pulled her already stiffening body in the direction of the warmth.

*

'You're cold,' Marion said, touching Howard's hand, her voice over-full of solicitude.

'I don't feel it,' he said. He was lying back on the sofa, his face ashen.

'Freezing.' She kept her fingers on his hand a moment longer. Again she took comfort from the touch of another human but this time the language of the contact was different, unconsciously she was conveying gratitude for what he had done and apology for her own guilt in being unable to help.

'I'm all right.' He felt her hand hesitate then move away and again the sadness flashed over him. He liked her touching him, and in a way was grateful for it. She must know what it had been like, she dealt with snakes all the time. Well, perhaps she didn't know. No one who had not searched a house as he had searched this one for a deadly snake could possibly *know* what it was like to pull back a hanging curtain, to move a chair, look under a table — never certain from where it might strike. It was like playing Russian roulette except that a bullet was quicker and cleaner. He closed his eyes and again the huge slab-sided building that was called Shakespeare Close flashed across his inner vision. But now he saw it with the rain beating slantwise against the red-brick walls. He had stayed there once, years ago on long leave from the Colonial Service. When had that been? Early fifties? Must have been. That was when he'd met Jane.

He'd had a service flat in Wordsworth. She had been in Shelley. They'd met in unromantic circumstances. He had been buying a newspaper in the arcade of shops on the ground floor of the administrative block and she had been standing next to him. She'd had a fat dachshund on a lead. He had just bought his paper and was pocketing the change when he saw that the dachshund had defecated on the floor next to the shop counter. As he looked up his eyes met those of the girl holding the lead. They were filled with frightened embarrassment. The shopkeeper had not seen what had occurred, nor had the only other customer who was looking at a rack of paper-backs. In a second Howard had dropped his *Times* on the pile of stiffish dung, bent, scooped it up and marched swiftly from the shop to the nearest litter basket. The girl hurried after him pulling the dachshund after her like a miniature hippo.

'God, I'm sorry,' she said.

He smiled. Part of an old joke flitted through his head. He began to say, 'It's all right, I thought it was the dog.' But he shut his mouth with a snap. 'Don't worry,' he said. 'I had a terrier once that brought lions home. Nothing more embarrassing than an unwanted lion.'

She had stared at him as though he were raving, then slowly a smile of relief had spread over her face.

That had been the beginning. Her name was Jane Lasser, Mrs Jane Lasser, and she was twenty-three. Blonde. Good figure. Heavy bust. And the most beautiful grey eyes he had ever seen. She had been married for eight months to a man nearly twenty years older than herself who ran an international exhibition business and spent most of his time in Europe organizing trade fairs, boat shows, book fairs, wine shows, anything that people wished to exhibit. It meant almost constant travelling and she had not seen him for nearly five months.

She lived with her dachshund in a flat in Shakespeare Close. She had been ready for a liaison and, he supposed, he had been ready for the great love affair of his life. He had spent the past years in various isolated posts in Central Africa, deprived of any female companionship other than African women whom he had left untouched for fear of undermining his position of authority, and the District Commissioner's wife whom he had left untouched for fear of the DC.

He and Jane had fallen on each other like cannibals, devouring flesh and emotions as though they had been on the brink of starvation — which, he supposed, they had. Time had no meaning. They lived in her great double bed in a room with a view of the Thames and only emerged to eat or go to a show in the evenings. She used to get letters from her husband. She never opened them and after a few weeks there was a small pile on the table in the hall.

They lived like that for six weeks, almost inside each other's skins. Until then he had been a virgin, and in those six weeks his body exploded with the pent-up lust of enforced celibacy, and his senses demanded and received all the softness and tenderness of which the years in the bush had deprived him. They were in love as no two people had ever been in love, or so he thought. They talked. They planned for the future. They spoke of marriage. They could not do without one another. She would divorce her husband. Howard would leave the service and get a job in London. They would never be parted.

And then had come the terrible telegram from the family solicitor in Nairobi telling him that both his parents had been killed by Mau Mau terrorists.

He had flown back immediately and the only plane he could get was an elderly Dakota which had taken him down Africa with the leisureliness of a flying-boat, coming down for coffee, lunch, and tea and landing every evening so that the passengers could sleep in hotels. The first night he'd spent at Malta, the second at Wadi Haifa in the Sudan, the third at Entebbe in Uganda. He had finally reached Nairobi on the fourth day and his parents were already buried. It was only then he had realized with shame that during most of the flight he had thought very little about anything but the pain of his parting with Jane.

The first few evenings alone in the big stone-built farmhouse were among the worst of his life. His parents had been cut down while at the evening meal by one of the young gardeners who had burst into the room with a *panga*, and Howard could still see the blood stains on the rug around the table legs. The gardener had had to get past old Luke the cook, and had killed him too. Howard knew none of the servants, and each one looked a potential enemy. At six o'clock every evening he had closed the heavy shutters on the windows and barred the front and back doors and the servants had gone to their dwelling-huts half a mile away and he had been left alone with his thoughts and the crackling static of his radio.

The arrangement had been that Jane would follow in a few weeks. First she had to tell her husband and then she had to make arrangements for a divorce; it did not matter either to Howard or to her who divorced whom just so long as it was done. She would come out to Kenya and they would live together as man and wife until such time as they could marry. That was the arrangement. But as he sat in the farmhouse night after night writing to her, he was torn by need for her and by the thought of bringing her out into an area of danger. He had finally compromised by taking a flat in Nairobi where she could stay and where he could join her for weekends or for longer periods depending on work at the farm.

All this he put into his letters, together with suggestions for what clothing to bring — she had assumed Kenya to be overgrown with steamy jungle and he had had to convince her that at six thousand feet their farm was cool enough even on a summer evening to wear a jersey. They were letters full of longing, full of allusions to what they had enjoyed during those six weeks. He found himself also alluding openly to their sexual life, something he would normally have been inhibited from doing. As he recalled the days and nights in which they were drunk with each other's sexuality he would be overcome with desire for her and the empty farmhouse would become a prison.

He wrote every day, she wrote once a fortnight. He told himself that his own letters were as much to pass the long evening hours as anything else, and that the brief rather hastily-written letters he received from London were fruits of a normal correspondence. But then weeks began to pass without a letter from her. The ones that did arrive were even briefer than before. He became anxious. He wrote asking if anything was wrong. She did not reply. He sent a telegram. She did not reply to that either. He telephoned. It took him six hours to get through to Shakespeare Close and when he did so the line was bad.

But not so bad that he couldn't hear the man's voice who had answered the phone and who had told him Jane had just gone down to the shops for a few minutes. Howard steeled himself, then plunged.

'Is that Mr Lasser?' he had asked.

The man had laughed. No, he said, it wasn't Mr Lasser. Howard could suddenly visualize the scene: the big double bed; the telephone on the table next to it; the man lying naked staring out at the rain dimpling the Thames; and Jane shopping downstairs. What for? A couple of steaks so she could make steak and chips as she had so often done for them? 'To keep your strength up,' she had said. And he had seen in that instant another picture. The hall table. A pile of unopened air-letters; this time they were from him. He had put down the phone and tried to put Jane out of his mind. It had taken more than a year before the pain began to diminish.

'Here,' Marion Stowe said, 'let me put some of this round you.' She had taken off her coat and was trying to tuck it round his body.

'No. No,' he said, sitting upright. 'I'm not cold. Really.'

'Of course you are. Frozen. And it's big enough for two.' For the past few minutes she had been watching him. His face, already grey, had become thinner, the cheeks more hollow, the flesh more tautly stretched.

He's sick, she thought. Either sick or physically drained from fear. *Don't drift away*, she thought, *don't leave me here alone*. She had begun to fuss with her coat and when that did not seem to wake him, had taken it off and begun to wrap it round both of them. To do this she had to move much closer, until their bodies were touching. Her soft and rounded limbs met sharp angles and bony protuberances and she realized that under his clothing he must be very thin. Her heart went out to him again. They used him, these people, like some sort of ... her mind tried to search for the exact word and a picture arose of a man holding a mine detector. That's how they used him. A piece of machinery, with no feelings. But he did have feelings. He was terrified and yet he had been kind to her, gallant almost in an old-fashioned way. She found herself immeasurably touched but at the same time frightened lest he slide away into some capsule of his own for his own self-protection. She wanted him in her dimension. She needed him.

'Which part of Africa are you from?' she said brightly. 'Kenya.'

'Oh, I've never been there. Except just to land at Nairobi.' He did not reply. 'You can't see much from airports. I mean you can't really get a taste of the country, can you?'

'No, I suppose not.'

'Have you a family out there?'

'I'm not married.'

'Oh.'

Supposed to have been, he thought. Should have been.

The District Commissioner's wife had always said, 'Dick'll make someone a marvellous husband.' And each time she said it she had eyed him with a speculative look and he knew he could have had her any time he liked, when the DC was away on tour. Harry Marshall had had her. He'd said it was like going to bed with a python. But going to bed with your DC's wife was a cliché in the Colonial Service — it was where most divorces stemmed from and Howard had steered clear of that. He'd been ambitious then, although he liked to think he wasn't, and he had not wanted anything to blight his career. Half an hour between the sheets with the DC's wife one hot afternoon was just the sort of thing that might do it.

He *would* have made a good husband; Jane had missed something there; she'd never know how much she'd missed; he'd have given her everything. Now, remembering the amused voice of the man on the telephone he felt again a twinge of anger and jealousy. In all this time he had never said to himself that he was lucky, rather the reverse; if he'd stayed on in London it would never have happened; he had left her; she was lonely; he had finally come round to the conclusion that it had been his fault. After Jane most women he'd met seemed like flat soda water. He'd taken them to bed as he needed to but there had never been any very strong feelings. There had been a time when he had been in with the BOAC lot, different air hostesses arriving in batches twice and sometimes three times a week — and he still had the flat in Nairobi. He'd taken them out to the game-park on the edge of town and then to drinks or dinner and then back to the flat. It had been almost too easy. Some said it was the altitude; that it went to their heads. Whatever it was these blue-skirted, white-bloused, coolly attractive girls suddenly seemed to become nymphos once they landed. It had been good for a while but then for financial reasons he'd had to give up the flat and driving all the way into Nairobi for a date and then sneaking up the hotel stairs to the girl's room hadn't been quite the same. He'd had an affair with a widow on a nearby farm; neither had wanted marriage and that had been soothing; no tensions. They'd talked about books mainly and then gone to bed without much passion, but with a need for therapeutic contact. Most of the time he stayed on the farm by himself. He was lonely and thought about marriage often; the only trouble was that no one he met looked like Jane. Then when he had sold the farm and gone into the safari business he'd been glad there was no wife to leave behind. There had been stories that white hunters always took along a double sleeping-cot so that their clients' wives could bag the hunter while their husbands bagged a rhino. It was rubbish. Firstly, you slept on a canvas cot in the bush and two people humping up and down on it would have flattened it in a minute, secondly, you were too bloody tired at the end of a day for that sort of caper, and thirdly and most important of all a white hunter was only as good as his reputation and that spread out to cover a multitude of things; apart from anything else you didn't want an irate husband armed with an elephant gun poking his head round your tent flap while you were at it. It wasn't on, no matter what the novelists said.

'My husband was a South African,' the voice next to him said. 'That's why I knew the accent.' She'd said it before and it sounded silly said again, but what else could she say? He seemed to disappear within himself. Somehow she had to bring him out and keep him out.

He did not react. 'What did you do in Africa?' she said remorselessly.

'Quite a lot of things. Colonial service. A bit of hunting. Farming. Looked after a safari park.'

She was aware that Jacmel had half turned and was listening, but she ignored him. 'Tell me about it.'

'What?'

'You.'

'Me?'

'Yes. Why not?'

'What sort of thing?'

'I don't know. About your life.'

'It'd take all night.'

'We've got all night.'

'Yes, I suppose we have. But you don't want to know about me.'

'For God's sake,' she said. 'Talk to me. Don't close your eyes. Don't drift away. Talk. Tell me.'

He pulled himself upright and swung round to look at her, seeing the face as a soft pale blob in the dim light, the dark eye sockets. 'Give me your hand,' he said. She put out her hand and took his and brought it back on to her warm lap under the coat. 'You'll be all right,' he said. 'Don't worry.'

'*We'll* be all right.'

'*We'll* be all right. Where d'you want me to start?'

'You said you were in the Colonial Service. Start there.'

So he told her about the Service and the DC's wife, and going on tour of his district, and to Salisbury on leave, and sometimes home to Kenya. But he didn't tell her about Harry Marshall or Jane Lasser. He spoke in brief jerky sentences and as he went on the sentences grew longer, the detail more varied and after a while what had started as a kind of *curriculum vitae* was fleshed out into autobiography. He, too, became aware that Jacmel was listening but, like Marion, he did not care. He told her about being in London when the cable had come about his parents' death and he realized that she had only barely heard of the Mau Mau terrorism in Kenya which had marked the early fifties with bloodshed, when white farmers by the tens and black people by the hundreds were slaughtered by Kikuyu tribesmen who had taken blood oaths. He told her of the farm and how, after Kenya had gained independence from Britain, he'd had to sell it at a quarter of the true value; how, after his debts were paid off, he had only enough money to equip himself for the hunting business — the only other business he knew. He told her about going down to Mozambique with Michel Blanchet and how he had started the safari park hotel.

And when he had finished she said, 'Why did you leave?'

'Kenya or the hotel?'

'Both.'

Here it was. She had asked the question innocently enough but in fact this was where everything had been leading. It was unavoidable. Again, as in a dream, he felt the lion on top of him and involuntarily his hands went to his stomach where the lacerations burned at the memory.

'I had an accident,' he said.

'What sort of an accident?'

'With one of the lions. One gets too confident and then they turn on you.'

'What happened?' This time it was Jacmel's voice from the window.

'Someone was taking a photograph of it and it charged,' Howard said.

'At you?'

'At me.'

'Why did you not shoot it?' Jacmel said. 'You had a gun, no?'

'Yes,' Howard said wearily, 'I had a gun.'

They waited but he did not explain and finally Jacmel shrugged and said, 'English. You love animals even when they kill you.' Howard's silence seemed to get to him for he came away from the window and stood near the sofa and said, 'You let them take this place away from you.'

For a moment Howard was confused and then he realized what Jacmel meant.

'The British Government decided to give independence to Kenya,' he said. 'Nothing we could do about it.'

'You could have fought against the Mau Mau *and* against the British Government. In Algeria we fought for our country. Do you know what is a *pied noir*?'

'The settlers. The ones who fought against France.'

'Yes, but not France, only against those Frenchmen who wished to give Algeria independence. We, the *pieds noirs*, were patriots. *Algerie française*. That was our banner. We fought against the French army and we fought against the Moslems. And we fought against de Gaulle. He did what you call a sell-out, no? Do you know what is the O.A.S. and the F.L.N.? Do you know of the Delta Commando? Of the *plastiquage*? The *barbouzes*? Do you remember the Week of the Barricades? Salan? Gardes? Maurice Challe? What do you know of a colonial war? You gave up the country to the black people. You gave up your farm. I too had a farm. I did not *give* it away. But you — you did not even fire a gun.'

Jacmel looked down at the sofa and saw two frightened people. What could they know of his life? How could they understand the war in Algiers and Oran? You could not take a cup of coffee at a sidewalk cafe for fear of bullets from a passing car; you could not go to a cinema for fear of plastic explosive in a brief-case. Death was all around you in those days. Friends, brothers, fathers — one day you would be all together, the next, half would be arrested or dead.

No, he had more in common with the big policeman who waited in the cold. He would have been a good man to have on one's side in Algeria.

He saw again in his mind's eye the shattered glass that so often crunched underfoot in the streets of Algiers, the blood, the twisted wrecks of bombed cars; he saw again the vineyard near Miliana bursting into flames, erupting in smoke as he set it alight. Then he saw Louise and himself, hand in hand, running towards the car. Driving away. Never looking back. At that moment he had thought that his life was over. He didn't care. Let the F.L.N. take him. But the O.A.S. looked after their own.

He and Louise were smuggled aboard a freighter bound for Barcelona and a new life for them began in Spain. Franco had from the beginning adopted a lenient attitude to members of the O.A.S. and Spain became a haven for those on the run from the French police. Jacmel and Louise drifted along the coast to Malaga where the establishment of semi-permanent foreign colonies allowed them to submerge from view. They rented a small villa at Monte Mar and he tried to put what savings remained into land deals. But he was five years too late. Development on the coast was so fast and on so massive a scale that there was no longer room for the small entrepreneur. Instead he turned his attention to the Coin valley some miles inland expecting this to be the new centre of the building boom. He bought a run-down orange farm and waited for the hotel companies and the apartment-house builders to come out to him. But no one wanted to live that far from the sea, especially holiday-makers, and the holidaymaker was God.

It was while they were living on the decaying *finca* near Coin that he and Louise broke up. Their affair had been born in a hothouse of tension and excitement and now it foundered on the rocks of routine domesticity. Unlike Jacmel, Louise had been on no one's wanted list and she was free to move in and out of France at will, so two years after they arrived in Spain she went to live in Paris.

Jacmel sold the farm at a loss and took a small flat in the Calle San Miguel in Torremolinos, which was just beginning to be torn apart and changed from a beautiful fishing-village into a concrete disaster. He met an American woman, heiress to a soft drink fortune, who had a villa on the outskirts of the town. She was ten years older than he and drank herself into a coma by seven each evening. She made very few demands on him — she was hung-over in the daytime and too drunk at night — and that suited him. In six months he went to bed with her three times. After her there had been a German countess who had fled from Prussia before the advancing Russians at the end of the war. This time there was less money and more sex. With his American lady he had been fed steaks specially brought in from Madrid; with his German countess he ate a great deal of crumbly goat's milk cheese and large green olives. But that didn't bother him and he became quite fond of her two flaxen-haired young daughters. After the German countess there was a young blonde Swede who had come to southern Spain because Sweden and Swedish men bored her. She had less money than the American, more than the German, but a better body than either, and one day she had left him for a young Italian who played the guitar. The last he saw of her she was heading along the coast road with her new friend in the direction of Marbella.

He might have gone on like this, drifting from one woman, one house, one bed to the next — his capacity for self-disgust was buried in the ruins of Algeria — but he met two other former members of the O.A.S.

He knew there were ex-officers living farther up the coast around Nerja and Motril but he had never sought them out. One January morning after he had bought his *oleo* for the paraffin stove that kept his small apartment warm he had gone up to the square, to the Bar Central, for a cup of coffee and there they were, two men he had last seen on a bank raid in Bone. There had been a reunion. Champagne, couscous at a French-Moroccan restaurant on the Malaga road, brandy, then back to his apartment late in the afternoon for red wine. By evening it was apparent that the two had not met him by chance but had come to look for him, and by midnight he knew what they wanted. The following month they relieved the Banque de Roussillon in Perpignan of just over a million francs, and re-entered Spain by the smugglers' paths through Andorra in a snow-storm.

After that life became better; there was money, and he could pick his women instead of the reverse. In 1970 they held up the Credit Golfe in Montpellier, this time taking nearly two million francs, re-entering Spain by fishing-boat which put them ashore near Cadaques.

Jacmel had grown tired of the south coast, of the continual noise of concrete mixers, and after the second bank robbery he went north to Madrid, bought an apartment not far from the university and kept his money in a safe-deposit box in the Banco de Viscaya near the Plaza del Sol. Through former O.A.S. members he heard occasional news of Louise.

Things had not gone well with her in Paris. The French police were on constant alert for O.A.S. action, especially after the de Gaulle assassination attempts. Many of the old groups had split up and dispersed. Louise had gone to Cannes as the mistress of a former O.A.S. officer turned yacht broker. Cannes, with its old and new harbours stuffed with expensive craft, was a yacht broker's paradise and it was possible that they might have made a success of the new life had they had sufficient capital to last until they had built up contacts. But they did not and to rectify that they had robbed half-a-dozen holiday villas closed for the winter between Cannes and St. Raphael before they were caught. Louise had spent two years in gaol in Nice and when she came out she was alone once more. This time she teamed up with a Marseillais, first smuggling American cigarettes into Italy and then, as the late sixties turned into drug heaven, smuggling hash from Morocco to France. When the American Government exerted pressure on France in the early seventies to clamp down on the drug trade, she had been picked up in Toulon and put away for three years. This time she served her sentence in Marseilles and when she came out she knew a great deal about the French underworld.

While she was spending her three years in prison, Jacmel's life had also undergone a change in Madrid. He had met Isabel. She was half-Spanish, half-Venezuelan. Thirty-one years old, the widow of a textile manufacturer in Caracas who had left her enough money to make her comfortable for life if she was careful. She was not.

She had an apartment off the Alcala, drove a Lancia coupé, spent her weekends at the sherry *bodegas* in Jerez, or on someone's yacht at Barcelona, and generally lived life at an expensive and rapid pace. She was deeply tanned and while no conventional beauty — her Venezuelan ancestry had given her the high cheekbones and flat planes of an Indian — she was attractive in a vital way. She was small and big-breasted, a combination that fascinated Jacmel. He met her at the Banco de Viscaya where she, too, kept her loot in a safe-deposit box.

To have her it was necessary to keep up with her: this he realized from the start. And while he still had a good deal of capital tucked away he knew it would not last long at the pace he was living. He tried to reach his former associates but they had left their old addresses and when he got in touch with a former O.A.S. colonel in Nerja he received the disquieting news that they had been deported from Spain for illicit currency dealing.

His capital diminished rapidly. There were dinners at Botin's and lunches down on the river at Aranjuez. Five days at the *feria* in Seville had cost him nearly a hundred and fifty thousand pesetas. There were weekends at the Granada Palace and the Reina Christina in Algeciras and trips from there to Tangiers, and skiing at Puerto de Navecerrada. And presents. But there was no thought of giving Isabel up. He had become too infatuated, not only with her, but with her life-style, for that. The problem must therefore be solved by the other route. If he needed money then he would get more money. It was at this point, when he was at his most receptive, that he had received a letter from Louise bearing a London postmark. It had gone first to his old address in Coin where they had lived together, then to his flat in Torremolinos, then to Madrid. It had taken nearly a month to reach him but when he saw its contents he knew it might be the answer to his problem.

He had read the letter several times before coming to a decision and even now he could recall whole paragraphs. It had been cleverly written. She had not used either his name or hers yet there was enough private knowledge to make it obvious that the letter had come from Louise. The first part had given him news of her. Things had not been good since she had left prison after the second conviction. She had been ill with hepatitis and been in bed for nearly two months. Almost a year had gone by before she felt well enough to face the world again. She had moved back to Paris but all her friends were either dead or in hiding, so she had taken a position as a maid in a moderately well-off household. She had moved after a year, getting a good reference. She took another job. This time the reference meant she could aim higher and she began work for the Due de Cherbourg. Again she stayed a year, again she was given a good reference. Now she was able to put into operation the first step of a plan which had been forming in her mind: a position of trust in a rich household where there were children. She had to wait nearly half a year before her opportunity came. M Michel Blanchet, the hotel millionaire, wanted a personal maid for his new wife in London, someone who could also look after a small boy. References had to be of the highest and a knowledge of English was required. Louise filled both prerequisites admirably.

Gradually Jacmel began to see where the letter was leading. He had been involved in political kidnappings as a member of the Delta Commando but had never liked them much. They were often messy. By their nature they were complex and had a way of going wrong.

It was the last part of her letter that had decided him. 'Do you remember that night we burnt the vineyard?' she had written. 'As though you could forget! When we drove there you told me how the rich Moslems from Algiers and Oran were offering you less and less for the vines.' He remembered, for the need to sell had by then been one of the central facts of his life and he had just realized what was happening to him. It had started nearly three months earlier and it had worked this way: an expensively dressed young Moslem had arrived in a new Mercedes and had offered him a sum which they both knew to be too low. He had refused and the young man had said insolently that the way things were going politically that sum would soon seem enormous. Three weeks later another Moslem had arrived, this time in a not-quite-new Citroen and offered him a lesser sum. This, too, he had refused. A month later a farmer in a dusty Renault had offered him a sum still smaller. Again he had refused, but this time with a feeling of panic. It was only by chance that he had told the story to another vineyard owner, also a member of the O.A.S. and found that he had experienced something so similar that it had to be a calculated psychological game which must already have yielded a goodly number of vineyards, farms and businesses. The subtlety lay in the first bid: it had to be low enough for the owner to refuse yet high enough to make him frightened when he saw how it was being eroded. Most farmers had sold on the third or fourth bids.

All this he had explained to Louise as they drove out to the vineyards that day. But now her letter told him something he had not known, which swung his mind towards her plan. Behind the Moslems, she had written, was a syndicate of French businessmen, hotel owners, land speculators, developers, who had callously waged a psychological war on the *pieds noirs*. It was their money which had bought the Mercedes cars and the expensive clothes and it was their money that paid for the cheaply-bought hectares. The head of the syndicate, she had found out recently, was

Michel Blanchet, the man for whom she now worked. She told him this, she said, lest he had any qualms about what she was suggesting.

Deep down in Jacmel, in the very deepest and darkest area of his psyche, was the caul of knowledge with which all whites in Africa are born, the knowledge that one day they will be forced to leave, to give up what they have created and get out. The knowledge is a kind of built-in spectre that accompanies them to every feast. What made it tolerable was that even the most hardened *pied noir* could recognize a kind of justice. But what enraged Jacmel as he read Louise's letter was the cynical arrangement of white businessmen. It was one thing for his vineyard to be turned over to a Moslem village co-operative; quite another that it should be owned by white speculators using Moslem front-men. If anything was needed to sway Jacmel it was this. Three days after receiving the letter he left for London on his first visit.

Now he was on his second and all the careful planning of the first visit had gone wrong. But he had grown used to that in Algiers during the final phase. He had become an expert at extempore action. The two situations were not dissimilar in at least one respect; in the last days of the Algerian war he had been alone against the forces of the French army *and* the F.L.N. He was alone again. In a way there was a kind of parabolic logic about it. He was not enjoying himself in the sense that what was happening was pleasurable; but at least it had a tension and a vitality he had missed for a long time. There were no thoughts of morality to cross his mind and muddy the picture. In that respect he was much like Bulloch. Had he been asked to rationalize what he was doing he would not have hesitated: the life he had been brought up to had been wrenched away from him; he knew only one other way.

He stood in the icy room of the house off Eaton Square and looked down at the couple on the sofa. They were pitiable. In another place at another time he might have felt sorry for them. Now they represented counters in a game he was playing with Bulloch. If they had to be sacrificed, he would do what was necessary. It was time now to put another section of his plan in action, but first eh must find whether there was an alternative way out, just in case. It had not been possible before. Dave would never have gone through the house an hour ago even with Howard leading. But now the house was as cold as a tomb and if they were right the snake would already be too chilled and stiff to move. There might be something in the cellar, a door, a window; perhaps boarded over; hidden behind a cupboard; a false wall. These old houses had many such things. He needed to know, for the really dangerous time was when the money was handed over. If the police were going to make a move it would be then. He did not think they would, not with a woman and a child in the house as hostages. However, he wished to be sure, for if there was a way out it meant that there was also a way in. He turned now to Dave, hardening his face, preparing his tone, so that when he spoke it would ring like iron.

*

'The leggings, sir?'
'Yes, the leggings.'
'And the helmet, sir?'
'And the helmet.'
The traffic policeman had parked his motor-cycle by the side of the road and he and Bulloch were standing near the police Rover. The traffic policeman looked large and menacing in his black uniform, almost as large as Bulloch.

'Can I ask why, sir?' the traffic policeman said.
'No, you cannot ask why.'
They stood staring at each other in the light of the cars, the smoke coming out on their breaths. Rich stood to one side of Bulloch and on the other side was a short, rotund gentleman who had arrived a few minutes earlier by police car. He was Mr Beale and they had had to fetch him from Orpington. Mr Beale was from the London Zoo. He gave the impression of having been woken suddenly and having dressed hurriedly; pyjama bottoms could be seen peeping out from the ends of his trousers. In one hand he held what looked like a fishing rod but was in fact a pair of long catching tongs, and in the other a box about three feet long and eighteen inches wide containing a canvas bag with draw-string top. He looked as though he was about to leave on a butterfly-catching expedition.

'You'll want the gloves, too,' he said.
'And the gloves, Williams,' Bulloch said to the traffic policeman.
'And the goggles,' Mr Beale said, addressing himself to Bulloch and not the traffic policeman.
'And the goggles,' Bulloch said.
Williams first took off the heavy, stiff leather leggings and Bulloch began to fasten them round his own legs covering his calves from knee to ankle. But whereas the traffic policeman was wearing large black boots

Bulloch had on a pair of soft suede shoes and the combination was ludicrous. No one laughed.

As Williams divested himself of each piece of clothing he passed it to Rich who held it for Bulloch and soon Bulloch began to take on the appearance of some eccentric lunar explorer. After the leggings he put on the helmet, then the goggles, then the heavy gauntlets, and closed as much as he could the thick sheepskin collar of his coat. The only flesh visible when he had finished were small areas on either side of his face near the jawbone.

'The gun, Rich?'

'Yes, sir.'

Bulloch clipped the holster to the waistband of his trousers and pulled out the revolver. It was a Smith & Wesson short-barrelled .38 holding five shots. He broke it and checked that each cylinder was loaded. Then he replaced the pistol in the holster under his coat but left the buttons open so that he could get at it.

'You want a shotgun,' Mr Beale said. 'That thing's no good.'

Bulloch turned and looked down into the chubby face, from which the fragrant bowl of a shell-briar emerged.

He was tense now and he had to keep a strong grip on his temper.

He spoke softly as to a child: 'We haven't got a shotgun, Mr Beale. I am not allowed to use a shotgun. I am what is known in the police force as an authorized shot, which means that I can use a hand-gun. If we wished to use a shotgun, I would have to apply for someone to come here who is qualified to use a shotgun, Mr Beale.' Each thought was spelled out. 'I am not going in after the snake. I am probably not even going in. I'm going to have a look around and am protecting myself while doing so. Is that clear?' He did not wait for Mr Beale to reply but went on. 'There are at least two men, two women and one child in the house, Mr Beale. Those are the ones that I am interested in. Once they are out of the way the snake is your responsibility. Understood?'

Mr Beale removed his pipe and stared up at Bulloch for a moment before he said, 'In that case I think you'd better let me come with you, Mr Bulloch.'

'By all means, Mr Beale, but keep behind me.'

A few minutes earlier when Rich realized what Bulloch was about to do he had gathered himself to open the argument once more, but Bulloch seemed to guess what he was going to say for he pre-empted an outburst by saying, 'This is the only time we've got left. Once they've got the money it'll be too late. If there's any chance of doing something it's *before* we hand over the money.' Rich watched Bulloch as he finished dressing and then said, 'I'm coming too, sir.'

'No, you're not.' Rich ignored him.

The three of them walked round to Sloane Mews at the back of the house. Sampson and Hodges were waiting for them at the door of a small building that had once been a ground floor garage and was now *Eaton Dressmaking. Wedding gowns a speciality*.

Bulloch went in the door and Sampson said, 'Over against the far wall, sir. Behind the pressing-machine.' Someone switched on a torch and guided Bulloch through a maze of sewing machines and tailors' dummies. He negotiated the pressing machine and stood looking at the wall as Hodges played the torch over it. At first he saw nothing then when Hodges moved the torch he could make out a faint shadowy outline under the floral pattern of the paper.

Now that the moment had come he paused and looked about the shop once more. A door led away to the right. 'What's that?' he said.

'Leads to a small kitchen, sir,' Hodges said.

'And that?' He pointed to another door.

'Toilet, sir.'

'Nothing in either?'

'No, sir.'

He turned back to the wallpaper. He couldn't postpone it any longer. 'Anyone got a knife?'

'Try mine,' Mr Beale said.

Bulloch slipped the blade under the paper and cut around the outline. The paper was dry and old and peeled away quite easily. In a few minutes he had stripped away enough to reveal what was underneath. The doorway, if it was a doorway, had been covered by a large sheet of hardboard. He pushed the blade of the knife under one side and attempted to lever it away. But the pins holding it down had embedded themselves in the wood over the years and with a slight click the blade of the knife snapped in two.

'Sorry about that,' Bulloch said, handing it back to Mr Beale, who held it in his hand and stared down at it for some moments without replying.

'Try these, sir,' Rich said, holding out a pair of heavy dressmaking shears he had picked up from one of the tables.

Bulloch opened the blades and pushed one under the hardboard and when he exerted pressure it began to come away. Until then they had been talking in whispers, now as they watched him prise up each side of the hardboard, no one spoke. They were children again and this was like the door in *Alice*. It must have been boarded up for thirty or forty years and they stood there, not knowing whether it might open on to a magic garden or the pit leading to the centre of the Earth. Bulloch gently pulled away the hardboard and passed it back to the men behind him. There it was: a door. It was an ordinary door with an architrave surrounding it. Long ago it had been painted white but London's air had penetrated paper and hardboard and had turned it a brownish cream.

Bulloch looked at it carefully. It had an old Yale lock which would not give either Sampson or Hodges a moment's difficulty. He also noted that it opened into the house so that if, as was likely, the door had been boarded over in the same fashion on the inside, then pressure from the outside would push away the hardboard. He moved away from it and motioned to Sampson. He spoke close to his ear. 'Can you open that lock?'

'I think so, sir.'

He searched in the torchlight until he found a can of Singer sewing-machine oil and squirted it into the lock and also along the parts of the tongue he could see. When he was satisfied he took the heavy sewing scissors, this time keeping the blades together, and prised away part of the architrave, exposing the rounded end of the lock tongue. He inserted the point of one of the blades and forced it round the end of the tongue. Slowly the tongue moved backwards, stiffly at first but then more easily as the oil flowed over it. Sampson kept the scissor-blade in place and turned to Bulloch. 'It's open, sir,' he whispered.

Bulloch pulled out the revolver and held it in his right hand then took the scissors in his other hand to keep the tongue of the lock from returning. All he had to do now was exert pressure. What would he find on the other side? Would they be waiting for him with guns? Or would the snake be there? Which part of the house would he enter? A cellar? The kitchen? Or would it be a forgotten room, itself boarded up? Flashes of childhood nightmares entered his brain. Stories he had read. Of houses where the number of windows did not correspond with the number of rooms; of cupboards filled with human bones; steps that disappeared down into the dark void; *The Cask of Amontillado*; *The Prisoner of Chillon*; rats ... creatures of the primeval ooze ... the sweat was cold on his face and neck.

He nodded to Sampson who took hold of the brass door handle and began to turn. As he did so Bulloch put his weight to the door. As with the lock it seemed at first to stick and Hodges leant his own weight. Slowly it began to move. They could hear the slight tearing sound of the paper on the far side. Then ripping as the hardboard pins came loose. Bulloch knew he could open the door by himself now and he waved both Sampson and Hodges away. He held the gun ready and put his left shoulder to the door. He eased it forward, opening it half way, wide enough for him to see round and go through if need be.

'The torch,' he whispered.

Sampson passed him the torch and he held it in his free hand. Then slowly he put his head round the door and switched on the torch. As he did so he heard a woman scream. It was so loud, so near, that it froze his blood. At that moment light suddenly flooded through the half-open door.

The pupils of his eyes had grown large in the dim torchlight and now, as they rapidly contracted under the impact of a fluorescent strip in the cellar, he was momentarily blinded. He could hear voices and see shapes dimly. Then his vision cleared. He found himself on the threshold of a cellar. One at least of the shapes he had expected to be that of a woman, for his mind had placed her there after the scream. Instead he saw two men and in the background he could still hear the woman screaming. It had to be Dr Stowe and something inside him cringed again at the thought of continued mutilation. In the remaining few seconds before the cellar became a battlefield he registered the picture before him. The men. One in semi-uniform. The chauffeur. With shotgun. Must be Alec Nash's killer. The second: the Frenchman? The screaming rang continuously in his ears.

*

Howard and Dave were also aware of the screaming. It had begun as they made their way down towards the cellar door after having searched the remaining rooms of the house. For a horrible moment Howard thought it was Marion and that she was being attacked by the snake but at the same moment Dave paused and listened and said, 'That's Mrs Blanchet.'

Howard knew he was right. As she screamed again he could make out the word, 'Ph-i-l-i-p!' drawn out in anguished ululation. She must be in the street. But how did she know? How had she got back? Dave motioned him forward with the shotgun and he opened the cellar door with care, switching on the bright strip light.

'Get on,' Dave said.

It was then that something odd began to happen to the cellar wall ahead of them. It seemed to bulge. They stood transfixed. Automatically Dave pushed past Howard and stopped on the bottom step. Then, like in a movie Dave had once seen of an earthquake in Tokyo, the wall split and began to open. A figure appeared in the opening. He saw the strange leggings, the huge goggles, the helmet. He thought of Frankenstein's monster, of Dracula, of some dreadful being entombed in the cellar walls and now breaking loose. His nerves, drawn to fine threads, snapped. He began to raise the shotgun and as he did so the figure, too, raised a gun and pointed it at him. He felt sick with fear. 'No!' he cried. He heard the crashing sound of the revolver in the confined space and felt something smash into his chest. He tried to say, 'Stop! You're wrong. It's not me you want,' but all he could hear of his own voice was a mumble.

Then he was falling forward and, too late, his fingers were pulling at the triggers of the shotgun, both together, but the barrel was already swinging up to point at the ceiling. He seemed to fall very slowly and while he fell he heard the sound of his own gun firing. It came from a long way away, more of an echo than the original explosion. He did not feel anything as he crashed on to the hard cellar floor, for by that time all feeling had left him and life itself was hastening away.

For a few seconds the tableau remained then the gun in Bulloch's hand swung to cover Howard, who was half way up the cellar steps. The two men stared at each other. 'For God's sake,' Howard cried suddenly. 'Don't shoot, I'm not one of them!'

'Who are you?'

'I live here. They took me when they took the boy.'

'Is he still alive?'

'Yes.'

'How many of them are left?'

'Only one. The Frenchman.'

'Where's the boy?'

'In his bedroom.'

'Can you get the light on in the sitting-room?'

'I don't thi — Watch out!'

There was a movement at the far end of the cellar and both men swung towards it.

Dendroaspis Polylepis had been curled around the asbestos flue-pipe, seeking to absorb every therm of heat remaining in it. The cellar had been growing colder and colder. She had been drugged by the freezing air, unable to rouse herself properly even when Bulloch had begun to force the door in the wall. But then had come the tremendous reverberations of the gunfire, the crashing body, the dangerous movement of shapes, the smell of humans — all her sensors were flashing danger signals to her brain. A mixture of aggression and fear warmed her muscles. Stiffly at first, then with the lubricity of flowing oil, she uncoiled herself from the flue pipe and launched her shining black body into the centre of the room. It was her shadow thrown upon the wall by the light which Howard first saw.

'Over there!' Howard shouted.

Bulloch saw it at the same moment. He fired wildly at the snake then leapt back through the door and slammed it shut. Howard fled up the few steps to the cellar door, closed it hurriedly, locked it and leaned back on it for a few precious seconds as the sweat dripped down his crutch and the inside of his thighs.

In those few seconds the snake also acted. Filled now with the energy born of fear, she fled the cellar. Territory and safety were one in her primitive brain and she did what she had done the first time she had been threatened: she sought the dark safety of the air-ducts. During those brief moments when Bulloch stood on one side of one door and Howard on one side of another, the snake thrust herself up into the open airduct and flowed along the system until her whole body was inside. As she drove upwards, making for the junction where she had earlier lain and where her smell still lingered, her sensors began to pick up, very weakly at first, a slightly higher temperature. She moved along the system in its direction. Then her tongue 'heard' faint vibrations. She paused. The vibrations were dangerous, but the heat was life. She moved in the direction of the heat.

Part VI

Saturday 5.38 a.m – 7.01 a.m.

'... out of nowhere, sir,' Detective Sergeant Glaister was saying apprehensively. 'Taxi came up and out she jumps and before we could do a thing she was running towards the house screaming at the top of her lungs.'

'Gave me the fright of my life,' Bulloch said.

'Very sorry, sir.'

'Where is she now?'

'Control room, sir. D'you want to see her now, sir?'

They were standing at the end of the street and Bulloch was taking off the leggings and the helmet and goggles and handing each piece to Williams the traffic policeman, who accepted the return of his clothing with obvious relief. No, Bulloch thought, he did not want to see her. The last thing in the world he wanted was to see an hysterical woman. She had sent his blood cold with her screaming. But you couldn't blame her. You come home out of the blue and find your house surrounded by police and no sign of your kid — enough to send a statue into hysterics.

'Have you given her anything?'

'I made her some coffee, sir. Borrowed a drop of your rum, sir.' Glaister looked as though he had been caught dipping into the collection plate, but Bulloch was too preoccupied to notice.

'Shall I bring her to the car?'

Bulloch thought of the inside of the mobile control unit. People in and out; no privacy. People ... people ... Dr Stowe ... Mr Beale ... the man in the cellar (who the hell was he?) ... now Mrs Blanchet ... the place was crowded with unwanted people ... complications. He became aware of yet another person: a tall man standing in the street light twenty yards away. He was clutching a brief-case to his chest.

'Who's that?'

Glaister looked round then said, 'Office manager, sir. Mr Prothero. He's brought the money. He's waiting to see you too, sir.'

'Let's have the woman first. And coffee. And tell Rich to bring me some fags.'

They brought Ruth from the mobile control unit to the car. Her legs were unsteady and she was crying; it was a soft, uncontrollable weeping. It had followed the outburst of wild hysteria which had swept over her when the taxi had pulled up at the end of the cul-de-sac and she had found the house in the midst of a police siege. After the events of the day, after the failure of her two telephone calls, after the growing unease of the return journey, it seemed to have an horrific logic; it was as though all the hours of frustration were building up to this denouement — no, not only hours, but all the months and years of worry about Philip. She had been right to worry; right to cosset him, right to be pessimistic — and everyone else had been wrong. That was the desperate irony that kept the tears squeezing from her eyelids and filled her with such hopeless despair that she wished she was dead. All the energy of that first dash to the house, when she would have smashed through the ground-floor window to get inside and get to Philip if two of the policemen had not restrained her; all that force, that strength to get to her child, had evaporated and now she felt hollow inside.

They helped her along the road, one man on each side of her, and she was hardly aware that her legs were moving. She seemed disassociated, like a spastic, unable to control her movements, and she wondered whether it was the liquor they had given her. She never drank rum and had no idea how much had been in the coffee. They helped her into the car and someone gave her another cup of coffee. Her gorge rose as she bent to meet the rum smell but this time all she could smell was the coffee.

'Help me,' she said to Bulloch. She spoke in a dull, hopeless tone. 'They've got my child.'

'Yes, I'll help you. We'll help each other. But first ...'

'They've got Philip.'

'I'm afraid that's so. What we've got —'

'He's sick.'

'Sick?'

'Sick. For years.' She seemed to be drifting away and Bulloch brought her sharply back.

'We'll need your help,' he said.

'Help. You've got to help Philip.'

'That's right. Philip. Now tell me. Who was in the house when you left?'

He dragged it from her little by little. She didn't understand why he was asking her so many questions. Especially about Dick Howard. Howard ...

a brave man, Michel had called him. If he was brave, how had he let this happen? But this big man was asking if he was one of them; one of who? The ... she could not even bring herself to think of the word kidnappers ... the 'dirt' the man had called them. Dirt. Yes. But not Howard. Whatever you said about Howard he wasn't dirty. Not one of them. What was he doing there, the man was asking. Why was he there? Why? Why? Questions. Questions. And all the time Philip was in the house.

'Excuse me, sir,' a voice said.

Bulloch wheeled angrily round in his seat. 'What the hell is it?'

A man leant down and spoke through the half-open window. 'It's me, Smith, sir, lab liaison officer.'

'Can't it wait?'

'It's about the ... the exhibit, sir, the one that fell from the house.'

'All right, Smith, what is it?'

'Just wanted to show you something, sir.'

Bulloch opened the door. He did not particularly want to see the finger again but there was nothing he could do about it. Smith held the grubby handkerchief in his hand and opened the folds. In the weak light from the inside of the car it looked ghastly. 'Well?' Bulloch said.

'Don't know if you noticed the ring, sir.' He held the ring out in his fingers.

'What about it?'

'Doesn't fit, sir.'

'What d'you mean?'

'There's no mark, sir. It hasn't been worn on this finger.' Bulloch's mind was turning over very slowly. The ring didn't fit. Or at least it hadn't been worn on the finger. No mark. Therefore the ring had been placed —

'What are you doing with my ring?' Ruth said dully.

'*Your* ring?'

'What are you doing with it?'

Bulloch stared first at the ring and then at Ruth and then back at the ring, finally he handed it back to Smith. 'Give it to the exhibits officer,' he said. 'Tell him to take it to Lambeth with the other thing,' he indicated the finger in the handkerchief. 'Tell him to tell forensic I want to know if they can say whether it was cut off a live body or a dead one.' There was a pause as the words seemed to hang in the cold misty air. 'Get cracking!'

'Yes, sir.'

A live body or a dead one, Bulloch thought. That was the point. Either Dr Stowe was alive or dead, *or* ... it hadn't come from her at all, for why would she have been wearing Ruth Blanchet's ring?

He levered himself out of the car and called over one of the constables. 'Look after her,' he said. 'Get a doctor if necessary.' He began to pace up and down. A live body or a dead one. He knew of one dead body. The chauffeur. He'd lay odds that he was dead. He'd seen where the bullet hit. Seen the sudden splash of blood over the heart like a red rose opening in time-lapse; then spreading on the white shirt. Couldn't have been *his* finger. And it wasn't the boy's, that was certain. You could tell a child's finger. Everyone thought it was Dr Stowe's. But wasn't that —

'Sir.' This time it was Glaister.

'What?'

'It's Mr Prothero, sir. What do we do about him?'

'Take him to the control room. Sit with him or get someone else to sit with him. Don't take your eyes off him.'

Bulloch was hardly aware of Glaister leaving. Or Rich arriving with more coffee and a cigarette. He accepted both without thanks. Then he looked at Rich.

'Well?' he said. It was a challenge.

'Well, sir?'

'You'd have got the money into them hours ago, wouldn't you, Rich? And they'd have vanished by now and we'd have been looking for them all over bloody London.'

'It's only money.'

'It's only money, is it? It's not your bloody money, Rich, that's why you're so generous with it.'

'I don't see that it matters one way or the other, sir, we've still got to give it to them. Doesn't matter whether it was a few hours ago or now.'

'Christ, Rich, sometimes I despair of you. By postponing the hand-over we've got one of them. The chauffeur. Now there's only one left.'

'I wasn't thinking of the chauffeur, sir. I was thinking of the woman and the child.'

'Don't get all pious with me, sonny, not before you know the reasons.'

'Yes, I'd like to know the reasons ... sir.' There was a hint of angry mockery in Rich's voice.

'Thought you might. Smith says the ring doesn't fit the finger. Mrs Blanchet says it's her ring. D'you think Dr Stowe pinched it?'

'Mrs Blanchet's ring!'

'No mark on the finger. There'd be a mark, you see. Indentation. But nothing on this one.'

'Then ...' Rich groped for the thought. '... Then what you're saying is that it mightn't be Dr Stowe's finger.'

'You're getting there, Rich.'

'And if it isn't hers then it must be what's-her-name's, the maid's, Louise something. She'd stolen the ring.'

'Right.'

'You mean they'd mutilate her? I thought she was one of them.'

'Why not if she was dead?'

'But why would they kill her?'

'The snake, Rich. The snake. They said she'd been bitten. We believed them. Then they grabbed Dr Stowe and we thought it had to be a trick. We never thought it might be both.'

The two men paused, staring at each other but not really seeing, looking inward at their own ideas.

'Right at the beginning,' Rich said. 'That's when it could have happened. She could have been bitten right at the start when the kid came back with the snake. She might have been dead for hours before Dr Stowe arrived.'

'What does that tell you?'

'Tell me?' It told him a dozen things.

'Surely to Christ it tells you *one* thing!'

Rich looked puzzled. 'I'm not sure what —'

'Well, it tells me something. It tells me he's soft.'

'Soft!' The word came out with enough force to bring Bulloch's head up sharply. Anger had flared in Rich again. 'Soft! It's still a game to you. It's still Detective Chief Superintendent William Bulloch. The Dirt. Aren't you forgetting that Inspector Nash was killed? That Frenchman's never going to give way. You think he's soft because he mutilated the maid instead of Dr Stowe. It was more convenient, that's all. You don't say the Nazis went soft when they pretended to the train-loads of Jews that they were just going to have hot showers. It was more *convenient*, that's all.'

Bulloch had never seen Rich like this; had never been spoken to like this before and was not sure how to react. He took refuge in sarcasm. 'Lovely, Rich, a really lovely speech.'

But Rich had gone too far now to stop. 'Don't you see what you're doing. Even now you're trying to buy time. To delay. Because you just can't visualize a situation where he wins and you lose and the woman and the child are caught in the middle. Well, this isn't an Irish gunman or a Greek-Cypriot willing to die for God and country. There's a clever bloke in there who's in it for the cash. He's out-thought you all along the line and he's still got a woman and a child in there and when he's finished cutting Dr Stowe into little pieces he'll *still* have the boy and there's no way —'

'Stop it! You're tired. You're saying things you'll regret later.'

Bulloch had dropped his voice and both men were whispering fiercely.

'The only thing I'll regret is seeing Dr Stowe's body or the kid's body. Because that's what we'll see if you go on like this. And then who'll you get to hold your hand? Or sit with you? Or wipe up after you've puked? Because it bloody well won't be me!'

They stared at each other in silence. The words had been spoken, no one could take them back. Bulloch turned on his heel and walked down the street a few paces. Rich stood where he was, waiting for the onslaught. But it didn't come. After a moment Bulloch turned and said, 'Get a message to the marksmen. There's a chance the light may go on in the sitting-room. The boy's in the bedroom so there'll only be the two men and the woman in the sitting-room. Tell them they won't have more than a few seconds but they're not to fire until they're absolutely certain. Got it?' Bulloch's tone was flat.

'Yes, sir.' Rich had been hot, now he was very cold and shaking slightly. It was as though he had undergone a great catharsis. He told himself that he should be terrified at this moment but found he wasn't. He turned on his heel and went to deliver the message. As he did so he saw Bulloch's massive hunched shape moving towards the house. It stood dark and cold in the early morning and from a distance it looked like a stage-set on an empty stage.

*

Inside the house fear hung in the air like a dirty smell. Howard was afraid; Marion was afraid, and now, and this was new, Jacmel was afraid. Or at least Howard guessed he was. He could not see him clearly, only his feet as he paced up and down, up and down the icy room. One ... two ... three ... four ... five ... turn. One ... two ... three ... four ... five ... Turn. Back and forth like Howard's leopard in its enclosure in Kenya.

He and Marion were lying down on the floor, on their stomachs with their hands clasped behind their necks. It was hideously uncomfortable and the muscles in his shoulders were beginning to cramp. He watched

Jacmel's feet move away. Counted to three and then whispered, 'Are you all right?'

Their bodies were almost touching and he felt her move towards him.

'Can you hear me?'

Again he felt the slight pressure of her body and realized she was using it to answer for her. The steps came nearer and he lowered his head to the carpet once more. He was lying over the television aerial cable and it bit into his chest. The smell of dust rising from the carpet was suffocating.

One ... two ... three ... four ... five ... stop. The feet were only a matter of inches from his face. Jacmel was standing over him. What was he doing? Staring down at them? Looking across the room into the black of early morning? Making up his mind what he was going to do? He had to do something, hadn't he? Or was he still in the driving seat? He still had the boy. He still had Marion. And for what he was worth he still had Howard. Would the police try again, or had that been in the nature of a reconnaissance? Would Jacmel *force* them to act and if he did, by what method? The easiest way would be to show them he wasn't fooling and for that he might sacrifice one of his counters. The least valuable. The one he would be sacrificing anyway, the one who knew about Shakespeare Close.

Howard was under no illusions about the Frenchman. After the gunfire in the cellar he had come upstairs in answer to Jacmel's shouted order to find him and Marion on the landing. Jacmel had forced the barrel of his revolver into her mouth. The slightest movement and the top of her head would dissolve. Howard would never forget the sight of her. Lips pushed forward and rounded like some New Guinea native using a blow-pipe, eyes bulging with terror, blood dripping down her chin where the gun-sight had nicked her lip.

He had made Howard tell him what had happened, all the while keeping the gun in Marion's mouth.

'The shotgun?' Jacmel said.

'The policeman got it after he had shot the chauffeur.'

The lie hung in the air. It was safe enough, Howard thought. No one was going back down there to disprove it. Jacmel made him push a heavy Jacobean chest against the cellar door. If the police made a move now they'd have to batter their way in and they were not going to do that, not while the boy was in the house. Not while Jacmel had Marion.

It had been a piece of pure bad luck that he and Dave had been entering the cellar as the police broke through the wall. They'd have been in there now, perhaps even in the house itself, hidden in rooms, in walk-in wardrobes, awaiting their chance. But then he remembered the snake. Would they really have come in knowing what was loose in the house? Of course, the big policeman had been wearing protective clothing. That made a difference.

Knowledge of the snake was his one weapon. He had thought of telling Marion that it was safely locked away in the cellar but something stopped him. It seemed to him that if he was to have any chance at all of getting out alive he needed every weapon he could grab. The knowledge of the snake was his entire armoury. Jacmel would think that wherever it was in the house it must be close to death by now. Or at least inactive. But he couldn't be sure. Not absolutely. And therein lay Howard's only chance. Only chance of what? His mind kept picking at the problem but nothing came. Then he heard Bulloch's voice through the open window.

'Can you hear me?'

The shoes in front of Howard's face turned sharply and Jacmel crossed to the window. He stood behind the heavy curtain in his usual place. 'I can hear you,' he said.

For Bulloch the walk from his car to the front of the house had been a very long one, not physically but emotionally.

His mind still surged with Rich's angry outburst. Phrases zoomed in and out of his thoughts unwanted, and where he blocked some, others popped up to harass him. It was all so unfamiliar. The carapace of anger which for so many years he had been able to draw over him like a shield, was now curiously missing. He had not been able to use it when Rich spoke to him nor, as he walked towards the house, was he able to reawaken it for his own protection.

'He's out-thought you all along the line,' Rich had said. It wasn't true.

'It's more convenient,' Rich had said. 'Just like the Nazis.' It wasn't true.

'It's still a game to you. You can't stand the thought that he might win and you might lose.' No. It wasn't true.

And the pictures that Rich had evoked. The woman's body. The child's body. The man's body.

As he walked he shook his head, trying to clear it of thoughts like those.

Rich was a kid. He didn't understand. But the rationalization did not work. It wasn't true either.

Other pictures rose unwanted in his mind. His flat. The loneliness. The desperation that last time after the Sutherland Street siege, when he'd felt as empty as a paper bag. And Rich had stayed with him. He'd needed him then, no one would ever know how much. Now he'd flung it back in Bulloch's face.

Where was the anger? Where?

He stopped in front of the house and raised his head and shoulders. The effort was enormous. 'Can you hear me?' he called.

The pause before Jacmel answered was like eternity. Bulloch had begun the walk towards the house with the knowledge inside him that the Frenchman was not the man he had taken him for. Deep down there was a soft core and it was this knowledge that had refurbished his own confidence. But as he walked, as Rich's words came back to him, the whole complex structure of his attack crumbled, all the confidence that had reawakened in him, seemed to seep away, draining out of his body like old bathwater. As he waited for Jacmel's reply he did not know how to play the game any longer.

'Yes, I hear you,' Jacmel said.

He heard a different quality in the voice. There was anger, but cold and deep. Was there fear? Was there a slight edge? The Frenchman was alone now. He must already know that the chauffeur was dead. And if Bulloch was right, Louise was also dead. It was then that he admitted what he had not been able to before, what he had never acknowledged before — the similarity between the two of them. He asked himself what he, Bulloch, would do if he were in the Frenchman's situation: it was when he had answered the question to himself that he knew what to say.

'The money has come,' he called.

Again there was the slight pause. 'Good. Do you have it?'

'In the car.'

'Bring it.'

But the factors that had made Bulloch the man he was still lurked to influence his thoughts. He was incapable, inherently unable, to let things go; at the last he was ineluctably held by his own character, fastened by the web of his own life, and now, against his own wishes almost, he played out the final moves.

'It's all there,' he said.

'Do you hear me? Bring it.'

'There's something I've got to do first.'

'What is that?'

'I want to see the boy.'

Even as he said it he knew the Frenchman would never agree. He, Bulloch, would never have agreed. He didn't even know why he was asking except that it delayed, it wasted time, it added seconds, minutes perhaps.

'No,' Jacmel said.

'The woman, then. Dr Stowe.' Bulloch hardly recognized his own voice. He tried to sound in charge. 'There'll be no hand-over unless I see that Dr Stowe is all right.'

Again the pause.

'All right,' Jacmel said. What had he to lose now? It was simply a matter of speed. Bulloch heard the growing confidence.

'You know what will happen to her if your men try anything.'

'Yes.'

'No lights.'

'All right.'

'No questions.'

'How will we know she's okay?'

'She will tell you so.'

Pause. 'All right.' The tone was tinged by hopelessness. 'Stay there.'

In the house Dick Howard heard Jacmel turn from the window and felt the vibration of his steps across the carpet. The black shoes stoped near his head.

'Did you hear?' Jacmel said.

Howard knew Jacmel wasn't talking to him and felt Marion's body move closer. 'Yes,' she said.

'Get up.'

She got to her haunches and then straightened. 'Give me your scarf.' There was a pause. 'So,' he said.

'Why?' Marion asked.

'Because I say so.'

Howard craned sideways and looked up, seeing first Marion's legs disappearing up into the dark recesses of her skirt and then above that one of her arms being tied in a sling across the front of her body.

'You heard what I told him?'

'Yes.'

'He will ask no questions. You say you are all right. That is all. Understand?'

'Yes.'

'If you make to climb the railing, if I think you are trying to jump, I shoot. You understand?' He turned to Howard. 'If you move I shoot her. Understand?'

'Yes,' he said. Jacmel turned back to Marion.

'You go out. Very slowly. You stand where the policeman can see you. You come back very slowly. Understand?'

'Yes.'

Howard watched her legs as she began to move. He knew that if there was a moment, any moment at all when he might do something, it was while she was on the balcony. Jacmel's attention would be on her almost wholly. If Howard tried to get up or fling himself at Jacmel the Frenchman would have ample time not only to shoot Marion but Howard as well, for Howard was near the fireplace some ten feet away from the window. In any case, he knew he had neither the strength nor the nerve.

He heard Jacmel say, 'All right,' and saw Marion's feet step over the sill. It had to be now. But what?

The TV aerial cable was hurting his chest and he moved slightly to a new position. He could no longer see what was happening. He turned and lowered his hands, rolling over so that both Jacmel and the window were visible. He could just see the Frenchman squatting by the curtain, completely hidden by its folds. Again he moved from the discomfort of the cable and in doing so rolled it underneath him and he heard the faint plop as its end fell from the input socket at the back of the TV set.

What happened next was without conscious thought but seemed to be born not so much in his mind but directly into his muscles. He found himself acting without thought. Just as his mind had directed his legs to run when the lion attacked, now, by-passing the decoding device in his brain which would have made them subject to delay and scrutiny and possibly rejection, the thoughts first appeared as impulses in the muscles of his arms.

He pulled the end of the thick cable towards him and as he did so his mind seemed to split: one part guiding the action; one part trying to stop it; one part screaming at him that no one could be fooled by such a thing; the other that he had been fooled by it himself, that he had seen what he had expected to see. Then, even as he heard Marion's voice on the balcony saying what Jacmel had told her to say, his thoughts were cartwheeling ahead: it wasn't the *thing*, not the substance, but the symbol; not reality, but shadow. It was the *shadow* that had terrified Dave; the *shadow* they had seen in the cellar.

His hands grasped the end of the cable, bent it in a crook, then he looked round wildly for somewhere to place it, somewhere it could stand upright with the light behind it. Next to him was a big bowl of stiff dry grass, beech twigs and honesty. He leant sideways and placed the cable in the bowl. It caught in one of the beech twigs and by pushing slightly he managed to get the crooked end above the display.

'Come back now,' Jacmel was saying to Marion.

Howard heard her steps on the tiny balcony. Behind him on the floor and to his right, out of reach, was the second big lamp in the rough glass carboy. Again his muscles reacted seemingly without conscious thought; for this time the realization of what might happen to Marion would have stopped him. As she came through the windows and stepped between himself and Jacmel he slithered the few feet to his right and felt for the light switch. At the precise second she moved past Jacmel, Howard switched on the light. He had wanted to shout something. Anything. But he crouched frozen in the brightness and the cry died in his throat. He found himself looking, with terror, into the barrel of Jacmel's gun. Then it shifted briefly to the left as the Frenchman saw the rearing, snakelike shadow. He fired, swung the gun back towards Howard as though realizing he had been cheated. At that moment there was a tinkling of glass as the top of one of the big windows shattered. Jacmel fell forward. As he did so Howard saw a small jet of blood spurting from the back of his head.

The last thing Jacmel ever saw was the huge shadow on the wall; the shadow of the snake, head curved, waiting to strike.

*

There was complete silence in the room. Marion stood quite still. Howard crouched on the floor. In the midst of the carpet Jacmel lay on his face, the small jet of blood pumping up six inches in the air, then, like a hosepipe after a tap has been switched off, drooping, stopping. They stared at him, unable to believe him dead, yet knowing that he was. The silence, which had rushed in from the walls after the loud explosion of Jacmel's gun, seemed almost as loud as the noise of the gun itself. Then it too was broken. The weight of the aerial cable was finally too much for the beech twig which had been supporting it. The twig bent, snapped, and the aerial fell with a plop on to the floor. The shadow vanished. The slight movement brought life back into the room. Howard rose to his feet. Marion moved towards him. He stepped over Jacmel's body. She put out both her hands and he took them. 'It's all right,' he said. 'It's all right now.'

She touched him on the cheek. 'Are *you* all right?'

'Yes.'

She looked down at Jacmel. 'How did it happen?'

Howard shook his head. 'They said they wanted the light on. Must have been a police marksman.' He waved a hand at the night. 'On one of the roofs probably.'

'Can you hear me?' Bulloch's voice floated up into the room.

This time it was Howard who answered. 'Yes,' he said. 'I'm coming to the window.'

He held Marion's hand and took her with him. They stepped out on to the balcony. Bulloch waved his arm at them and first one then another car switched on its lights and the front of the house was lit up.

'Are you all right?'

'Yes.'

'Doctor?'

'Yes,' she called. Others were coming towards the house now and some were running.

'And the boy?' Bulloch called.

'He's asleep,' Marion said. 'Fast asleep in his room.'

'Is the snake still in the cellar?'

'Yes,' Howard said.

'Right. We're coming up.'

'I'll let you in.' He felt for the door-key in Jacmel's suit then went downstairs. Marion came half way with him as though unwilling to be parted. Bulloch and Rich came into the hall.

'Who's that?' Bulloch said, pointing to the covered lump on the floor. 'Maid?'

'Yes.'

He lifted the blanket and he and Rich looked underneath.

'You were right,' Rich said.

Bulloch turned. 'Yes, I was, wasn't I? Let's have a look at the other one.'

Marion and Howard went into the room which had been their prison for less than twelve hours but which seemed like twelve days. Bulloch turned Jacmel over, then shook his head. 'Doesn't mean a thing to me. Rich?'

'No, sir.'

'Well, it doesn't matter now. Let's have a look at the boy.'

As he said it, the air was cut by a scream.

'What the hell's that?'

As Howard followed Bulloch from the room he saw Ruth in the passageway. She was holding back the curtain that covered the passage window looking into Phillip's room and scream after scream was coming from her throat.

Bulloch put his arm around her and said, 'What's happening?' Then he saw what she had seen and said, 'Oh, Jesus!' Howard, coming up beside him also looked through the window and felt his body freeze with shock.

Philip lay on the bed fast asleep. He was on his side, facing them, knees curled up. Beside him lay the mamba. It too was curled up. Its head was on its coils facing the foot of the bed. Below it, on the floor, stood the fan-heater, sending waves of warmth over both the reptile and the boy. The vibration of their feet in the passage had unsettled the snake and its head came up from its resting place and hovered in the air.

The screams had also unsettled the boy, penetrating the cells of his mind which had been curtained by the drug. He opened his eyes. It took him some moments to focus, to realize where and who he was, and then, as the drug left him, he saw his mother in the passage window. And Dick. And other faces. He was about to shove himself up on his elbow when he felt an unaccustomed weight on the blankets next to him. He heard a low, warning hiss. Then he saw the snake.

Howard put his lips to the glass. 'Don't move,' he said. 'Please don't move.'

'For God's sake do something,' Ruth said.

Bulloch lifted her in his strong arms and carried her bodily away from the window. 'Leave me,' she shouted. 'You've got no right ... !' She struggled in his arms for a moment as Marion came to her.

'He's all right, as long as the snake isn't frightened,' Marion said, taking her arm. 'We're making too much noise.' Ruth said, 'Why doesn't someone *do* something?'

'Rich, get Mr Beale up here,' Bulloch said. 'Tell him what's happening.' He turned to Ruth. 'I've got an expert down in the street. Mr Beale from the Zoo. He knows there's a snake in the house. Got everything he needs to catch it.'

Then Marion said, 'Where's the main switch? If you switch off the electricity the heater will stop. Can you get the outside window open?'

'What'll that do?'

'Make the room cold. Immobilize the snake.'

'All right.' He turned to Howard. 'Where's the fuse box?'

'In the cellar.'

'Glaister, you get down there and switch off the mains.' Then back to Marion. 'What if the window's locked? What about the noise it'll make?'

'Couldn't you cut out the panes?'

Bulloch paused, then trotted heavily down to the street where a constable was on guard. 'Tell Rich I want someone with a glass-cutter, fast as you can.'

'Right, sir.' Upstairs they heard the hard crash of the constable's running footsteps.

Ruth had returned to the window. She was quiet now, her face set in a mask of horror.

Howard said softly, 'Don't worry, Ruth. We'll get him out. If the room gets cold enough the snake —'

'You did it!' she said. 'It was your idea, wasn't it, to bring this thing into the house. Philip would never have thought of it by himself.' Howard quailed before her ferocity.

Marion, standing next to him, said, 'It wasn't his fault. They made a mistake. He'd ordered a harmless —'

But Ruth had turned away and leant her forehead on the glass pane, staring through it, cutting herself off from the others, letting her eyes lock with the terrified eyes of her child, trying to send through her vision love and strength and courage.

Now all they could do was wait; watch and wait for the air in the room to grow cold, wait for Mr Beale; wait for the glass-cutter; wait … and at any moment the snake might rear up. Howard looked at his watch. It was showing a few minutes to seven. It would be an hour at the very least before the room got really cold. Less if they could cut open the windows. But say an hour. He glanced at Ruth, could she last that long without breaking? Could Philip? Wouldn't the cold start him coughing and fighting for breath? Wouldn't that make him move? No one had thought of that. But what else was there? Anyway, Mr Beale was on his way. He was the expert.

Just then Ruth turned away from the window and he felt her hand grip his. Her long nails sank deeply into his flesh. He looked into her face and saw a skull.

'The clock,' she whispered.

She did not have to explain. The alarm clock on the bedside table was usually set for seven o'clock so Philip could clean the animals' cages before he had breakfast and went to school. Howard could see the clock's Mickey Mouse face, could see the hands pointing a little before seven, could even see the smaller dial set into the large one. And on top of the clock he could see the two brass bells and the little brass striker that would, in a matter of a minute or two, vibrate between the bells, setting up the clanging that would echo through the house.

'Did you set it?' Ruth said.

Had he? Tomorrow was Saturday, no need to get up early. But that was in normal times. Everything was abnormal. Had he set it without thinking? He could not remember. All he could recall was winding it after Philip had mentioned it. It was just done to reassure the boy. Had he done something more? Had he actually set the alarm? He looked round desperately. Bulloch was still downstairs. Mr Beale had not arrived.

'Did you?' Ruth shouted.

'I don't —'

'Help him!'

'Mr Beale will be here in a minute,' Marion said.

'For God's sake — !' Ruth tore at Howard.

He held her for a moment before she flung herself off. She ran to Philip's door and dragged at the handle. Every fibre in Howard's body was protesting. He had coped in the sitting-room. He could not be expected to —

'The key!' Ruth yelled.

It was on the telephone table.

'Give it to me,' Marion said. 'I've had experience with snakes.'

Howard reached for the key. He held it in his hand. It was unfair. Dreadfully unfair. Ruth grabbed it and began fumbling at the lock. Marion tried to hold her but Ruth shook her off. Howard finally moved. He ran back into the sitting-room, scooped up the long poker and the largest cushion.

'What the hell are you doing?' Bulloch said, coming back up the stairs.

Howard did not hear. He pushed Ruth aside and opened the door very slowly, inching it back. When he got his head through he said, 'Listen, Phil, I'm going to try and distract its attention.' His voice was high-pitched. 'I'm hoping it will come down off the bed. If it moves towards me, get your head, arms, everything under the blankets.'

The snake had turned towards the new figure. Howard closed the door behind him. He was so frightened now that he was numb. The snake lifted its head higher. Howard held the poker in his right hand and tried to cover himself with as much of the pillow as he could. He took another step. The snake swayed, but did not seem willing to leave the bed. Instead it moved slightly towards the boy.

The alarm went off. In the room it sounded like a million whirring pieces of metal. The little brass tongue between the bells moved backwards and forwards, vibrating so quickly that the human ear could not take in anything but a continuous noise. The vibrations entered the snake's brain. It reared, a gigantic moving shadow on the wall. Then it struck. It struck at the alarm-clock, sending it crashing down from the bedside table on to the floor. The clock continued its vibrations. The snake struck again from the bed, shooting forward, smashing the glass, stunning herself on the whirring mechanism for a brief second. That was enough. Howard brought the poker down on the long black body. He broke the mamba's spinal column within a foot or two of her head, paralysing the whole of the back section. She had nothing now to grip with, no muscles left to launch her body. Only the front two feet of her body had strength and she raised herself defiantly as Howard hit again. And again. And again ... again ... again. He hit and hit until there was nothing left but a long strip of orange pulp where once the head and throat had been and he was still striking with the poker, smashing down wildly, when Bulloch came in and took his arm.

*

Saturday 9.14 a.m.

Rich stood on the pavement and watched the sound engineers from the BBC and ITN trucks begin to pull in the cables and pack up. The TV interviews were over, the reporters had gone, the cars had gone, the police notices had been taken away, the barriers removed. Everything was over. The night was over and the morning was a replica of the previous one, grey, cold, misty. He turned and looked at the house. The front door was closed, the windows were closed. It was shut up. Locked. There was nothing to tell of the horrors it had been host to.

Rich was so tired he could hardly stand. He walked slowly to the car and got in. He put his head on the back of the seat and closed his eyes. Just ten minutes and he'd feel better. But he did not sleep. His mind was filled with racing images: he saw again the orange stripe on the carpet in the boy's room that had once been a venomous snake; he saw Mrs Blanchet, face taut like a skull, eyes far back in her head, carrying her child to the ambulance; he saw the shell of the man called Howard being helped down the stairs by Bulloch and Glaister, his feet hardly touching the ground as they took him to a second ambulance; he saw Dr Stowe, with tears wet on her cheeks, watch as the ambulance slowly turned from the cul-de-sac and made off into the traffic; he saw Bulloch in front of the TV cameras, big, ebullient, aggressive once more, making jokes with the reporters. He saw Mr Beale being interviewed about the deadliness of the snake and how such a thing could have happened. And above all he saw the dirty handkerchief and the etiolated horror it had held. The night unrolled in hindsight, like a black and white movie, made grimmer by chiaroscuro.

He thought of Bulloch. He turned in his seat and looked through the rear window of the car. The sound trucks were moving away. Bulloch stood at the end of the street giving one last interview. He must have been interviewed by every TV reporter, every national daily crime man, every agency, every provincial journalist. It wasn't that Bulloch got much satisfaction from the interviews, Rich knew he had never sought the Press, it was just that he seemed to feel so good. He had erased any doubts, forgotten anything that Rich had said.

As Rich watched him the reporter finished the interview, got into his car and drove off. Now everyone had gone and Bulloch was left on the pavement. And suddenly Rich saw a different man from the one he had watched over the past hour. Bulloch looked right and left. He was alone. For a few moments he seemed lost. Then he saw Rich in the car and came striding towards it. He dug his hand into his pocket and tossed a sheet of paper on to Rich's lap as he got in.

It was a dossier on Jacmel from Interpol. Rich flicked his eyes down the list of political murders, bombing and robberies.

'Glad I didn't know that,' Bulloch said. 'Sometimes it's best not to know too much about the dirt. But I'd have done him anyway.'

Still Bulloch. The Dirt, Rich thought. Still the one-man show. The game he had to win.

'Coming for a drink?'

There was nothing Rich wanted less than a drink. He wanted coffee. Bacon and eggs. A warm bed. Sleep. Nor did he want to spend another minute in Bulloch's company.

But underneath the seemingly casual question he knew an effort had been made. Bulloch did not forget, no one forgot such things. And so his effort had been a great one.

'My place first until the pubs open,' Bulloch said, starting the car. 'Right?'

'Right,' Rich said, and they headed out into the London traffic and the long, long day ahead.